Patrick Loves Love

LLL Book 2

Sophie Sinclair

PATRICK LOVES LOVE

To Owen, the best writing partner a girl could ask for.
We did it, buddy.
Forever in my heart.

"I think I'll just go down and have some pudding and wait for it all to turn up – it always does in the end."
– Luna Lovegood

Chapter 1

Patrick

The Wedding Dance

THE CROWD ON the dance floor sings along with the song blasting from the speakers as they throw their arms in the air. It's your typical wedding playlist with all the celebration songs belted out by drunk family members who have saved up all year to be at this event so they can let loose for one night.

I walk along the edge, a whiskey in my hand as I look for her. I'll admit, I'm a little tipsy. Watching my two best friends get married today was one of those moments I won't forget. Seeing them so happy in love made me want that for myself. The ceremony, set on the white sandy beaches of Hilton Head, was a fairy tale.

I love love, and I can't wait for the same magic to strike me someday.

"Patrick, you were wonderful up there today. Your speech was amazing! They are very lucky to have you." Lindsey's aunt Ginny squeezes me into a tight hug.

"Thank you, Mrs. Love. It was a beautiful ceremony."

"Oh yes, dear, it was, wasn't it? I never thought Lindsey would marry. I wish she had waited until after she had the baby, but Linda told me they insisted on getting married before the baby was born. Each to their own, but if it were me, I wouldn't have wanted a beach ball under my wedding dress."

"I thought she was stunning, absolutely glowing with love," I grumble as I spy Lindsey and Nick across the room talking to some guests. I've never seen her look happier or more beautiful.

"Oh, well, of course she was! That's our little Lindsey! She's very...spirited! Oh, there's Linda. I'll see you later, dear." Thankfully, she bustles off to talk to Lindsey's mom before I'm forced to say something rude.

I pause as I finally see her dancing with her sisters. She's the most beautiful woman in the room tonight. Tendrils of apricot gold slip from her chignon as she lifts her arms in the air and moves with the beat. She smiles as she spots me and waves me over to join them. I set my drink down on a vacant table and smoothly dance my way over to her. Unfortunately, someone has spilled their drink along the path I'm dancing. My tuxedo shoes have no grip on the shiny parquet floor as they slip out from under me. I reach out and grab for the closest thing next to me before falling on my ass.

Beads rain down on the floor as I take down Lindsey's great-aunt Mildred with me. Her damn dress is so slippery because of all the icicle beading hanging off of it. Luckily for her, I manage to break her fall as she lands on top of me. Someone quickly helps her up to her feet, unscathed. Unlucky for me, she thinks I'm a pervert who tried to attack her on the dance floor. I apologize profusely as she repeatedly hits me with her matching handbag until Lindsey's cousin manages to drag her away. I feel like such an idiot as I rub my aching lower back.

"Oh my god, are you okay?" Kelsey giggles as she helps me up. "That was amazing!" she gushes as she leads me over to her sisters, who are dancing up a sweat.

"Really?"

"Yes, you did this backspin thing." She gazes up into my eyes and blushes. "Oh, never mind, I don't know what I'm saying. I'm a little tipsy." The music suddenly changes to a slow song, and half the people make their way back to their tables to rehydrate. We stand there awkwardly watching people slow dance, neither one of us sure what to do. I'm about to suggest getting a drink when she turns to me.

"Wanna dance?"

"Sure, I'd love to."

Her whole face lights up when she smiles, and I'm completely mesmerized by it. She wraps her arms around my neck, and I hold her to me. I breathe in her light floral scent and wish I could run my lips along her bare shoulder.

"So, you're Lindsey's best friend, Patrick. The one that's really into Star Wars?"

"That makes me sound weird. I'm not obsessed if that's what you're thinking."

She gives me a wink. "It's cool."

"And you're one of Nick's sisters."

"Kelsey."

I return her wink. "I know."

Her cheeks stain a pretty pink as I glide her slowly across the dance floor. "You're a terrific dancer, and you look handsome in your tux." She ducks her head. "Oh my god, I can't believe I just said that."

"Thanks." I blush as I try to tamp down my nerves clawing at my stomach. "I wanted to wear my converse, but Lovie wouldn't let me. If I had, I wouldn't have taken down her great-aunt Mildew."

"Aunt Mildew?"

"It's Aunt Mildred, but Lindsey and Shannon call her Aunt Mildew because she's old and not very nice."

"Well, I'd personally like to say thank you for de-beading her dress. She looked like a disco ball out on the floor. It made my eyes hurt." Her warm smile makes my heart want to burst out of my chest.

"Glad to be of service. So, where do you live?"

"In New York, outside of Ithaca. You?"

"Charleston."

"Oh, I've always wanted to go there. Now that Little Di—I mean, Nick and Lindsey are living there, I'll have a reason to come visit."

"Will you look me up and say hi?"

Her eyes dilate as I count the little golden flecks misting into lapis blue. Her lips curl into a coy smile. "Maybe."

She feels so right in my arms. My hands tighten on her waist as she trails her fingers up my neck. I can't take my eyes off her gorgeous mouth and how badly I want to kiss it. She gasps as I tug her closer, the heat from her body melting into me. I've lost track of time and space. I couldn't tell you what song is playing or that other couples share the floor with us as we sway together. I have no idea where Lindsey, Nick, or the Elliot sisters are, and I don't care. I bend my head as I feel her breath hitch. I'm going to taste the champagne on her lips if it kills me. She looks up at me from under her lashes as she laces her fingers into my hair.

The music suddenly changes to a fast-paced tune as Kelsey's eyes widen. She quickly untangles herself from me before I can kiss her. "Oh my god, I love this song! Do you know how to do the body roll?"

"The what?" I'm momentarily stunned as if Aunt Mildew whacked me in the head with her purse again.

She's dancing like a hula girl on crack, her hips gyrating and arms all over the place. I'm pretty sure that's not the body roll, but she's making a fool out of herself, so I join her, doing a horrible rendition of the robot.

"Kelsey Elliot, I think I love you." I laugh as she tries to do an Irish jig.

"Oh, sorry, Patrick, I'm not looking for love. Just a good dance partner."

"I…wasn't seriously saying I love you, only that I think you're fun."

She flashes a smile at me right before her sisters join us on the dance floor. "Oh my god, you guys look so cute together!" Bridget croons. "You *have* to do the scene from *Dirty Dancing*, Kels."

"Yes! Come on, Patrick, it will be awesome!" Arden grabs my arm. All escape routes are blocked by her three sisters.

"Uh…okay, I guess. I'm not sure—"

"Patrick, you come down here." Bridget pushes me to the other side of the dance floor as MK and Arden clear a path.

Lovie's made me watch the movie once or twice so I kind of know what to do. I roll my sleeves up and nod to her

SOPHIE SINCLAIR

exactly like Patrick Swayze does to let her know I'm ready as I'll ever be. She flings off her heels, and takes a deep breath before taking a running start. She launches herself at me like a flying squirrel and I scream as she barrels toward me. I'm tipsy, and I don't really know what I'm supposed to do with a woman running full-force at me. She smashes into me like a linebacker, shoving me back a few steps into a table before slowly sliding down my body into a puddle of tulle on the floor. The room is engulfed in silence.

"Good effort!" someone behind us shouts before the crowd resumes dancing.

"Oh god, how bad was it?" she mumbles from the floor.

"Not bad. No one saw it." Everyone saw it, but she doesn't need to know that. I help her up and hold her steady.

"Thanks for catching me."

"Sorry I couldn't hold onto you."

"Did I make it above your head at least?"

"Uh, no, not even close."

"I think I need some air." She bends to straighten out the poufy skirt of her dress and tug up her strapless top.

"Sure, let's go."

I grab two bottles of water as we head toward the French doors. I sit down on a bench underneath a ceiling of twinkling lights as the ocean waves roll over the moonlit sand down below. Kelsey sits down next to me and groans.

"Oh my god, my feet are killing me."

"I'd offer to rub them, but I don't want you to think I have some creepy foot fetish."

She giggles. "That's okay, that's what I get for dancing in heels."

I hand her a bottle of water which she greedily drinks. "Are you here with anyone tonight?"

"No." She frowns. "You?"

"No, I'm single. I thought about bringing a date, but I didn't want the girl to get the wrong impression."

"I know what you mean. I feel like a wedding date is setting her up for some serious letdown, especially to your best friend's wedding. To you it's just a date, but to her it's a lifetime commitment ceremony. And then you're surprised when she wants to move in with you two weeks later because love is in the air, blah, blah, blah."

I smirk at her as I take a sip of water. "Not into commitment?"

"No, I am! I was…" She shakes her head and sighs. "I don't know anymore."

I lean back and put my arm around her shoulders. She scoots closer to me and rests her head on my chest. "It's nice to sit here and talk and not have my sisters yammering in my ear. You smell good, by the way, like rain and fresh-cut grass."

"Thanks, so do you. Like a field of meadow flowers."

Her fingers trail up the buttons of my tux, and my abdomen clenches.

"Patrick?"

"Kelsey."

"If you did have a date here, what would you say to her now?"

"I'd say, wanna get out of here?"

"And where would you go?" She peers up at me.

"Maybe a walk on the beach."

"And what if your date said, it's too windy."

"Then I'd ask her what she would want to do." I trail my fingers on her shoulder in slow circles against her soft skin.

"What if your date…" She hesitates a beat. "What if your date said she wanted to go back to your room?"

I swallow as nerves sizzle low in my belly. "Then I'd say, let's get a bottle of champagne and go."

She sits up and looks at me, her blues swirling with hesitation. "Why champagne? What would you be celebrating?"

"Oh, I don't know. Life, love, blah, blah, blah."

That beautiful wide smile lights up her face as she leans in and gently presses her petal-soft lips to mine. She stills as if she's afraid to kiss me wholly, her breath a soft pant on my lips as she touches her forehead to mine. Needing more, I take over the kiss as I gently thread a hand into her hair, holding her to me. I nip her bottom lip and then her top, running my tongue along her seam, begging for entrance. She tastes like strawberries and champagne, and it drives me wild. Our kisses quickly grow hungry and frantic as she clings to me.

She tears her lips from mine, her crazed eyes mirroring my own, our chests heaving for air. I nod as I pull her up from the bench and go in search of a bottle of champagne.

THE CLINKING OF glasses and giggling dissolves into the background as I concentrate on sticking the plastic key card into the slot. We both had a glass for courage downstairs before we agreed to come up to my room. The lock clicks, announcing that I'm free to step inside as I slide the card back into my coat pocket. Shadows and anonymity welcome us into the hotel room. Her giggling quiets as I set the glass and bottle of champagne down on the table.

"We shouldn't be doing this," Kelsey says, a note of indecision hanging in the air as she pauses unbuttoning my shirt.

"We most definitely should, but I'll stop if you want me to."

"God no, keep going," she whispers as my lips glide along her neck. Satin slides over her smooth, silky skin as I kiss along her collarbone. The damn zipper sticks as I roughly tug it down, cursing as she pants in my ear.

"I've never done something like this before. I want you to know that. Promise me something."

"What?"

"Promise me you won't forget tonight. Don't forget me...I mean...never mind, I don't know what I'm saying."

"Okay." I lift her chin. "I won't forget." I swallow her words with kisses, not wanting to talk anymore. We've said plenty tonight. Her dress rustles as I slip it down her body. She urges me with her hands to hurry up.

But I don't want to hurry up. I want to take my time with her. She threads her fingers through my hair and tugs hard, directing me right where she wants me to go. I chuckle against her skin, and she gasps as my fingers find her velvety heat. I breathe in a trace of her floral perfume as I glide my nose along her skin. She urges me on, but I don't want this to end quickly. I'm drunk on her and the wine, so I give in.

SOFT BLUE LIGHT filters in through the window where I forgot to close the curtains. I grunt in protest as I turn my head. My hand reaches, but my fingertips only glide against cool cotton sheets. She's gone.

I lie there for a moment and wonder if I had dreamed it. I sit up and hold my head in my hands as I try to quiet the raging headache thrumming against my skull. I call room service and order a carafe of coffee and some scrambled eggs and bacon.

The only thing that takes forefront of my brain as I look around the empty room is the fact that Lovie is going to fucking kill me when she finds out I slept with Nick's sister at her wedding. Because she *will* find out.

Chapter 2
Patrick
Palpatine the Maleficent

Six Months Later

SHE RUNS THE cart into my leg for what feels like the bajillionth time as she picks up something that caught her eye on an end cap.

"Lovie, will you watch where you're going? I'm going to have to be admitted to the ER after this."

Lindsey rolls her eyes as she reaches up for a unicorn piggybank, standing on her tippy toes. "Trick, stop being so dramatic and help me get this down."

I reach impatiently for the piggybank, handing it to her as I pick up a Star Wars Mandalorian Baby Yoda bank. "This is so cool. She needs this one." I gently put it in the cart, causing Lindsey to huff. She takes it out and replaces it with the unicorn.

"When you have a baby someday, Trick, you can give it all the Star Wars crap in this world. In fact, I'll go to Pottery Barn and buy out their whole collection, but Olive's room is unicorns. So, I'm getting her a unicorn piggy bank to match."

"I'm not having kids, so I need to spoil yours. Baby Yoda

is so much cooler."

"Says the man-child who is probably wearing Mandalorian days-of-the-week boxers." She wheels the cart down the next aisle. I peel down the waist of my jeans. How does she know this shit?

"They're not days of the week," I mutter. "So anyway, about tonight, Ca—"

"Ah shit. Man down!"

I immediately drop to the ground like I'm about to do a push-up. An older woman down the aisle looks at me like I'm completely deranged as she quickly wheels her cart away from us.

"What are you doing?" Lindsey looks down at me. "Get up. That employee just called someone on his walkie-talkie."

"You said man down. I thought we were under attack." I slowly get up and dust off my hands.

"Under attack from what? My boob? Here, hold this." Lindsey starts unpacking plastic tubes from her diaper bag and shoves them into my arms as Olive happily coos in her car seat. "I know, Uncle Trick is a complete lunatic," Lindsey says to her in a happy sing-song voice.

"I can't help it that I have PTSD from your husband." Ever since our trip to Paris, where Nick and I had to rescue Lindsey from the Russian Mafia, I've been super paranoid they're coming back to exact revenge. "What is this?" I look down at the small plastic funnel.

"My boobs are leaking. I need to quickly pump a bottle."

"I did not sign up for this when I said I'd go to Target with you."

"Trick, it's a leaking boob of milk. Get over it. It's not

like I'm going to make you watch me, or god forbid, ask you to help me pump." She maneuvers the cart over to the dressing room as I shiver in disgust at the image she planted in my head. "Watch Olive for me."

"Why don't you, er...breastfeed her."

Lindsey laughs as she takes in my expression. "God, it's so much fun watching you get all splotchy and squirmy. I can't get her to latch on, so I'm trying to use breastmilk as long as I can until I have to switch to formula. These puppies are like milk warlords. They go off like a geyser when they get full, demanding to be pumped. You look like you're about to pass out." She smirks as she leaves me with sweet Olive, who has her mom's delicate features and her dad's midnight-blue eyes.

"Your mama is a booby monster." I grin as she kicks her little arms and feet out. "So anyway, this Friday night, can your sister watch Olive?" I call to Lindsey on the other side of the dressing room.

"I can ask...why?"

"Candy wants to have you and Nick over for dinner."

"Oh...okay. Why can't we bring Olive?"

"I don't know. She said something about it only being adults only. Can you do me a favor and see if you can get a sitter?"

"I guess."

Olive starts to fuss, so I pop a pacifier into her mouth and move the cart back and forth. "How long is this going to take?"

"I don't know, like ten minutes...maybe longer. Just walk her around. I'll find you."

"Fine." I push Olive and the cart back over to the children's section. "Let's go check out the Star Wars stuff." I pass by the end cap with the piggybanks and quickly exchange the unicorn for the Baby Yoda. "Uncle Trick has your back."

Olive gurgles and kicks. She's so darn cute, and even though she's not mine, I'd do anything for her because she's my family. I throw in some Darth Vader crib sheets and a wookiee blanket. I pause and throw in a second one for myself.

"Patrick? Patrick Healy? Oh my god, is that you?"

I whip around, my eyes widening as Janice McKinavitch stands in the Carter's aisle with her hands on her hips.

"Wow, Janice…" I swallow audibly. "You haven't changed a bit."

"I know! Neither have you! It's been what…ten years?"

"Yeah, something like that." I step back as she advances. Her eyes flicker down to my cart and then to my hand.

"Oh my gosh, you have a baby? She? He?" Her eyes ping-pong between Olive, my face, and my hand. "I don't see a ring. Does this mean you're single?" she whispers naughtily.

Oh, Jesus, I'm going to have to start wearing one of those rubber wedding bands I see guys at the gym wear. I can't count the number of times someone has cooed over Olive and then over me because they think I'm a single dad with a new baby.

Janice is the last person I would want to go out on a date with…not that I'm interested. I have a girlfriend, but the Janice I used to know, that little tidbit wouldn't deter her.

She lived on our co-ed floor during freshman year of college and was always hanging out in my room trying to hook up with my roommate David. I'll never forget her annoying habit of putting on Chapstick and then making kissing noises.

I look over my shoulder toward the dressing rooms hoping Lindsey stays put. She and Janice were like oil and water. "So, Janice, what have you been up to?"

"Oh! What have I been *in to* is more like the question!" She winks and giggles, causing my brain to go places I don't want it to go with Janice. "I'm in real estate and recently moved to Charleston from Charlotte. So yeah, very exciting! Are you in the market for a new house? I have some fabulous listings and we could spend lots of time together trying to find the perfect place for you and your baby. You didn't answer my question, are you married?" She keeps touching my arm, which makes me take a step back.

"Oh, uh…"

"Well, well, well…if it isn't Janice McKinabitch."

I sigh. Great, here we go. Why couldn't Janice have just said a quick hello and been on her merry little way?

Janice's razor-sharp eyes trail down Lindsey's small frame like a snake appraising its prey. "It's McKinavitch. I'm sorry, have we met?"

"I see a leopard never changes its spots," Lindsey mutters.

"Easy, tiger." I gently push her behind me. "Janice, you remember my friend Lindsey? You guys lived on the same floor freshman year."

"Oh, she remembers me," Lindsey grinds out.

Janice pulls out a tube of lip balm and glosses her lips. I

cringe as she kisses the air. "Oh right, Lindsey Love...I didn't recognize you. Patrick and I were reminiscing about the good old days. Funny, I don't have any memories of you."

Lindsey's nostrils flare like a bull about to charge the red flag. I need to diffuse this meeting pronto before Lindsey starts shouting *Olè* as she takes Janice down.

"Okay, well, good to see you, Janice. We've got to get going. Welcome to Charleston." I wave as I grab Lindsey's hand and yank her along with me.

"Call me if you are in the market for property!"

"Sure thing, Janice." I wave to her as I steer the cart around a corner, pulling Lindsey along with me.

"What is she talking about? You're in the market for property?"

"She just moved here from Charlotte. She's a realtor."

"I seriously hope you're not considering using her. Do you remember how awful she was in college?"

I shrug. "I'm sure I'll never see her again. Besides, I don't plan on moving."

"What are the odds of running into Janice McKinabitch in the middle of Target?"

I release her hand now that we're a safe distance from her, but Lindsey continues.

"She teased you relentlessly about your love for all things Star Wars. She spread the rumor that I was sleeping with our Resident Assistant after watching me leave his room one night. When in reality, I was picking up an essay he was helping me correct. Someone drew 'Randy hearts Lindsey' on my door in Sharpie...I know it was her. It was so humiliating. She's pretty much the reason you and Katie broke up."

"Nah, Katie and I had nothing in common. I stuck around because of you."

Lindsey stops walking and places her hand over her heart. "Aw, Trick, because of me? That's so sweet that you would date my roommate to spend more time with me."

"Well, you had a car and wanted to try fun new places to eat. You were every freshman guy's wet dream." I laugh.

"Eww, gross. Please don't ever refer to me as that again." She shivers as she moves the cart down the aisle. "Red alert, red alert! Oh my god," She breathes, spinning in a panic, confusing the hell out of me.

"Are you having another boob leak? What the hell is wrong with you?" I look around, bewildered as she drives the cart into a bunch of dog food cans while trying to turn around in the aisle, cursing as they clatter to the floor.

"No, no, no, no! I can't escape this woman! Don't let her see the baby! She'll place some kind of hex on her."

"What the hell are you talking about?" I turn around to see if Janice followed us, but there's only a sweet elderly woman hunched over a cart wearing a cardigan, pearls, and a pleated floral skirt. She looks up at us as she's reading a list, but there's no hint of recognition in her rheumy eyes behind the glasses perched on her nose. "What is going on?"

"Whatever you do, don't make eye contact, don't talk, and for fuck's sake, don't say my name." She tugs my arm and tries to propel me to the opposite end of the aisle.

"I guess even establishments like Target let the trash in."

Lindsey exhales loudly, turning around to shield Olive

with her body. "Hello, Mrs. Bixby. I hoped I'd never see you
again. Sadly, that's not the case. What brings you into such a
mundane establishment such as Target?"

"Lovie, don't be rude," I hiss.

"Trick, she's evil."

"If you must know, I'm here with my granddaughter,
Elinora. I see you're here with a different man...again. That
poor sap that impregnated you didn't have a clue what a
hussy you were, did he?"

"What is she talking about?" I whisper out the side of my
mouth.

I've heard Lindsey drone on and on about how awful
Mrs. Bixby was, but in classic Lindsey fashion, I thought she
was overreacting. Suddenly a tall woman with hazel eyes and
glasses turns the corner. She beams at us when she realizes
her grandmother is talking to us.

Her smile slips a little as she notices Lindsey's grimace as
she faces off with Mrs. Bixby. "Is everything okay, Nana?"

"Nana Beelzebub. Has a nice ring to it."

"Hi, Patrick Healy," I quickly intercede, trying to talk
over Lindsey.

"Hi, my name's Ellie. Do you know my grandmother?"

"Nice to meet you, Ellie. Lindsey used to live above your
grandmother."

"Oh! That's wonderful! I always worry she gets so lonely
in that big old apartment. But her new neighbor has been so
helpful." She winks at me, and I goofily grin back at her.

"Yeah, that's great."

"Earth to Patrick! We have to go. *Now.*"

I look over to tell Lindsey to give me a minute when I see

Mrs. Bixby sourly looking down at sweet Olive.

"She doesn't look anything like you. Are you sure she's yours? Back in my day, babies were switched all the time at the hospital. She looks jaundiced, and her head is shaped peculiarly."

"Put a stocking in it, you old bat. She's mine, and she's perfect!"

I laugh nervously. I look at Ellie's horrified expression as Lindsey tries to run the cart over Mrs. Bixby's foot.

"Harlot!"

"Devil's spawn!" Lindsey yells over her shoulder as she quickly turns the cart causing more cans to fall off the shelf as she exits the aisle.

"Ha, well, I guess I have to go." I quickly pick up the cans and place them back on the shelf. "It was nice to meet you, Ellie. Mrs. Bixby." I nod in her direction then turn and jog after Lindsey. "What the hell was that?" I catch her arm.

"*That* was Mrs. Bixby. And by the way, you suck. When I yell code red, that means hustle out of the building like we have the Russian Mafia after us."

"Well, I can't keep up with all your code reds, man-down, crazy talk."

"Ugh, man-down is boobs, or Olive poops green sludge in her diaper. Code red is we're about to die, or Mrs. Bixby has materialized out of thin air."

"Like Darth Sidious."

"Exactly. That's the perfect name for her. Palpatine. I need to stop by the Catholic church on the way home and sprinkle some holy water on Olive."

"Seriously?"

"Yes, seriously! While you were flirting with Elinora, she whispered something over Olive. I'm pretty sure she just went all Maleficent on her ass, and now Olive will die from a spinning-wheel needle at the tender age of sixteen."

"Does Nick ever comment on how exhausting you are to be around?" I look over at her as we check out.

"You have no idea." She holds up the piggybank. "What the hell is this?" She scans Baby Yoda, and I feel triumphant. "You're lucky this time, Uncle Trick, only because Palpatine the Maleficent and McKinabitch are lurking the aisles, and we have to bust a move. I mean, who would have thunk Target attracted all the weirdos today?"

I eye her surreptitiously. "Yeah, who would have thunk?"

"Next stop, church."

"Of course." I smile down at my most favorite weirdo of all.

Chapter 3

Patrick

Pattycakes

I ENTER THE kitchen and slide up behind my girlfriend Candy, wrapping my arms around her waist as I nuzzle her neck.

"Patrick, not now! I'm cooking. I want everything to be perfect."

"Why? It's just Lindsey and Nick. They're family."

"Exactly! I want them to like me."

I pick up a carrot stick and dip it in the ranch. "Of course they like you." I don't understand why she's so nervous. It's not like she hasn't met them before. "Remember when we went out to dinner a couple of weeks ago? Everything went smoothly."

"I don't think Lindsey likes me."

I scoff. "Trust me, if Lovie didn't like you, you'd know it. She's not exactly subtle."

"Nick is so intimidating. I swear, with one glance, it's like he's figured out my whole life history. He stares at me like I'm trying to hide something."

"Nick can be intense sometimes." I wrap my arms around her again. "It will be fine. My friends like you. Is that what this slaving over a hot stove is about?"

Candy shrugs but continues to stir the Bolognese sauce. "Why do you call Lindsey 'Lovie' anyway?"

"It's just a nickname from college. I call her Lovie, she calls me Trick."

"Does it bother Nick?"

My eyebrows scrunch in confusion. "No, why would it?"

She wiggles out of my grasp. "No reason. I mean, don't you think it's kind of strange having a girl for a best friend? There's always that fine line that can't be crossed."

"You know Lindsey and I aren't like that. She's like a sister to me."

"But at some point, you were, right?" She slyly eyes me over her shoulder. "You're telling me you two have never thought about it?"

"I mean, sure, at first. Lindsey has this personality that kind of bowls right over you. Still, we both agreed that physically it would never happen and definitely wouldn't get in the way of other relationships. Nick isn't threatened by me."

"He should be, from what I've seen."

Before I can delve into this line of questioning further, the doorbell rings. Candy and I have been dating for about two months. I met her in a bookstore when I accidentally bumped into her and made her spill her tea on her favorite Minnie Mouse t-shirt. A fact she relentlessly chides me over. I was reading the back of a fantasy book, and she was looking through a book about Walt Disney. We immediately hit it off over a cup of coffee. She's exactly my type—a woman who loves to read and understands my obsession with Star

Wars, because she's equally obsessed with Disney. She keeps dropping hints that we should move in together and have our wedding at Disney World, but I feel like she's trying to make this train go too fast into the station. It's probably what's been causing this niggling feeling in the back of my brain over our relationship. I'm having fun with Candy, and I'm happy with that. I don't need to take things to the next level right now, especially with all the traveling I do for Lindsey's show.

I swing the door open and hug my best friend, and fist-bump my sidekick. "May the force be with you."

"Yeah, yeah, thanks for having us." Lindsey rolls her eyes and shoves her coat and purse at me.

Nick slaps my shoulder and arches an eyebrow. "Drunk already, dude?"

"Oh, it's an expression of goodwill."

"Ah, got it. What's the phrase to ask for a beer?"

"Ah, a grog or a Starfire skee." I drop Lindsey's coat on a chair.

"I'm not sure either of those sound good," Nick mumbles. "Can the force get me a regular beer?"

Candy rushes out of the kitchen. "Pattycakes, stop talking in *Star Wars* lingo, it's so juvenile," she chastises. "Hi, guys! I'm so glad you could come!"

"*Pattycakes?*" Lindsey mouths to me and smirks as Candy hands Nick a beer. I shrug as I shake my head. This nickname is new to me, and I can't say I like it, but I'm going to go with it for tonight because Candy is a little on edge.

"Hey Patrick, JD wants to talk to you and me about

working on his new project. Can you meet Monday?"

"Yeah, totally! That would—"

"What's this about a new project? Are you going to be traveling *again*?" Candy's eyes dart back and forth between the three of us.

Nick's eyebrow arches in that intimidating way he saves for Lindsey when she's acting like a lunatic, which is most of the time. "I'm sorry, Candy, but I can't discuss the details at this time."

Candy snorts. "What is it, *classified?*"

Sweat breaks out along the back of my neck as Nick gives me a hard stare. God, I wish I had the Jedi force to use on Candy and make her forget what we're talking about. Little does she know that Nick used to be a secret agent for a group called The Syndicate. He was drafted into it after serving his country as a Navy SEAL. He was granted release from the group in exchange for top-secret recorded information from a Russian spy named Claudine.

"Classified, ha! It's not like we're filming *Mission Impossible*, Candy," I chide, but the air is thick with tension. I laugh to try and put everyone at ease, but it falls flat. "Classified, that's funny."

Lindsey's smile is frozen on her face as she places a hand on Nick's arm, subtly squeezing it. "Candy, please excuse my husband's gruff delivery. He sometimes forgets he's not in the SEALs anymore. Isn't that right, Nick?"

He shifts in his seat as he looks at Candy. "Sorry, I didn't mean to sound rude. We don't know what JD wants to discuss, but yes, it will probably involve traveling." Nick picks up his beer and gulps it.

Candy drops down onto the armrest of my chair and pouts. "Pattycakes, I don't want you to travel again. I feel like you just got back from New York. I get so lonely here without you."

"Candy, I went to New York for a weekend." I laugh nervously as Lindsey gives me the *are you fucking kidding me* look. "It's my job."

She suddenly pops up and claps her hands. "We'll discuss it later. Let's eat dinner, shall we?"

"Sure. Is there anything I can help you with, Candy?" Lindsey trails behind her, giving me one last pointed look over her shoulder. *What?* I mouth to her. She rolls her eyes and disappears into the other room.

Nick finishes his beer and smirks. "Pattycakes?"

"Dude, I don't know. She came up with that one tonight."

"It suits you."

"So, do you have any idea what JD wants to do?"

"He didn't say, but he's dropped a few hints that he'd like to go back to Africa to work with a team of conservation wildlife vets. He also wants us to come down to Miami and check out his new facility first."

"Yes! That would be amazing."

"Come on, Pat! I need you to open the wine!" Candy calls out from the kitchen.

"I'm in, Nick. Whatever you need." I reluctantly get up.

"Oh, I can open it for you, if you want. Where do you keep your wine opener?" Lindsey gets up from the kitchen table.

"Oh no, sit down. It's Pat's job to do it. He and I are

25

SOPHIE SINCLAIR

hosting this little soiree after all." She shoves the wine bottle in my hands and plates the pasta. "Lindsey, I made the pasta and sauce from scratch from my favorite Disney cookbook. I hope it will stand up to your culinary tastes."

Nick snorts as he pulls out the chair next to Lindsey. "Have you met Lindsey? She'll eat a burrito in an alley from a rundown...ow!"

Lindsey beams at Candy as I set a wineglass down in front of her. "I'm sure it will be incredible, Candy. You did not have to go to all this trouble for us."

"No trouble, I've only been cooking for *four* hours!" she says dramatically. "Nick, do you need another beer? Pattycakes, don't just sit there like a bump on a log. Get him another beer." Candy pulls parmesan cheese out of the fridge. She could have easily plucked a beer out, but she's obviously trying to prove a point. I just don't know what it is.

"Patrick, I can get it." Nick starts to get up, but I wave him back down. I can feel Lindsey's eyes burn a hole through the back of my shirt. She knows I hate being called Pat. She also knows I look like a complete tool as Candy orders me around, but now is not the time to make waves.

I sit back down after I grab two beers. "Wow, this smells great, doesn't it?"

Candy sits down and deposits a platter of rolls on the table. "It's going to be awful."

I run my palm over her back. "Don't say that. It's going to be amazing."

"I'm starving, Candy. Trick's right, it smells delicious." Lindsey picks up her fork and twirls it in her pasta.

"It's Pat."

"What's Pat?" Lindsey looks up, her fork midway to her mouth.

"His *name* is Pat."

Lindsey chooses to ignore the steely look Candy shoots her as she puts her fork back down and arches an eyebrow at me. *Yes, I know, Lovie. I'll do something about this later.*

"Pattycakes, can you pass me the rolls?" Candy asks sweetly. I hand them over.

Nick takes a bite, and his eyebrows draw together. He looks pained as he swallows. "It's...good, Candy." He takes a long pull on his beer. I follow suit and immediately want to spit it back up in my napkin. It takes all my brainpower to tell my esophagus to push it down. The Bolognese sauce tastes sweet like she poured honey in it. I hope Lindsey can fake it. If not, I'm doomed.

"*Merci beaucoup!*" Candy smiles as she takes a bite. The table falls silent as Nick and Lindsey give me a questioning look. I hadn't told Candy anything about Paris, but the subject always makes us nervous. "What? Did I say something wrong? Don't you all *love* to go to Paris?"

"Why? What have you heard?" Nick gives her a hard stare as Lindsey starts to babble.

"Paris? It's okay, I mean, we were there for such a quick time. I don't even remember it. Food, bleh. Sights were good, but Italy was so much better, right Pattycakes?"

I choke on my roll and take a drink of beer. "Right."

"Why are y'all acting so weird?"

"We're not acting weird. *Jinx, you owe me a coke,*" Lindsey and I shout at the same time. Nick snorts and shakes his head as Lindsey shimmies in her seat. "I still got it, ha!"

"Uh, I believe I won that one." I bite into a roll. Candy looks at me like I've grown two heads.

"Just ignore them." Nick says. "So, Candy, what's in this?" He stirs his pasta with his fork.

Lindsey's eyes widen as she tries the pasta. "Oh wow, so…good. Is this Goofy's recipe?"

"Oh, it's called Pasta at the Park. The recipe called for some beef, red wine and onions, red pepper flakes…but onions upset my stomach, so I put in sweet pickles. Oh, and I added some sugar and ketchup to cut the red pepper's heat. I detest spicy food."

"Oh wow. That's…different." Lindsey stares at her bowl.

"Oh my god, you hate it, don't you?" Candy bristles next to me.

"No, babe, it's amazing." I try to soothe her by shoving a forkful into my mouth, swallowing it down without chewing. But she's not buying it, throwing her napkin on top of her food. Abruptly, she stands and storms out of the dining room. Nick and Lindsey's shocked faces mirror my own as I sigh and reluctantly get up to follow her into the kitchen.

She's violently scrubbing dishes as I place my hands on her arms and kiss her neck. "Candy, come back in and enjoy dinner. I know how hard you worked on it. Everyone is having a great time."

"Stop trying to coddle me, Pat! Your friends are so fucking hard to please. I can't take it! Do you know how hard it is to cook for a food critic?" she seethes.

Lindsey's eyes bug out as she enters the kitchen. I shoo

her away before Candy sees her.

"Candy, please calm down." I squeeze her waist and bend to kiss her shoulder. "No one said they didn't like your food."

"I'm not going to calm down. I have feelings, Pat, and I'm going to express them however I please. I hate it that she calls you Trick. It's not your name. I don't like that you'll be traveling again. What about *me?*"

Nick pops his head into the kitchen. "Uh, we're gonna head out, give you two some privacy."

I look up helplessly at my friends. Nick sets their plates down on the counter and steers Lindsey into the living room to grab their coats.

Lindsey pops her head back into the kitchen as I turn to lean against the counter. "Call me tomorrow. Thanks for dinner, Candy." Her eyes scream *run* as I nod in acknowledgment. I wait until the front door closes before I say anything.

"Want to tell me what the hell that was all about?" My skin feels hot as I turn toward Candy, who is still stewing at the kitchen sink.

"I don't like your friends, Pat. They're rude, and I think it's weird Lindsey and you are so close. Your best friend shouldn't be a woman, and there's something strange about Nick. He was staring at me with an odd expression during dinner. It made me super uncomfortable like he was hitting on me with his eyes."

What the fuck? I back away to get some space between us. "Just because Lindsey is a woman, we can't be friends? I've already explained there's nothing between us." I fold my arms over my chest. "I don't know what's gotten into you, Candy, but your behavior tonight has been completely erratic."

She turns to face me, her cheeks flushed. "Are you saying I have a substance abuse problem?"

Jesus, if I could use some Jedi mind trick on her right now and end this crazy night, I would in a heartbeat. "What? No, I never said that. Look, Lindsey is like a sister to me, nothing more. Nick only has eyes for Lindsey. Trust me, that man is completely besotted with her. It pains me that you don't like them. They are my family—you need to accept that."

"I don't want you to take whatever job Nick wants you to do next."

I look at her incredulously. "Candy, it's my *job*. Nick recently made me a producer of *Lindsey Love Loves*. It's not like I can say, nah, I'll catch you on the next one. If they replace me with someone else, then that's it. I'll be hanging out in the wind with nothing to fall back on."

"Please. Lindsey won't let that happen. She's your *family*, right?"

I scrub my hands down my face as I lean back against the counter—Lindsey was right. *Run.* "Where the hell is this coming from? It's like a switch has been flipped, and you're acting…" I press the heels of my hands into my eyeballs before I say something I'll regret. "Look, Candy, I enjoy my job. I love traveling. My friends make me happy."

"What about me? Don't I make you happy?"

I thought she did. Now I'm not so sure. "I want this to work between us, but I'm not going to give up my job or my friends."

She turns and wraps her arms around my waist. "I want a family, Pat. I want to get married and have lots of mini Pattycakes running around. I don't want you to travel anymore. Why can't you get a normal job and settle down? It's like I'm dating Peter Pan, the boy who doesn't want to grow up!"

I blow out a breath as I internally shut down, and the walls go up like a steel fortress. "My job is important to me, Candy. We've only known each other for two months. It seems a little premature to start talking marriage, don't you think?" I sound like a robot as I step out of her embrace. Decision made, I walk into her bedroom and grab some clothes and shoes I've kept here and shove them into a backpack.

"What are you doing?" she shrills from behind me.

"I think we want different things, Candy." Damn, my voice sounds so calm compared to how I'm feeling—like a volcano ready to blow. "Call me what you will, but I'm not ready to settle down and have kids. I'm taking whatever job Nick throws my way because I want to. I'm going to travel with Lindsey and her show because it makes *me* happy."

"Well, that's pretty fucking selfish."

"Yeah, I guess it is."

She tries to block my way out of the bedroom.

"Candy, don't." I sling the backpack over my shoulder and raise an eyebrow. "Let me leave, please."

Her eyes dart around the room nervously. "We'll talk about this tomorrow. You're upset. Take some time to breathe." She reluctantly steps back so that I can pass. I look at her over my shoulder as I open the front door.

"I don't want you to call me tomorrow or the next day. I think this relationship has run its course."

"You can't end this, not right before the holidays! My parents are expecting you for Thanksgiving!"

I shake my head as I walk through the door, feeling like I dropped a massive weight off my shoulders. "I just did."

Her shrill scream pierces the otherwise quiet hallway as I jog down the stairs and out of her life.

Chapter 4

Patrick

Gates of Hell

LINDSEY OPENS THE door, and I shuffle in, holding a bottle of wine. "Yay! I'm so glad you decided to come!" She throws her arms around me and squeezes me into a big hug. The noise coming from the family room and kitchen are loud and boisterous. I unwind my Millennium Falcon print scarf and shrug out of my jacket as Lindsey takes the bottle from me.

"I thought you said it was going to be Nick's parents and your family." My eyes dart around nervously.

"Oh, well, when Nick's sisters heard we were hosting Thanksgiving, they all decided to come! Fun, right?" Lindsey's eyes tell me it's been anything but. "I'm so glad you're here." She pulls me into a tight squeeze.

"It's going to be okay, Lovie." I chuckle, and then my face falls as I hear a buzz of women chatting in the kitchen. "Uh, look, there's something I've been meaning to tell you."

"Patrick, my man! So glad you could make it!" Nick walks into the foyer. He wraps Lindsey into his arms and kisses her neck. "Please don't make me go back in there."

Lindsey giggles. "Maybe the three of us can leave now. No one will even know."

"Uncle Little Dick, where's the bathroom?"

"Charlie! I told you not to call Uncle Nick that! Sorry, Nick." Nick's sister MK rushes in after a tow-headed boy holding his crotch. "Hi Patrick, nice to see you again, please excuse us! I have to make sure he doesn't pee all over the wall." She steers Charlie out of the foyer and into the guest bathroom.

"Wow, dude, I had heard the story, but they actually call you that?" I smirk.

Nick grimaces. "They even have a song about my little dick."

"Ouch." I hang my coat and scarf on the rack by the door.

"What did you want to tell me, Trick? Now's the time before we enter the gates of hell. You won't get a chance to get a word in from here on out."

"Yeah, I remember from the wedding." I grimace. "Thanks for inviting me to such a *fun* holiday event. A true best friend would have given me a heads-up on the way here so that I could have turned my car around and enjoyed a quiet peaceful night by myself."

Lindsey loops her arm in mine and laughs. "You're funny."

Nick claps my back, keeping his hand on my shoulder as they steer me toward the kitchen. I wouldn't be able to escape even if I tried. "Remember, dude, sidekick. I need you tonight."

"Beer me up."

"On it."

"What did you need to tell me?" Lindsey whispers.

"Patrick!" the kitchen choruses.

"Uh, it can wait."

Right now, I wish I were invisible. My eyes dart around the room. My shoulders sag in relief when I don't see her. I thought I heard her laugh, but it was probably her sister Bridget. All the Elliot sisters sound alike.

Lindsey tugs me farther into the kitchen. "Here's your mission if you choose to accept it. Can you find Shanny and ask her if Louisa wants turkey or if I need to make some chicken nuggets? I think Charlie wants chicken nuggets."

"Yes." I exhale, not even realizing I was holding my breath. "I can handle that. Is Aunt Mildew here?" I arch my neck, looking for the old bat that hit me with her purse at the wedding when I accidentally bumped into her. She kept referring to me as The Pervert at the farewell brunch the next day.

"No, thank God."

I spot Lindsey's sister, Shannon, talking to Nick's mom and make my way through the throng of women. Shannon squeezes me into a side-hug as she continues her conversation without missing a beat. "So that's the reason the channel is dry and creates pain."

"Oh, that explains everything." Nick's mom nods her head thoughtfully.

I pop a piece of cheese into my mouth from the tray on the counter. "What are you ladies talking about?"

"Oh, just talking about what creates vaginal irritation and dryness in older women during sexual intercourse."

The cheese gets lodged in my throat as I choke on her words. I start to thrash, trying in vain to get it to come back up.

"We've got a choker!" someone yells behind me and then bludgeons my back with their fist.

"No, you don't do it that way. Use both fists." Another pounding on my back results in me pitching forward into Shannon, but the cheese remains lodged. My vision starts to waver with the lack of oxygen going to my brain. I desperately claw at my throat as I turn in circles.

"Jesus Christ, get out of my way, you two." Nick gives me the Heimlich, and the cheese flies out of my mouth. Gasping, I bend over, thanking the heavens above for fresh air.

"Oh my God, Trick, are you okay? What happened?" Lindsey reaches me and lightly pats my back, handing me a bottle of water.

"Cheese…" I gasp, "Old lady dry channels…" I shiver in revulsion. "I saw a bright light, and then someone tried to kill me with a sledgehammer."

"That would be Arden and Bridget." Nick gives them a scathing glare.

Bridget bounces up to me and squeezes me into a big hug. "Patrick! Glad you're okay! You'll be sitting next to me tonight, but first, I need your predictions for the football games this afternoon. I'll need a twenty to enter the pool. Oh, and you'll need a spread, and because you're the last, you can't pick what someone else has unless that person is willing to split the pot, but I doubt it with this crowd. We're kind of competitive." Bridget holds out her hand and looks at me expectantly. I'm trying to keep up with what she's saying with all the chaos and conversations humming around me, not to mention that I almost died. I reach in my back pocket for my wallet and pull out a twenty.

"Put me down for whatever," I say hoarsely before gulping water.

"Jesus, B, give the guy a second to breathe before hitting him up for the football pool. He almost choked to death," Nick admonishes. Bridget ignores him as she plucks the twenty from my fingers. "Here's a beer, dude. Come on, let's go into the family room with my dad and brothers-in-law. It's too crazy in here."

"And then she said my dildo's stuck!" All the women in the kitchen erupt in laughter.

"Oh my god, Shanny! That's *not* a story for Thanksgiving Day!" Lindsey screeches as her face turns bright red. "Or any day!"

I've heard the story before because it's her sister's favorite about the time Lindsey called her because she couldn't get a dildo unstuck. I turn to Nick, who looks about as traumatized as I feel. "Great idea, dude, lead the way out of here."

We enter the family room, and my heart skips a beat when I see her.

Chapter 5

Kelsey

Foreplay

I SHRINK BACK against the couch cushions as Nick and Patrick enter the family room. Maybe he won't see me. When I heard Lindsey talking to him in the foyer, I hid in their downstairs bedroom to calm myself down. *Why is he here?* Okay, I know why he's here. He's Lindsey's best friend. He was in their wedding. *I* was in their wedding. He's practically family, which makes what we did kind of incestuous, right? Not really. We're not family. We're not anything. *Calm the fuck down, Kelsey!* We're just two people who had a hot drunken one-night stand. We were the typical cliché of wedding party *what not to do's*, and we haven't spoken since I snuck out of his room in the early dawn. The chances of me running into him were slim to never.

Now he's standing here in Nick's living room holding a beer looking sexier than I remember. He's tall and lanky with broad shoulders, but under that lean build are muscles that made my fingertips dance with delight. His silky chocolate-brown hair is curled and mussed, but short on the sides. He's wearing glasses tonight, and they bring a whole new level of hotness I wasn't even aware I found attractive. But I do. I find him incredibly attractive. I shift uncomfortably in my corner of the sectional. His long legs stretch out as he folds himself into a chair. He waves hello to all the men in the room before his eyes land on me, and he nods.

"Kelsey."

"Patrick."

Awkward. As. Fuck.

I immediately shift my attention to the game on the big screen, but I can feel his stare lingering. It makes me feel naked, exposed, and incredibly more turned-on than it should. It was a one-time thing. I haven't thought about it at all.

Liar.

I take a healthy sip of the whiskey in my tumbler. My sister Arden raised her eyebrows when I poured it earlier, but what she doesn't know is that I'm barely hanging on by a thread.

My eyes have a mind of their own as they wander back to Patrick. He's like a magnet I keep pinging back to. No matter how much I try to ignore him, the laws of physics override. I suck my bottom lip between my teeth. *Those glasses.* My brain procures naughty images of him with his shirt off reading with his sexy glasses on. *No, Kelsey, bad!* Think of the cleaning products you have to write about for your new job. I sink lower into the couch cushions, suddenly feeling depressed.

"When did you start wearing the glasses?" I blurt out. My eyes zip around the room wondering if anyone heard me. *Did I say that out loud?* It's like the whiskey temporarily rewired my brain into thinking I needed to talk to him. I immediately focus on the game, praying he didn't hear me.

Out of the corner of my eye, Patrick leans forward and clasps his hands. "Are you talking to me?"

I look over at my brother Nick, his brows knitted in confusion. My eyes slide to Patrick, and my heart starts thundering in my chest. "You're the only one wearing glasses, so…" Damn, I can be such a prickly bitch. What am I even doing? Why am I flirting with him? I snort and look away when he raises an eyebrow. You are a sad, sad case, Kelsey Elliot, if this your idea of flirting.

He didn't mind it at the wedding—the little annoying voice in my head whispers. We were drunk at the wedding. We danced like we were in the final rounds of *Dancing with the Stars*. We even tried to do the scene in *Dirty Dancing*.

I stand up suddenly, knocking back the rest of the whiskey. It rolls in my stomach, burning my throat. All eyes turn to me, so of course, I open my big fat mouth.

"Going to the bathroom," I mumble as I stalk toward the hall bathroom. I'm almost to the promised land when I can feel movement behind me.

"Kelsey, wait." I try to shut the door in his face, but he stops it with his quick reflexes. He leans into the doorframe. "What gives?"

"What do you mean?" I ask innocently. Ugh, I wish he'd stop staring at me so intensely. It's making my knees turn to jelly.

"I mean, are we going to talk about what happened between us?"

Good God, no. "I don't think there's much to say…"

"I disagree." His voice is smoky and deep. He leans into

my personal space, and he smells of ocean and green grass. "There's a lot to say."

The sound of his voice and his smell evoke a disturbingly erotic memory that I haven't been able to erase from my brain for the past six months. I sway toward him and then shake my head. I can't sleep with Patrick again, drunken mistake or not. He's Lindsey's best friend. He *works* for my brother and Lindsey. If things went sour between us…well, it would end up exactly like this. Every family gathering, I'd have to sweat it out, not knowing if he'd show up or not. Awkward moments shared across the dinner table. Good god, if my sisters ever found out about this, I'd never live it down. No, thank you.

"Patrick, look…you're a really sweet guy."

"Cut the crap, Kelsey. Don't give me some lame *it's not you, it's me* speech."

"Wow, okay then. *It's you, not me.*"

He rears his head back, and I take the opportunity to slam the door shut, almost taking off his hand.

"Can I please pee alone now?" I gripe obnoxiously. I check myself out in the mirror and take in my flushed cheeks and wide eyes. Maybe I was a little too harsh. Guilt washes over me as I swing the door back open. "Patrick, look, I'm sorry…"

I sigh at the empty hallway and bang my head on the doorjamb. Regret needles my heart like a thousand tiny pinpricks. It's for the best, I tell myself as I head toward the kitchen where I can get lost in the chaos of my sisters.

Chapter 6

Patrick

Who Wants Pumpkin Pie

BRIDGET BEAMS AT me as she passes me the dish of stuffing. She's extremely sweet and likable, unlike her sourpuss brooding sister across the table, who is doing everything in her power to avoid my gaze. What happened to the fun sweet Kelsey from the wedding? She keeps calling me Star Boy, and I'm a hundred percent sure it's not a term of endearment. It rankles me because I'm thinking maybe she can't remember my name, although it would be hard to miss since Bridget keeps calling me Patrick every fifteen seconds.

"So Patrick, what are you and Lindsey planning on doing next?"

I look down the table at Lindsey, who sits with a frozen smile on her face as Shannon explains hot flashes to Nick's mom. *Yes, Alex, I'll take Bridget peppering me with a thousand questions about Lindsey Love Loves over her obstetrician sister for two thousand, please.*

"Well, we were supposed to go to Africa, but that trip has been postponed."

"Oh no, why?"

"Severe hurricanes are coming off the coast. JD, the veter—"

"Oh, I know all about JD! I follow him religiously on Instagram. He's so dreamy…"

"Uh, yeah, well anyway, he wants to do that this summer, so he's set up a new sho—"

"Oh my god, no!" Bridget squeals, causing me to jump in my chair. Everyone stops their chatter and looks at us. "*Lindsey Love Loves*, and Dr. JD Evans are doing a show together?"

"No, uh…no, I did *not* say that." I look around for someone to help me out.

"Lindsey, you didn't tell me you'd be leaving again!" Lindsey's mom gives her an annoyed look. "Where are you going? Who's going to watch Mac? Who's going to watch Olive? Your father and I are going to be cruising the Med!" Lindsey's parents 'gifted' her their cat Mac when they retired and started traveling. He is the most cantankerous cat I've ever met.

"Mom, calm down. We're going to Miami for a few weeks." Lindsey glares at me. I shovel a forkful of mashed potatoes into my mouth, averting my gaze. "We got a house sitter to take care of Mac, and I'm going to bring Olive with us. Can you pass the brussels sprouts?"

Kelsey's fork freezes in midair. "You're going to Miami? When?"

"Lindsey, you can't bring that baby on tour with you!"

"On tour?" Lindsey smirks at Shannon. "Mom, I'm not a musician."

"We could take Olive back to New York with us," Nick's mom chimes in. "Oh wait, we're leaving town after the holidays for Utah…"

"Oh, that's very nice of you to offer—"

"No, no, no, if Olive is going to stay with someone, it's going to be with us." Shannon smiles serenely.

"But you're so busy with work and the girls, and Dan has to check on Mac…he likes to be pet while he eats." Lindsey's mom worries her napkin.

"I adore Olive, I'd be hap—" Dan tries to intercede.

"Olive can come to New York and stay with us for a week, and then we can ship her over to MK's or Arden's house when we go to Utah." Nick's mom looks over at MK for approval.

"Olive is not an animal to be passed around!" Lindsey shouts, causing the table to fall silent again.

"Olive will be coming with us," Nick says with quiet finality.

"Well, that's nice, dear, but what about when you guys are filming? Surely you can't bring her along with you to the restaurants," Nick's mom frets. "Oh, wait! I have the perfect plan!" She snaps her fingers. "Kelsey, didn't you say you wanted to go visit Kiernan in Miami before you started the job at the paper? This is perfect! You can help with Olive!"

Kelsey spits out her wine all over her plate. "What?! No, no, I don't even—"

Nick glares at his mom. "Absolutely not! She taught Charlie that song—"

"Wait, what do you mean, absolutely not?" Kelsey stares at Nick indignantly. "You don't trust me?"

Nick rubs his forehead. "Remember the time when Kelsey was sixteen and she 'accidentally' reversed the car over Bridget's prop doll for the school play?"

"Oh yes, that was a shame. Poor Polly Pullup's head kept falling off, and she never did quite cry the same after that."

"And remember she left Lizzie in the stroller outside that boutique in town with the old pigeon-feeding lady, because she saw a hot guy inside?"

"Totally did *not* happen like that, Arden." Kelsey rolls her eyes at Nick. "I mean, it was for a split-second. She was fine! She liked the birds."

"And remember the time she taught Charlie and Emma to say the word shit-balls or the song about my little dick? Hello? Have we already forgotten *that* little gem?"

Mr. and Mrs. Love cough into their napkins.

"Now, Nick, that's enough. Really dear, that's just sad the way you're trying to throw Kelsey under the bus when she's already feeling nervous about this new job," Mrs. Elliot chastises. "And let's not talk about your little appendages at the dinner table, please."

Nick's face turns beet red. "But, she...they...it's *not* little!"

I almost burst out laughing but manage to cough into my napkin instead. I've never seen Nick this flustered before.

"Oh no, I think Patrick is choking again!" Bridget thumps my back hard.

"No, I'm good!" I rear away from her. Damn, she has a lethal blow.

"Lindsey, a little help here, please?" Nick looks across the table at Lindsey imploringly.

"I think it's a great idea," Lindsey says as she cuts her turkey. "Your mom is right, we will need help. Kelsey can be there—"

"Uh, hello? Don't I get a say in the matter?" Kelsey mutters.

Lindsey looks beseechingly at Kelsey. "It would be so great to have some help with Olive from a family member rather than having to hire a babysitting service." She turns her attention to Nick. "I feel confident that she won't run Olive over or teach her new words because she's not at that stage yet, and it will be nice to have some girl time while we're traveling, right, Kels? And according to your mom, you wanted to go. It's a win-win!"

"Sure, but—"

"Great, it's settled." Lindsey beams while Nick looks like he swallowed something sour.

I grudgingly look over at Kelsey as I raise my beer to my lips. I have mixed emotions about this new proposition. Having Kelsey with us will mean I'll see her every day. That in itself is enough torture, but the fact that she pretends like our night together didn't even exist cuts deep. I can't stop thinking about it. It's stuck in my head like a porno on repeat. Her blue eyes collide with mine, my stomach twisting because I can't tell what she's thinking.

Nick snaps his fingers. "Patrick can watch Olive for us! Kelsey said so herself—she'll be busy with Kiernan. Besides, she probably can't stay as long as we'll need her. She has a job at the paper she'll need to start."

Wait, what? I lean forward in my seat, glaring at Nick. "Uh, I'm not a nanny."

"But you're my sidekick..." Nick gives me a pleading look, and I crumble.

"I mean, I'm sure I can hold her in a Baby Bjorn during

filming…"

Bridget sighs next to me. "Aw, that's so adorable!" I flinch as she grabs onto my arm and squeezes.

Kelsey's eyes flash like lightning in a stormy sea as she glares at me. "You know what, Lindsey? I'll take the job. Little Dick, draw up the paperwork so I can sign on the dotted line or whatever you need me to do."

Lindsey's mom claps giddily. "Oh, thank goodness, having her at home was getting to be a little much. Who wants pumpkin pie?"

"Mom!"

"Fuck my life," Nick mutters as the mashed potatoes suddenly feel like lead in my stomach. I agree with his sentiments exactly.

Chapter 7

Kelsey

The Hot Nerd Next Door

LINDSEY GIVES ME a brief tour of the house they've rented in Coconut Grove that we'll all be sharing for the next few weeks. I envisioned a lumpy futon or a pull-out couch for my bed, but this ranch house has three spacious bedrooms, an office where Olive will sleep, a cozy living room, a huge kitchen, and a two-car garage. It also boasts a saltwater pool and a two-minute walk to the beach. It's incredible, and I feel bad that I haven't been completely honest with Nick and Lindsey as to the real reason I'm here. What they don't know is that I'm interviewing for a job.

After Thanksgiving, everything just kind of fell into place. I talked to my cousin Kiernan whose friend Marco works at *The Miami Times*. He pushed my resume into his boss's hands as a favor to Kiernan. The depressing part? I don't have much on there to boast over, so my hopes aren't high. A year of freelance writing for local magazines while I redecorated my house and twiddled my thumbs while my fiancé diddled his office manager isn't going to wow the socks off anyone. But as Marco reminded me, it's a chance. A second chance that could change everything.

There's no way I can go back to New York and work at that stuffy Ithaca newspaper writing a column about different cleaning products each week under the name of Miss Cookie. I mean, who the hell needs to read about how to make your grout sparkling white? Go to your local home improvement store, and they'll tell you what to get. But not in Ithaca, no siree. The blue-haired ladies want to read about the how-tos from Miss Cookie's housekeeping column. My dad was so excited because he helped me get the job. He's friends with Mr. Pennington, the editor in chief. How could I turn it down and disappoint him?

But I don't want to live in Ithaca. It's been bad enough that my fiancé left me, and I've been living at my parents' house for the past eight months. A few years ago, I thought my life was sailing along smoothly. After a brief stint at a local paper, I landed an interview with *The New York Times*, a job I'd always dreamed of, but a month later, my fiancé Todd was offered to take over a family medicine practice in Ithaca. An opportunity he couldn't pass up. So, I begrudgingly went along and put my dreams on hold. We were going to be married last year when he decided he liked giving his assistant tonsil checks with his tongue a little bit more than spending the rest of his life with me.

Lindsey opens a door, bringing me back to the present. "And this will be your room."

"Oh, I'm at the opposite end of the hall from Olive's room?" *Right next to Patrick's room.*

Lindsey mentioned that Nick and Patrick are meeting their veterinarian friend JD over at his clinic in South Beach, so luckily, I won't run into him right now. I've convinced myself that I'll have no problem avoiding him since he'll be busy with Lindsey's show and helping Nick. Miami is a big city, after all.

"Nick and I don't expect you to get up in the middle of the night with Olive, Kels. The office is right next to our room, so it's perfect. To be honest, we probably could have managed just fine on our own, but you seemed sad at Thanksgiving—"

"I'm not a charity case." I grind my teeth as I look around.

"Oh, I know you're quite capable, but I thought it might be a nice break from your mom and dad's, and I do think it will be fun to hang out in Miami together. Plus, it will be helpful not to worry about having a stranger from a babysitting service watch Olive when we go out for restaurant shoots. I mean, I know you need to see your cousin too, but we're grateful you could help us out."

I sit down on the bed. "I'm sorry, I don't mean to sound ungrateful. I appreciate what you and Nick are doing for me. I was losing myself on my parents' couch watching soap operas every day. I'm floundering, and everything is hinging on this…"

Lindsey looks at me curiously. I reach back and grab a throw pillow and fluff it.

"Well, anyway, I'm grateful to you guys for this opportunity."

She sits next to me and squeezes me into a side-hug. She is so sweet, and it's nice to get away from my sisters' constant badgering. I exhale slowly as I think about how it sucks to be the middle child. You're always the last to get your say, the last to get noticed. You have to be independent and confident in being a middle child, things I'm currently lacking. I feel like I'm quietly drowning, and no one in my family seems to care.

"Of course, we're happy to have you here."

I quickly wipe away a tear. Damn, I never get this emotional. Exhaustion and depression overriding my usual sensibilities.

"Aw, what's wrong?" Lindsey squeezes me again. "Is it Todd? You can talk to me."

"No, I'm done crying over that jerk. It's just…Bridget is finishing up her internship at the hospital. MK has her cute little gift shop in Ithaca, Arden is a successful lawyer, Nick is an Emmy award-winning producer, and I'm…" I flop my arms helplessly.

"And you are Kelsey, an amazing sister, daughter, aunt, and friend. You will be the queen of clean, the next Martha Stewart of cleaning products…or something. I'm not that good at cleaning." Lindsey squeezes me and pops up. "Wanna go eat and drink our feelings? I saw a cute little Mexican joint two streets over."

"What about Olive?" I look at the sleeping baby strapped to Lindsey's front.

"Well, I'll eat, you can drink." She winks at me. "We'll gossip about guys, and that awful new reality show *Miami Heat* starring that annoying Sonja girl. Ooh! Maybe we can find out where they're filming and try and sneak on set."

"That sounds like the last thing I want to do." I laugh as I swipe my cheeks free of tears. "Okay, let's go drink my problems away, but we're not talking about Nick. I don't ever want to know what he's like in the bedroom."

"No problem, I save all that for Trick." She laughs. "Oh, by the way, I hope you don't mind, but you'll have to share a bathroom with him. It's a jack and jill. Don't worry, he's tidy and doesn't leave the seat up," she says casually over her shoulder as she walks out of the bedroom.

"Sure, no problem," I murmur as I stop in the doorway of Patrick's room and look around like a creeper. The Star Wars blanket on his bed makes me smirk. The room smells like him, and it makes my pulse quicken. Woodsy and masculine. I take a deep breath and think back to our one night together. I want to wash my clothes in his scent and roll around in it until the day I die. *Geez, Kelsey, dramatic much?* Maybe, but I can't help myself.

So much for thinking I won't ever see him while I'm here. Not only do we have bedrooms right next to each other, but we'll be sharing a bathroom. *Forget about Patrick.* I can't let anything derail me this time—especially not a tall, brown-eyed, Star Wars-loving man.

"Kels? What are you doing?"

"Coming!" I call out as I close his door to whatever I'm feeling. Maybe a few drinks will help me erase this tangle of emotions squeezing my heart.

Chapter 8

Patrick

Dawn and Spike

JD CLAPS A hand on my shoulder, bringing my attention back to the present. "Isn't it great? I wanted you guys to see the facility first before committing to the project. Adventure Animals wants to bring you on, Nick. You have to say yes. Filming will start in a few weeks, and then I figure we'll head back to Africa for the rhino angle. I'm super pumped about this!"

"Whoa, whoa, let's slow down a little." Nick tries to calm JD down as a nurse walks by holding a six-foot boa constrictor. Not a fan of snakes, I immediately back up against the wall.

"Come on, let's chat in my office." JD leads us down a hallway and opens the door to a spacious, bright modern room. Files are stacked on his desk in front of a Mac laptop. He plunks down in his seat and motions for us to sit in the chairs opposite him. "Look, Adventure Animals isn't a big company, but if we can get this show rolling, a major network might want to pick it up."

"It sounds great, but what exactly is your goal for the viewers, and how do I fit into this?"

"Animal education is my number-one goal. I want to create something fresh. We see all sorts of exotic animals here. I want to show what it's like to give a snake a check-up, trim a cockatoo's nails, or give a cheetah a physical exam. I want to share how amazing these animals are with everyone." He bridges his hands as he looks at Nick. "I trust you, Nick. I don't trust the people at Adventure Animals. They must really want this, though, because I demanded that we bring you on as executive producer, and they said okay."

Nick looks wary as he takes the file on Adventure Animals JD slides toward him. "Why hasn't Adventure Animals contacted me?"

"They wanted me to feel you out first."

"I need to meet with their production crew to get with their producer and director. I think this has the potential to be great. Will you be the only one we're filming here, or will you have a supporting doctor and staff?"

"Mainly, it will just be me. I have two other doctors on staff here, but one of them isn't keen to be on camera. Something about personal integrity and turning into a reality star. Her prerogative. The staff has all signed off and are excited for filming to start."

Nick looks over at me and smirks. "Shame you're over-seeing the production crew for Lindsey's show now."

JD's face falls in disappointment. "No, Patrick? I can't do it without you, bud. Did you see Lucy out there? The one that walked by us?" JD waggles his eyebrows.

"The nurse that passed us? I mean, she was cute, but…"

JD laughs. "I was talking about the snake. Lucy is a yellow python."

"Oh, uh yeah, I'd have to pass on that one. Not much of a snake person."

Nick grins and arches an eyebrow. "Lindsey has a full production crew from Food and Travel now that her show has taken off. I asked Patrick to head it up since I'll be here."

I breathe out a sigh of relief. I loved filming with JD and Nick in Africa. The excitement was palpable, but the exotic animals and the vet clinic don't interest me as much. Snakes and lizards aren't my jam. I sense JD's disappointment. "Yeah, look, I'll help out any way I can, JD, but I am committed to Lindsey's show while we're in Miami."

A knock on the door grabs JD's attention as a brunette nurse pokes her head in and blushes when she sees us. "Sorry to interrupt, Dr. Evans, but your three-thirty appointment is in room six."

"Thanks, Carly, I'll be right there." JD stands up and swings on a white doctor's coat. "Duty calls. If you want to stick around, I'll be examining and determining the sex of Spike the iguana."

Nick chuckles. "Spike might be a girl?"

"Might be." JD wraps his stethoscope around his neck.

"Uh, I'm going to pass on that." I stand up and stretch my legs.

JD laughs and turns to Nick. "I see what you mean."

"Hey, I can handle watching Spike get sexed, but if given a choice, I'd rather not."

JD claps me on the back. "Come on, it will be a first for everyone in the room but me. It's my last appointment, and then we can go grab a beer after."

I look over my shoulder at Nick, but he doesn't look up

as he chuckles while texting something on his phone. Great, I'd prefer filming Lindsey gagging on a frog leg than iguana sexing 101.

JD knocks and then opens the door. "Hi there, I'm—"

"Dr. JD Evans! Oh my god, I am fangirling so much right now! Dawn Fitzburger, it's such an honor." She pumps his hand enthusiastically. "I have waited six months for this appointment. *Six months!* It's *so* hard to get an appointment with you. Agh! I can't believe you're standing right in front of me, and you're even more gorgeous in person! Oh my gosh, I can't believe I just said that. Eek! I'm so excited."

By the sound of overzealous Dawn, you would think she was a high school cheerleader, but no, she's a forty-three-year-old third-grade teacher from South Beach with a love of knitting, books, and scary movies. She's also a big-time coffee addict, a romance reader, and is *not married, just to be clear.*

Nick and I slide into the exam room as Dawn prattles on, still clenching JD's hand. He flashes his movie-star smile and tries to tug his hand out of her grip, but Dawn is not letting go. Nick coughs as he tries not to laugh and leans against the far wall.

As soon as Dawn pauses for a breath, JD jumps in. "Dawn, it's a pleasure to meet you, and I'm so honored that you waited six months to see me. Should we take a look at Spike? I'll need both hands." He winks at her, and she simpers as she sits back down. That's when she finally notices us.

"Oh my, you frightened me! I didn't even see you two standing there. Three handsome men in the same room, to what do I owe the pleasure?"

"Oh, I'm sorry, this is Patrick Healy and Nick Elliot. They will be helping with a television show we will be doing in a few weeks here at the cl—"

"STOP. IT!" Dawn slams her hand down on the seat next to her. She adjusts her glasses, her cheeks pinking as she stands up. "Do you think Spike and I could come back to be on the show? That would be so amazing! Wait until the teachers at Coconut Bay Elementary hear about this!"

"Oh...uh...of course, we'd be honored to have you on..." JD looks over at us, and I have to bite my lip to keep from laughing. "We'll set it up with Carly, my assistant, once we're done here." He turns his attention to Spike sitting docilely on the exam table. "Okay, so has Spike been behaving normally, eating, drinking..."

"Yes!" Dawn pushes her glasses up as she eagerly looks up at JD.

"That's great. Patrick, can you come here for a second?"

"Me?" I look between JD and Dawn. "Why not Nick?"

"I'm allergic, sidekick." Nick grins, but I know he's full of shit. Who's allergic to reptiles?

"Please?" JD looks at me imploringly.

Grudgingly, I get up and walk over to the exam table. Dawn beams at me as JD puts his stethoscope on and listens to the lizard's heartbeat and belly. The smile freezes on my face as I stare at the giant lizard. "I need you to hold Spike so I can show Dawn some things."

I swallow and look at Spike. Befitting its name, it has spikes down its back and a massive tail, not to mention its talon-like claws. Where the hell is Carly? "Maybe you should call Carly in here."

"Patrick, it will only take a minute."

I swallow. "Is it going to bite?"

"Spike is a lover, not a fighter, but don't touch his tail. He doesn't like it. Well, I call him a *he*, I guess we'll have to wait and find out! The kids will be tickled pink if it's a girl," Dawn gushes next to me.

"This thing is your classroom *pet*?" My voice cracks as I imagine this mini-dragon crawling around on the floor chasing after terrified screaming children. It has to be like thirty pounds of lizard. Dawn ignores me, all eyes on JD, sighing as she watches him perform his exam. He removes his stethoscope and winks at her.

Without so much as a 'here, hold this,' he picks up Spike and places him on my chest.

"Uh, JD? Nick?" I start to panic as I try to hold it away from me, but his claws are already embedded in my shirt. Its long tongue flicks the air. Oh my god, this thing will taste my fear and eat me. But no one is paying any attention. JD is talking about the spikes down his back and the bumps on his forehead on the meaty part of his eye. Nick is laughing as he types something on his phone, and Dawn is entirely enraptured by JD.

Spike is freaking heavy as he sits like a gargoyle on my chest as JD picks up the flappy-looking skin under his chin and then shows Dawn the bumps on the inside of his back leg, signifying that Spike is indeed a male. They start discussing diet as Spike's claws dig into me as he slowly starts to crawl up toward my shoulder, his tongue flickering out. He bobs his head.

"Uh, JD?"

He flashes me a quick grin, but his attention returns to Dawn, who *won't stop fucking talking.* Spike hisses, and I panic, my hand accidentally grabbing onto his tail which is swishing. Wrong move on my part. He scrambles up my shoulder, one leg poised on my head like he's going to climb on top of it. I scream as I feel his talons dig into my face.

"Get this fucking thing off of me!" I whirl around as JD tries to grab Spike while Dawn is screaming and Nick is doubled-over in the corner laughing his ass off. At least, I think that's what he's doing. It's hard to tell with the blood dribbling down into my eye. "Get it off!" I shout over and over.

"Is he having a seizure? What is he screaming?" Dawn yells over the ruckus.

I'm about to toss Spike into a wall when his tail comes off in my hand. I start screaming along with Dawn as I throw the tail on the exam table.

"What the hell is that? Why did his tail just fall off? Get this fucker off of me!"

JD finally manages to pry him off my head and safely wraps him in a towel on the table.

"I told you not to touch his tail," Dawn snaps at me. "It's going to take months for it to regrow, right, Dr. Evans? Poor Spikey, is he in any pain? Can that harm him? It will grow back, right? Oh, my poor Spike-a-doodles! Baby, it's going to be okay! Mama's here...shh...mama's here, Spikey Poo," she coos and snuggles the fucking dragon on the table like it's an adorable fluffy puppy. "Thank goodness the handsome doctor was there to save you. I sure hope that lizard killer won't be on the show, right, Spikey-bear? That might cause some lawsuits."

Something drips down my forehead. My fingers touch the area and come away with blood. I sway, feeling woozy as I turn.

"Dude, you might want to go have one of the nurses clean your forehead off." JD grimaces as he glances up at me while he checks Spike over for any other injuries. The damn dragon is getting more attention, and he's the one that turned into a full-on Godzilla attack machine. "Dawn, I assure you Spike is going to be okay. It's a defense mechanism. It will grow back."

"Oh, Dr. Evans." She starts to cry as she wraps him in a tight squeeze. "You're the best."

Nick apologizes to Dawn, who snivels into JD's lab coat, not letting him go. He follows me out into the hallway with a big grin on his face.

"That by far was the funniest fucking thing I've ever seen." He pauses and puts a hand on my shoulder. "You don't look so good. You look like you got in a fight with an iguana, and the lizard won."

"He was like fifty pounds! And his nails were five inches long! And his fucking tail can fall off? A heads-up on that one would have been nice! And that lady...she just wouldn't shut up!"

Nick laughs as he waves to one of the nurses working in the lab. "My friend here got a nasty gash from a lizard." He starts laughing again and walks away to compose himself.

"Some sidekick you are!" I yell as another nurse leads me over to a counter.

"Oh, this looks bad, but I don't think you'll need stitches. How did a lizard claw your forehead?"

"I accidentally grabbed his tail," I mumble, utterly humiliated as she tries to keep a straight face. She doesn't need to know the details of how he was on top of my head.

I rejoin Nick out in the hallway, and he laughs when he sees the Hello Kitty Band-Aid across my forehead.

"Not a word. It's all she had."

"Nice. Should we wait in JD's office and give him and Dawn a minute alone?"

"Yup." We walk back to his office, and all I can think is thank god I won't be working on JD's show.

Chapter 9

Kelsey

Spanx

I BURST OUT laughing as I stumble into the family room and spot Patrick with a Hello Kitty Band-Aid across his forehead. "Did you get in a lightsaber fight, Luke Skywalker? Or did an asteroid hit your head?" Yes, I'm obnoxious, but I'm also slightly tipsy. If I were the least bit sober, I would have pretended he wasn't there. I weave into the kitchen wall and bump my head. Ow, okay, I'm pretty sozzled.

"Lindsey, what the hell? Why is Kelsey drunk?"

"I'm not drunk." I hold up my hand but then think better of it as I start to lose my balance. Nick glares at me and folds his arms over his chest.

"Well, it was buy-one, get-one margarita night at the cutest little—"

"She had two margaritas?" Nick growls. "She can barely stand."

I silently tick the number of drinks I had off my fingers as my brother stews. "More like six." I shove off the wall and stand up straight but feel myself tilting over toward the couch.

"*Six?*"

"They were yummy." I stumble over to the couch and flop down next to Patrick. Lindsey goes into Olive's bedroom, and Nick follows her, crabbing about six margaritas.

"I don't know what his problem is. Six is my lucky number." I turn my head against the pillows and smile at Patrick. "Hi, it's good to see you again."

"Yeah, I hope it's as pleasant as the last time." He side-eyes me grumpily.

"Apparently, you and I are going to be next-door neighbors."

"Huh?"

"We're sharing a bathroom…you and me."

"Will you slam my face in the door in that one too?"

Ouch. I deserve that. I need to make Patrick my friend if we're sharing a house, but I don't have much finesse at the moment. "I like your Band-Aid. Meow." He ignores me, which spurs me on even more. "Does it have magical powers?" I whisper not so quietly.

"Does what have magical powers?" His jaw ticks in annoyance.

"Your lightsaber." I giggle and can't stop. *God, I'm funny.* Patrick doesn't seem to think so, though. "Oh wait, I've seen your sword." I raise my eyebrows up and down suggestively. "It *is* magical. Like unicorns."

"Did you just compare my dick to unicorns?"

"Maybe I did, maybe I didn't. It's been so long since I've seen one. Any guy's dick would be a unicorn to me."

Patrick looks over at me and laughs. "Wow, you should drink margaritas more often. They're like a Sith truth potion."

"Mmm, what's a sif?"

"Sith, truth serum."

"Never heard of it. Is this one of your *Star Wars* sayings?" My stomach lurches, and I know my night isn't going to end well. I try to sit up but instead, I roll off the couch and land with a thud on the floor. "Ow."

"Oh my god, Kelsey, are you okay?"

"Mm-kay," I mumble into the rug. Right here seems like the perfect place to sleep tonight.

His strong hands lift me from under my armpits. Nothing screams 'I've got my shit together' like having a guy haul you up from your armpits. I could think of a hundred other places where I'd like his hands. His fingers graze my boob, and I can't help but giggle because it tickles. He scoops me up like I weigh less than a bag of flour and walks down the hall holding me like a groom crossing the threshold with his bride. I try to suck in my stomach, but it's too much, so I let it heave out. I try again, but it makes me want to puke. My stomach pooches as I blow my breath out.

"Are you going to throw up? Your stomach is doing some weird shit." Great, did he see that little display of pretending I'm a size two?

"Spanx...spanxies are a girl's BFF," I ramble as my head lolls back on his shoulder, trying to convey that I wish I had worn my Spanx because they are a girl's best friend.

"You want me to spank you?" Patrick looks flummoxed, and I break out into hysterical giggles.

"Not spanks, Spanx! Spanx!"

"I uh...I don't know what you want me to do, but I'm going to take a pass tonight."

"Where we goin', Mr. Luke Skywalker?" I try to sound sexy using a killer British accent, but it comes out garbled.

Patrick looks at me funny. "Are you okay? Do you have something stuck in your mouth? Say 'ahhh' so I can check you're not choking on something."

"Ahhh…I'm fine. I was trying to talk Brish. I think I've had too many margs."

"Uh-huh. What exactly is Brish?"

"Brish!" I slur impatiently, annoyed he's ruining my game of friendly banter. "Ugh, just forget it. It's over. Over and done."

Patrick gently puts me down on my bed, and I curl into a ball. There's a light breeze coming off the ocean from my open window, which causes me to shiver. He pulls a throw blanket over me as he looks down, concern etched across his face. He lightly runs a finger down my cheek. His stare is too intense, too intimate. I close my eyes to escape it.

"I haven't been able to stop thinking about you." His voice is quiet and tender.

His words are a punch to the gut, knocking the air from my lungs. Is he crazy? He must be. I can't get involved with Patrick. He's my sister-in-law's best friend. He's *Nick's* best friend. It would mess up the symbiotic friendship they share.

The truth is, I haven't been able to stop thinking about him either. He made me feel things that night I've never felt with anyone else before. But I can't let his soft-spoken words tear down the wall I've built up around my heart. I'm not ready to get involved with anyone. I suddenly feel sober and depressed.

"Patrick, it's complicated…we were drunk."

"We weren't that drunk. I knew what I was doing." I hear his smile and catch a quick glimpse. He's right, he did. Dammit, I wish I could say screw it and see what it would be like to have Patrick touch me again. My fingers inch toward the sliver of exposed skin right above the waistband of his jeans.

"Trick? We brought back some food for you!" Lindsey calls down the hall.

"I'll be there in a sec!" He turns back to me, and I tightly squeeze my eyes shut, quickly tucking my hand under my chin. "Kelsey, I..."

I pretend to snore so that he'll leave me in my self-wallowing misery.

"I'm not giving up, Kels." He brushes a featherlight kiss on my brow.

I chance a peek as Patrick exits my room, my heart fluttering as fast as a butterfly trapped in a net. The real reason I never called Patrick burns a hole in the pit of my stomach.

The real reason is that I wanted more from him and that scares the ever-living shit out of me.

Chapter 10

Patrick

Bagels and Bitterness

I'M WASHING DISHES when the night of the living dead walks in and grabs a mug from the counter and fills it with coffee from the French press.

"Rough night?" I smirk as I run a plate under warm water.

"You have no idea." She takes cream out of the fridge and adds it to her coffee. "Where are Nick and Lindsey?"

"They took Olive for a walk."

She grumbles something unintelligible as she walks back out of the kitchen. I want to talk with her since we're alone, but now isn't exactly the best time to pull out a deep, meaningful conversation from her. I turn the water off and follow her.

"Hey, I thought maybe you and I could go grab dinner tonight?" I call to her retreating form.

"No thanks." She walks into her bedroom and slams her door shut.

"Well, that went well." I wipe my hands on a dishtowel and toss it on my shoulder as I pick up my cup of coffee and take a drink. The front door opens and quietly shuts.

"Hey Patrick, it's just us. We bought some bagels. Is Kelsey still sleeping?" Lindsey asks quietly as Nick lifts a sleeping Olive out of the stroller.

"She's up and got some coffee, but she's not real chatty."

Nick smirks. "She bite your head off? Bridget's the morning person."

"I think she's hungover. Nothing my super Saturday-morning eggs and bacon can't fix." I get out some eggs, whipping them in a bowl.

"We're going to check out some restaurants today the viewers of the show have requested. Sound good?"

"Oh, cool, absolutely. I can't wait to see where they want you to eat." I waggle my eyebrows at Lindsey, and she grimaces. We opened up a *Food and Travel* contest a couple of months ago for a viewers' choice. The popularity of it exploded, so we've asked viewers to pick some places in Miami for her to try.

"I know it's going to be some kind of weird shit. The ratings skyrocket every time I'm forced to eat something weird."

"I can't wait until we can go to Asia and Russia." I rub my hands together maniacally.

"Well, fortunately for me, that's not happening until Olive is a little older." Lindsey punches me in the arm as she pops a bagel into the toaster. "Everything bagel?"

"Nah, plain, please. I hate it when the poppy seeds get stuck in my teeth."

"I'll take his everything." I turn around at the sound of her voice and smirk. *I'd give her my everything if she'd let me.* Jesus, one night of fantastic sex, and I've turned into an obsessed maniac. She's clearly not interested. *Just let it go*, I tell myself as I turn back around and cook the eggs.

"Kelsey, we need you to watch Olive this afternoon. We're going to go check out some restaurants."

"Yep! Here to help…" She refills her coffee cup as she sits down at the kitchen island next to Lindsey. Nick spreads his newspaper out on the kitchen table. "Where is she?"

"Taking her morning nap."

"Bacon and eggs, Kelsey?"

"No thanks." She stares into her coffee cup. "I'm not a fan of eggs."

"That's because you've never tried my Patrick Saturday Special."

She places her coffee cup on the kitchen island with a thud. "I said no. No, thank you. I don't want any. Is that enough of a no for you?" Her cheeks flush, and she abruptly stands and walks quickly to her room.

Lindsey looks at me with wide eyes. "What the hell was that about?"

I shrug. "Guess she doesn't like eggs."

"Ignore her. She's been moody ever since…" Nick falls quiet and takes a sip of his coffee.

"Ever since what?"

"Todd."

"Oh yeah, poor Kelsey."

"Who's Todd?" I try to sound nonchalant as I take the eggs off the burner—curiosity inching up my spine.

"Todd was her fiancé. She moved heaven and earth to be with that jackass…gave up everything. The short of it is, they broke up, she ended up on my parents' couch devastated, and she hasn't been her old self since," Nick says. "That's all I know. We were filming in Africa, so I never got the details, and I never asked." He looks pointedly at Lindsey.

"What? I'm not going to ask her."

I huff out a laugh. "Yeah, right."

"Ask what?" The three of us freeze as Kelsey breezes back into the kitchen and refills her coffee cup. She steps over to me, and the scent of something floral and familiar overtakes my senses. "Hey, I'm sorry I was a bitch. I'm just…stressed."

"It's okay," I assure her as I scrub the pan. Her lapis-blue eyes hold mine for a second, her expression indiscernible.

She turns to Lindsey and Nick. "Anyway, you wanted to ask me something?"

Lindsey's eyes dart to Nick. "Oh, uh…ask you to watch Olive today while we go out and look at some possible locations for my show."

Kelsey looks at the three of us quizzically. "You already asked me, like ten minutes ago. It's no problem."

Lindsey claps her forehead. "Oh, I did? I'm so forgetful lately. Pregnancy brain."

I quickly take the eggs off the stove, my mouth hanging open. "You're pregnant? *Again*? Olive just turned a year old!"

"Wait, what? No! I meant, baby brain!" Lindsey's cheeks splotch pink as she tries to retract. "I meant having a baby makes me forgetful. Baby brain forgetfulness. It's a thing!"

"Lovie, that's not a thing." I look to Nick for confirmation, but he's smiling tenderly at his wife. Lindsey thunks her head down on the table, mumbling.

"What's that, Lovie? I can't hear you," I tease.

"Okay, fine! Jesus, you're relentless. I'm pregnant. Again.

Happy now?" She bursts into tears.

"Way to go, Star boy," Kelsey mutters as she pulls Lindsey into a side-hug. "Aw, don't cry. This is exciting! Patrick didn't mean to be a tactless jerk."

I flap my arms in exasperation as Nick shoves his sister over and reaches for Lindsey as she sobs into his shirt. He gives me one of his *you idiot* stares over her head as he rubs small circles on her back.

"Shh, Linds, it's okay. What can I get you?"

"A bagel and some juice." She sniffles as she rubs her nose on his t-shirt. "And maybe a foot rub, oh and some Peanut M&Ms."

I snort, knowing she's milking this little scene for everything she's got. Nick releases her to get her juice and a bagel. I lean against the counter and give him a fist-bump as he walks by me. "Congrats man, I'm happy for you guys. Just a little surprised."

"Thanks, Patrick. Yeah, so were we. We were going to wait and tell everyone after filming, but I guess the cat's out of the bag now." He ruefully looks over his shoulder at Lindsey and Kelsey talking, and shrugs. "Kind of puts a damper on our plans for Africa. I haven't told JD yet, so don't say anything."

"No problem."

"That's why you're my sidekick."

"Yesss! Did you hear that, guys? Sidekick, right here." Lindsey and Kelsey ignore me as I bring the bowl of scrambled eggs and bacon over to the island. Lindsey immediately dives in for the bacon while Kelsey takes her bagel over to the table. "You feel okay?"

"I'm great, actually." Lindsey beams at me.

"I was asking Kelsey, Lovie, but good to know you're tip-top after that little crying scene."

Lindsey throws a piece of bacon at me, and I catch it with my mouth. "It wasn't a scene. These damn hormones make me cry at the drop of a pin."

"You cry at the drop of a pin without the hormones." I grin as Nick sets her orange juice and bagel in front of her.

"Tread lightly, my friend. She can get wicked scary," he says quietly as he brings his breakfast to the kitchen table and sits down next to Kelsey, who has taken half his paper.

"Oh, Trick! I was thinking for your birthday next weekend we could go to Hollywood Studios and hang out in Star Wars land!"

"You mean Galaxy's Edge? Wow, yes, I'd love to do that! It's set on the planet Batuu at the Black Spire Outpost."

"Cool. Kelsey, you in?" Lindsey swivels on her chair. "Such a relief now that you know because I won't be able to ride the rides, but Kelsey can go with you!"

"Not exactly into *Star Wars*...ow." She glares at her brother. "Uh, yeah, sure, but I haven't watched any of the movies."

My fork freezes midair. "How have you never watched *Star Wars*?"

"Not high on my list of things to do. I'm more of a rom-com gal. Not really into space stuff."

"How did we...I mean, how did I?" I stumble. "How are we even friends?"

Kelsey snorts and snatches her bagel as she gets up from the table. "We're not friends."

"Ouch," Lovie whispers.

Kelsey slings her purse over her shoulder. "Heading out to the drugstore, but I'll be back before you all need to go." And with that, she stalks out the front door without a backward glance.

"Wow, Trick, she must *really* hate your Saturday-morning special."

"That was her being pleasant." Nick grins as he reaches for the sports section.

"She iced him out in front of us."

"Exactly. She likes him." He holds up the paper, effectively shutting us out as he reads.

"God, you Elliots are a strange bunch," Lindsey muses as she chomps her bacon.

I sit back and think about what Nick said. Her rebuffing me means she likes me? A spark of hope ignites. I love a good challenge.

Chapter 11

Patrick

Jedis, Spies, and Lies

I TAKE A sip of my Jedi Mind Trick as we sit at a table in Oga's Cantina at Hollywood Studios. Kelsey looks up at me, having just taken a sip of her Blue Milk. She's got a smudge of cream along her upper lip. I reach over with my thumb and glide it over her full lip before I realize what I'm doing. It's intimate, a move way too friendly for being acquaintances, but I can't help myself. Like a moth to a flame, I'm mesmerized by her sapphire-blue eyes that darken with my touch. Nick clears his throat, bringing me back to the present.

"You had some cream there."

She self-consciously runs the tip of her tongue along her lip and looks away. Desire burns in the pit of my stomach with an intensity I've never felt before. Why is it whenever I'm around her, she makes me forget there are other people in the room? It's unnerving and ties me up in knots, especially when she acts like I'm the last person she wants to be with. Nick's eyes are pinging back and forth between us, so I quickly change gears.

"I still want to get a picture in front of the Millennium

Falcon, and I don't want to miss the time slot for Rise of the Resistance."

"Are you seriously going to get a picture in front of a hunk of metal?" Lovie snorts into her drink. "It doesn't even fly."

"Do you even have to ask?" I arch an eyebrow.

Lindsey smirks as Kelsey eyes me curiously over her mug.

"Hey, it's Patrick's birthday. If he wants a picture, then let him," Nick grumbles.

I grin triumphantly at Lindsey. "That's why he and I are best friends."

"Traitor," Lindsey grumbles. "Let's go."

We gather our things and walk out into the hot sunshine.

"Oh, Trick, let's go in here. I want to get you a t-shirt for your birthday." Lindsey tugs my arm and steers us into a Star Wars gift shop. "Pick one out that strikes your fancy."

"Lovie, you know you don't have to get me anything. You guys already paid for this trip. Just being here with me today is enough. I know it's hot, and you must be bored out of your mind not being able to ride the rollercoasters."

"Hey, you'd do it for me in a heartbeat." She squeezes my arm and smiles. "I'm honored to be here."

Kelsey peruses a shelf of lightsabers. "Who on earth would buy one of these things? It's like a giant glo-stick. Holy shit, who would pay $114.95 for one of these freaking things?"

I feel my cheeks heat up as I busily look at t-shirts. *Please don't say anything, Lovie, please don't say a word.* I use my telepathy to her.

"Do you even have to ask? Patrick has at least six." Lindsey grins. "He once bought a Darth Vader one at an auction for four hundred dollars. He even got suckered into buying the cape and deluxe helmet that changes your voice with it. Spoiler alert, it doesn't."

Worst friend ever.

"You suck at telepathy," I gripe as I pass by her. "Definitely not your superpower."

"What did I do?" She looks all innocent, but I'm on to her. I join Nick, who is strolling Olive around.

"Dude, your wife…"

"What has she done now?" He picks up a Mandalorian helmut and glances at me.

"Just being herself."

"I'll try to tackle her down and put tape over her mouth."

I give him a wary look because he sounds very convincing. "You don't have to go to that extreme…"

"Dude, I was kidding. Jesus, what do you take me for?"

"An ex-spy that almost got us all killed by his crazy ex-girlfriend and business partner who happened to be working with the Russian Mafia."

A woman next to us nervously glances over at Nick and puts her merchandise down, quickly walking away.

"He's kidding!" Nick calls after her. "Are you ever going to let me live that down?"

"I don't know, it's kind of fun bringing it up now and again…"

"Between you and Lindsey, it gets mentioned at least once a day."

"Trick, how about this one?" Lindsey holds up a rhinestone-studded t-shirt. "Oh wait, never mind. I'm not spending fifty bucks on a t-shirt."

"Good, because I'm not wearing rhinestones."

Olive wakes up and starts to fuss. "I'm going to wait outside," Nick says as he tries to pop a pacifier unsuccessfully into her mouth.

"Here, I'll help. She may need a bottle." Lindsey pulls the diaper bag from underneath the stroller. "Trick, pick out something that catches your fancy. Happy birthday." She shoves her credit card in my face, flustered as Olive's cries get louder.

I look around for Kelsey and spot her on the other side of the store. She's looking at some sweaters and talking on the phone. I grab a t-shirt hoping she'll warm up to me if I ask her opinion on it. Her back is to me as I make my way over to her.

"I told you, I'll think about it." She looks around but doesn't spot me. "Fine, okay, but I'm nervous. No, I'm serious, it's…risky. I'm not sure I want to do it anymore." I pause my approach as she smooths a sweater out in front of her. "I'm worried my brother will find out. Ha! You don't know Nick like I do. He's suspicious of everything."

I melt into the clothes rack next to me. I feel lousy eaves-dropping, but I'm too curious by her end of the conversation not to find out what the hell is going on. She refolds the sweater, turning around as she scans the room.

"Look, I've got to go. No, no, don't do that. I promise I'll be there." She pauses as she listens to whoever is on the line. "It's crazy, but it might work. Ha, dangerous is my middle name. You might need backup. See you Wednesday night." She throws her phone in her purse.

I swallow past the lump stuck in my throat. Oh god, could it be happening again? Could Kelsey be in the same profession as her brother? Maybe she picked up where her brother left off. Kelsey…a spy? I start to sweat. Obviously, Nick doesn't know, or else he would have told Lindsey, who would have definitely told me. I glance around the store, lost in thought. This makes so much sense now. Her elusiveness, her unwillingness to have a relationship, her scary attitude… It would at least explain her cool demeanor toward me.

"Patrick? What are you doing?"

I jump and knock a display of a mannequin dressed as a wookie over, totally unaware that Kelsey had turned around and spotted me. *Stay cool, Patrick.* I have to pretend that I didn't just overhear her secret mission going down. I right the mannequin and turn toward her.

"Oh hey, didn't see you there. This thing is creepy," My voice cracks with nerves as I point my thumb at the mannequin. "Anyway, just looking at t-shirts. What do you think of this one?" I hold up the one I've been carrying.

Kelsey looks at the t-shirt I had been wringing in my hands seconds before. "I like big hutts and I cannot lie…Jabba got back? Uh…sure if that's your thing…" I whip the t-shirt around. It's a picture of a giant Jabba the Hutt looking extra slimey. *No, this isn't my thing!* I thought I had grabbed the vintage TIE fighter one.

"Yeah, no I—"

"Ready to go? We've still got to get you a lightsaber and ride a rollercoaster." She smiles as she grabs the t-shirt, breezing past me. I stand there speechless because there's only one thing I have to do, and that is to tell Lovie what I just overheard.

Chapter 12

Patrick

Cheese Orgasms

"LINDSEY, I SWEAR I know what I heard!" I open the door to the restaurant and usher her in.

Lindsey chews her thumbnail as we wait to be seated. "Maybe she's meeting her cousin?"

"What cousin? Cousin Kiernan? I don't remember him at the wedding. Do you know why I don't remember him? Because he's made-up. She hasn't mentioned him once since she arrived."

Lindsey arches an eyebrow. "So you think the whole family is in on this fictitious cousin, including Mrs. Elliot, as a ruse for..."

"I haven't figured that out yet." I snap my fingers. "Maybe 'Kiernan' is a code word for something."

"Code word for *loco poco*? I'm talking about you, by the way." She pats my shoulder gently like I've just made it out of an exhausting hour of therapy.

"Don't you think it's a little suspicious she was so eager to come down here with us?"

"I mean, who wouldn't want to spend time with sweet little Olive, her niece, and hang out with her awesome sister-in-law?"

I snort and fold my arms over my chest.

"Who knows, Trick, maybe she has a hot date?"

"She doesn't have a hot date." That thought makes me want to throw the mint dish sitting on the hostess stand across the room.

"Well, hear me out. Nick said she's been living at her parents' and mending a broken heart. Maybe she met someone online and set up a date..."

"In Miami?" I shake my head. "That's *not* what's going on."

The hostess comes back to lead us to our table. We sit down, and I immediately pick up my iced water, feeling parched.

"You're being very snippy about her having a date."

"No, I'm not."

"You are, and come to think of it, it's weird you aren't all flirty McFlirts with her like you were at the wedding."

"I don't know if you've noticed, but she calls me *Star Wars* Boy and isn't the friendliest toward me."

"Oh, I've noticed." She peruses her menu. "Your Jedi mind control is on fire."

I choke on an ice cube. "If I had Jedi mind control then we wouldn't be having this conversation!"

She waves a hand, already on her way to tuning me out. "Don't worry, I'm working on rectifying that situation."

I groan as I open my menu. "Lovie, please don't. I'm not interested, and it's crystal clear she isn't either."

Lindsey ignores me and looks around the restaurant as the waiter approaches our table. "I love the atmosphere in here. It's so authentic! Little Havana was a great choice!" She beams at me. "I'm going with the classic Cuban," she tells our waiter as he tries to take her menu. "Oh wait, and the ham croquettes…and the Cuban nachos. What's the difference between Cuban nachos and regular nachos?"

"We use plantain chips instead of tortilla, shredded pork, and mojo sauce."

"Sounds amazing! Okay, definitely those." She scans the menu one last time. "I seriously could order it all, but I'm good." She smiles at the waiter as she hands him the menu and then looks at me. "What? I'm eating for two. I'm starving."

I roll my eyes. "I'll have the *pan con bistec*, please."

"I love this place. Let's put it on our list for the show."

I look around the small restaurant and nod. "Let's try the food first, but yeah, I'll talk to the manager after dinner if it's good." It's bright and clean in here, if not a little on the small side. It's currently filled to capacity, making it hard to do the show with all the close chatter. We'll have to film at a time when it's not busy. Two men start to play guitar out on the patio, and I agree with Lindsey, this place is pretty stellar.

"Have you chosen the viewers' choice location yet?" She asks.

"Not yet, narrowing it down between two."

Lindsey rubs her hands together. "So exciting! Do I get a say?"

"No." I snort. "You wouldn't choose either of them."

Her face falls. "Great. Why do the fans like to torture me so much? The last place was disgusting." She wrinkles her nose. "Be glad you're not helping with JD's show. Nick says the director he's working with for Adventure Animals is a total diva."

I arch an eyebrow.

"Haha, very funny," Lindsey says. "The other doctor is a total snooze. They're bringing in an actor to play the role of another veterinarian to stir up drama. Nick is pissed. He wanted something genuine to produce, not some made-for-TV bullshit soap opera."

"I'm surprised JD is allowing that to happen."

"Apparently, in the beginning, he was against it, but the Adventure Animals director has convinced him the ratings will go off the charts. She's called him the Dr. Oz of the veterinary world. Don't think that hasn't gone to his head."

I take a sip of water, having a hard time imagining JD getting a big head. He's a down-to-earth, good guy. "Back to the situation at hand," I say. "I think we should follow her."

"Follow the director?"

"Lovie," I growl in annoyance.

"What?" Lindsey's eyes double in size as the waiter places a massive plate of nachos and croquettes in between us. "Oh, yes, come to mama." She immediately picks up a sauce and shredded pork-covered plantain chip and shoves it into her mouth, moaning. "This is the best."

"Lovie, I'm serious."

"So am I. I don't think I've ever had this kind of cheese before. What *is* this? It's like cheese crack." She moans. "It's gooey and salty and melts on your tongue. I need this every day for the rest of my life. Oh god, so good, like a cheese orgasm. We need to find out what this is for the show. I could eat a tub—"

"Lovie!" I bark out, irritated she won't stop talking about the fucking cheese. "Save it for the show. We need to follow Kelsey and see what's going on. What if she's in trouble?"

Lindsey eyes me dubiously as she shoves another chip in her mouth. "Trick, that's crazy, not to mention a total invasion of her privacy." She takes a long drink of her water, sliding me a look over the brim. I arch an eyebrow and she gives in. "Ugh, fine, I'll help you. Now let me eat my nachos in peace while I enjoy my cheese orgasm."

Sitting back in my seat, I smile triumphantly.

Chapter 13

Patrick

Date Night with Donna

I GROAN AS Lindsey yells down the hallway that we're leaving in ten minutes. I'm annoyed with her "scheme" to get Kelsey to like me better. She didn't come out and say that was her plan, but why else would she set up this double "date" for the four of us? I can handle Kelsey just fine on my own without Lindsey interfering like a pushy mother trying to marry off her forever bachelor son.

I grab a hoodie in case it gets cold. I sniff my armpits and then walk into the bathroom to grab deodorant.

"Oh my god, get out! I'm peeing! Why are you standing there? Get out!"

I quickly shut the door, my heart thudding against my ribcage—the echoes of a screeching banshee reverberating in my head. "I'm sorry." I swallow, my voice cracking. I clear it before I start again. "I didn't realize you were in there. Honestly, I'm surprised this is the first time—"

The toilet flushes, effectively shutting me up. I can hear her washing her hands before my door is flung open. I stumble into her since I was leaning against it.

"Were you listening to me pee? How about knocking next time?"

"What? No! I'm sorry, I was…I need deodorant."

She huffs as she reaches over and hands it to me before running a brush through her long hair. I'm completely mesmerized as she quickly braids the silky cascade. "Your armpits aren't going to deodorize themselves if you just stand there gawking at me."

"Right." I quickly walk back into my room, feeling like an idiot. I pull on my hoodie and close my door, bumping into Kelsey in the hallway. "Look, I'm sorry about the bathroom…I should have knocked."

"Patrick, look—"

"The sitter is here! Let's go!" Lindsey shouts from the kitchen. Nick meets us in the hall as he comes out of his room.

"Any idea what she has planned?" Kelsey asks him.

"Not a clue, but she's acting giddy, so prepare yourself."

We meet Lindsey in the kitchen as she shuffles us out to the car after giving the babysitter instructions. We pile in, Kelsey and I in the back seat.

"You know, Lindsey, I could have watched Olive tonight. That *is* why I'm here."

"Nonsense! This will be fun! Like a double date." She grins at us over her shoulder.

Kelsey tenses next to me as she drums her fingers on the leather seat, a fast-paced erratic rhythm matching my heartbeat. I place my hand over hers, gently squeezing, before she moves it to her lap. I ignore her rebuff as I turn my attention to the cruise director.

"Alright, Lovie, spill it. Where are you dragging us to tonight?"

"Bowling?" Nick asks hopefully.

"Eww, no. Do you know how many germs are in places like that?"

"A wine bar?" Kelsey clasps her hands together, praying to the wine gods.

"Nah, been there done that."

"Ooh, that new ax-throwing place we passed by the other day?" I throw in, hoping for something to burn off this nervous energy I'm feeling.

"No, I'm still waiting for our matching plaid shirts to arrive before we go there."

"Wait, seriously?" Nick raises an eyebrow before returning his attention to the road. I wouldn't put it past Lindsey to have ordered us matching shirts with our names embroidered across the pockets.

"I know," I say confidently. "An Escape Room place."

"That was my second choice, but I was worried someone might kill someone else in our group. We'll save that for a rainy day. Oh yay! We're here!"

Nick pulls into a little strip mall with a gym, a vitamin store, a nail salon, and a paint store.

"Ugh, Lovie, please tell me you didn't sign us up for a Zumba class!" I gripe from the back seat.

"We're not going to the gym. Although, that would be an interesting double date."

"Why do you keep calling it a double date? It's Patrick and my sister."

Lindsey opens the door. "Just...go with the flow, babe, okay? For me?" Nick grunts as we all file out onto the sidewalk. "Surprise! We're going to paint!"

"Paint what?" Nick looks around at the semi-empty parking lot. "Is this like a Habitat for Humanity kind of thing? It's supposed to rain later."

"No, silly, we're going to paint each other!" She winks before she laughs uncontrollably. "Oh my god, if you could see your expressions right now, it's priceless! Hold on, I need a picture."

"Um, Lindsey, what do you mean each other? Like *actually* painting our bodies?"

"Kinky...I like the way you think, Kels." She smiles as she takes a picture of us with her phone. "Unfortunately, this is a G-rated establishment. But way to bring your A-game."

"I wasn't trying—"

"Come on. Donna is waiting for us."

Kelsey, Nick, and I shuffle behind Lindsey, dreading what we're about to do.

"Do you think we're going to have a nude model?" I ask Nick.

Kelsey swats me in the stomach. "I hope it's a hot guy."

Nick surveys the building. "Places like this always have a back door we can escape out of, right?"

We enter the bright, cheerful paint studio. An older woman draped in a dark gray shawl with poufy shoulder-length white hair welcomes us.

"Hello and welcome to The Paint Store! My name is Donna, and I'll be assisting you with your masterpieces tonight! I have wine, beer, and soda. Oh, and I have a charcuterie board you requested."

"Excellent, Donna, thank you. I'm Lindsey, and this is my husband Nick, and this cute couple is Kelsey and

Patrick." Lindsey beams as she turns to us. "Isn't this exciting? Surprise date night, yay!" The only ones excited about tonight are Lovie and Donna.

"Donna? Give me your biggest glass of red wine, please, and keep them coming," Kelsey says as she looks around the room.

"Coming right up! Now, a friendly reminder, I encourage a little alcohol to loosen your arms up and feel one with the paintbrush, but if you drink too much, your painting gets sloppy."

"No worries, Donna, we're professionals." I smile tightly.

"Oh, you've painted before?" Her eyes sparkle with delight.

"No, I meant we're drinking professionals."

Donna's expression wobbles as she hands Nick two beers and a water for Lindsey.

"Oh my god, this olive tapenade is amazing." Lindsey greedily eyes the cheese selection as she stuffs a toast point in her already full mouth.

"If everyone can gather their plates and drinks and make their way over to the table, we can get started."

"Yeah, stop hoarding the cheese plate, Lovie, and let others enjoy it." I lightly shove her over. "And quit calling this a couples' date night. You're making Kelsey uncomfortable," I whisper, jabbing her in the arm with my finger to drive the point home.

"Wait, we're the only ones painting tonight?" Kelsey looks at the two tables set with four easels.

"Yes, it's a private affair," Lindsey sings as she sits at one table. "I thought it would be more fun to have a private class and not have some rando breathing down your neck comparing paintings."

"You just described you."

Lindsey sticks her tongue out. "Nick, you have to sit across from me so that I can see you. Kelsey, you sit next to your brother."

I smile as I sit down next to Lindsey and pick up a paintbrush, twirling it between my fingers. "This is going to be cake."

"Wow, someone's feeling a little cocky."

"It can't be that hard," I grunt, dropping the paintbrush on the floor. I lean over to pick it up and toss it on the table.

"These paintbrushes are not toys! They are crafted of willow wood and horsehair, so please be gentle with them." Donna takes the brush out of my hand and strokes it lovingly.

I lean into Lovie. "She's a little intense."

"Do I need to separate you two?" Donna snaps. Kelsey covers a laugh with a cough.

"No, ma'am." Lindsey glares at me as she picks up a paintbrush.

"Can we start?" Nick looks like he'd rather be zip-tied to a chair and held at gunpoint than begin painting. "If we get this over with, we might be able to catch the last quarter of the hockey game."

"Babe, seriously?"

"Oh, no handsome, art takes patience and time," Donna trills. "There will be no rushing tonight. You will become one with your paintbrush and canvas. The creativity will flow from your veins onto the canvas, your brush as your guide."

Nick arches an eyebrow at Lindsey, silently telling her she's going to owe him big time for this as Donna sways with her eyes closed. She suddenly opens her eyes and claps her hands causing us to jump.

"Let's begin. You will be painting your partner across from you. I want you to capture their essence with the colors you choose and your brushstrokes. Become one with your partner."

"I'm confused. Are we supposed to be one with the paintbrush or our partner? It can't be both," Nick whispers loudly.

Donna glares at him. "We're going to paint your background first. When you look at your partner, what color comes to mind? What is their essence, their aura color? Pick that color and cover your canvas with it. Do that while I go turn on some music to help your creativity flow."

I chuckle to myself because the first color that comes to mind when I look over at Kelsey scowling at her canvas is black. I choose a medium-blue mixed with greens instead and begin painting.

"Isn't this fun, you guys?" Lindsey beams as she slaps on paint.

"About as fun as getting cavities filled at the dentist." Kelsey grins back at her as an old country station pipes in from the speakers.

"Oh good, even better. Country music." Nick grimaces. Kelsey cracks up, causing us all to look up from painting.

"Sorry, but Nick chose baby-shit brown as his background color."

"That's the color you see when you look at me? The color of my aura is baby-shit brown?"

Nick shrugs. "I was going for pink but messed up mixing."

Lindsey rolls her eyes. "It's white mixed with red. How on earth you got baby-shit brown from that is beyond me. If you keep acting like a sourpuss, I'm going to give you a unibrow." She looks over at my canvas. "Trick, why does it look like a three-year-old is painting on your canvas? Fill in the white spaces."

"Stop looking at what I'm doing, Bob Ross. I've got this."

Donna floats back into the room and scowls when she sees Nick's canvas. "That's an interesting color. Perhaps add some white to soften it a bit? Okay, our next step is to mix the color for your skin tone. I want you to outline the shape of your partner's head in white first using the smaller brush." She passes behind Kelsey. "Oh no, dear, his head isn't the size of a lima bean."

"I need room so that I can paint him riding in a spaceship."

Lindsey snorts as I look up quizzically. "A spaceship?"

"Are you able to paint one?" Donna asks skeptically.

"I can wing it."

"Why don't we stick to head portraits," Donna says dismissively as she strides behind Nick's chair. "Hmm, her skin tone looks a little angry. And her head is shaped like a pear, maybe round out the top a little?"

"My head shape is not a pear," Lindsey gripes.

"Hey, it's my interpretation. Right, Donna?"

"Oh, well…I guess. Is this your first time painting?" Donna picks up a wineglass and guzzles it. "Let's work on facial planes and features."

I STRETCH MY back as I set down my paintbrush, surveying my finished masterpiece. Lindsey looks over and snorts. "Holy shit, Trick, I never knew you were artistic."

"I used to dabble in high school."

Donna gave up on us a while ago and is somewhere in the front part of the studio drinking and singing along to "Islands in the Stream" that she has blasting from the speakers. I look over at Lindsey's portrait.

"Why does Nick's nose look like a carrot?"

Nick sets his brush down and clears his throat. "I'm done." Kelsey peers over at his portrait and laughs.

Donna dances back into the room, clearly inebriated as she claps her hands giddily. "These are wonderful!" Kelsey shoots me a dubious look, and I can't help laughing. Clearly, Donna's vision has been impaired by the alcohol. "Are you ready to show your partner the big reveal? On the count of three. One, two, three!"

We turn our canvases and all burst out laughing.

"Why do I look like a parade balloon float?" Lindsey cries.

"Why does my nose look like that? And why is it orange?" Nick retorts.

"Wow, Patrick, that's seriously good." Kelsey swallows as she looks at her portrait.

"Did you paint me holding a light saber?" I laugh. "And why am I sitting on a dog that looks like it's puking?" She painted a figure sitting on a dog waving a wand in the air. The only thing that resembles me is the brown color of my hair and oddly shaped giant brown eyes.

"That's not a dog, that's a dragon. It's breathing fire." She points at the puke, and the four of us laugh harder.

Donna observes Lindsey's painting. "You could be the next Picasso. I like how you mish-mashed his face together." She quietly starts to hiccup.

Lindsey preens. "Donna just called me the next Picasso!"

"She's also three sheets to the wind," Nick whispers next to me. "I better call her a cab."

I nod in agreement as Donna throws an arm around Kelsey, squeezing her tight. "I love teaching couples. Don't you love love?"

Kelsey giggles nervously as she untangles herself from Donna, but she's not finished.

"The way you captured Patrick's essence is amazing. I'm not sure about the wand in his hand, but I can tell by looking at this painting how deep your love for him runs. To be one with the animal means he's a sensitive soul, his dagger raised in the air like he's going to defend your honor." Donna holds her hands over her heart as she sighs. "You are one lucky woman."

Kelsey's cheeks stain a pretty pink as she looks up at me.

"Geez, Donna, how much wine did you have tonight?" Lindsey laughs, dispelling the awkwardness in the air.

"Okay, gather together with your paintings so I can take a picture. Stand next to each other. A little closer, dear." She yanks Kelsey closer to me. I wrap an arm around her waist to steady her. "Say 'love is in the air'!"

We all smile as Donna deflates dramatically. "Come on! Love is in the air! Islands in the Stream that is what we are!"

"Just say it so we can get the hell out of here," Nick growls.

"Love is in the air!" we all shout.

"So wonderful!" Donna beams as she hands Lindsey her phone back.

We collect our paintings after Nick calls Donna a cab. Lightning zips across the sky as we open the door and run to the car, fat raindrops pelting down on us. Nick pops the trunk, and we throw the canvases in before piling into the car.

"I think Donna had a couple bottles of wine, don't you?"

"Considering she started the evening hating us and ended it by hugging us and giving us a free class, I'd say most definitely." Kelsey giggles.

"At what point did we drive her to drink?"

"Maybe after failing miserably to teach us how to draw eyes?" I venture.

"She yelled at me for drawing olives for eyes." Kelsey laughs.

"She snapped at me and said Lindsey's body looked like a baked potato and her eyes were too close together. If I never have to hear the term 'facial plane' again, I'll die a happy man."

"She crooned over perfect Patrick." Lindsey grins at me

over her shoulder.

"I can't help it that she likes Kelsey's face," I tease as I chance a glance at Kelsey's profile as she looks out the rain-splattered window. The hint of a smile tells me my compliment hit its mark. "Are you guys going to frame your portraits?"

Nick snorts at the idea. "No. It's going right into the trash."

"What? How can you say that about my potato portrait? I'm hanging them in the family room when we get back home."

Nick quickly glances at her. "You can't be serious. Mine looks like Olive could have painted it."

"Well, I'm not throwing it away. It was painted with love. Are you keeping Kelsey's, Patrick?"

"I wouldn't dream of throwing it away."

Her fingertips brush against mine. I don't dare make a move, calculating my response as if I were handling a skittish colt. She glides them over my hand with a featherlike touch. I swallow as I slowly turn my palm up. Kelsey's fingers trail away from my wrist, finding their groove as they lace with mine.

I look down at our joined hands with a tenderness I can't describe. I gently squeeze her hand in mine, not daring to let go. She doesn't either until we arrive back at the house.

Chapter 14

Kelsey

The Last to Know

I CLOSE MY door as I dig in my bag, looking for my sunglasses. Nick is out with Olive on a walk, so I have some time to relax by the pool. "Oof." A solid wall of muscle knocks me back as I run directly into Patrick in the hall. He steadies me as I lean back against the wall, my hands pressed against his chest. My fingers curl into his cotton t-shirt and I want to pull him to me and dip my nose into his neck, he smells so good. Nerves and excitement tangle together making my heart beat thunderously.

I've managed to avoid him since the "double date," making sure we're never alone together. I've exchanged pleasantries with him in the mornings when I quickly grab a cup of coffee, or I sit silently as the three of them tell stories about their day, avoiding his gaze through dinner until I can quickly excuse myself to my room.

It was a mistake holding his hand that night, but I needed that connection, it comforted me, and I wanted it. And even though it was only a simple hand-holding, it was wrong to give Patrick false hope. Who am I kidding? It gave me false hope. Hope that I could be Patrick's girlfriend. That I could pretend that night was an actual date, and he'd kiss me when we got to my door. I ripped that dream to shreds as soon as we got home. I locked myself in my room, staring at the painting he made me until I drifted off to sleep.

"Sorry," he says gruffly. He's wearing his glasses again, and damn if he doesn't look sexy as fuck with them on. Why does he have to be so hot and nerdy? It annoys me how his smile makes me all warm and gooey. He's still holding my arms, his touch searing my skin. I feel flushed, my heart beating erratically as he dips his head like he's about to kiss me. His breath is a whisper on my skin. God yes, I want him to kiss me.

He reaches up with his thumb and glides it over my upper lip. It's intimate, and I'm mesmerized by his golden-brown eyes. I want to pull him into me and wrap my legs around him. I want him to shove me up against this wall and make me moan like he did that one night we were together. I want to...*what are you doing, Kelsey?* I shove him away from me, and he effortlessly steps back as if I were in total control of this situation. Ha, that's laughable.

"Kelsey..." he murmurs as he steps into my space again. His arm casually leaning on the wall above my head. His woodsy scent permeates the air around me as I inhale a lungful of oxygen.

I try to get my head on straight, but I can't. I'm drowning in him. He bends, and I close my eyes, waiting for his lips to skate across mine. I don't have the strength or the will to push him away for a second time. Instead, he places a petal-soft caress on my neck, and it has my knees buckling. I grab onto his t-shirt again as I cling for dear life.

"Tell me why you're avoiding me."

"I-I haven't been avoiding you," I stammer. "I'm here to take care of Olive."

He nips my neck, causing a rash of goosebumps to rise on my skin. "Liar," he says huskily. "Tell me the truth, Kelsey. Was it really just a one-night stand for you, or does it haunt you like it does me?"

"You, me...what happened..." I swallow, trembling as he guides his tongue up to the shell of my ear. *Shut him down, Kelsey! You can't get involved!* "Oh god...it didn't mean anything to me. It was a one-night stand...a rebound night of hot sex that I desperately needed. Nothing more than that. I haven't thought about it at all." The lie spills easily off my tongue, poisoning the air around us.

His lips leave my neck, and I peel my eyes open, but I wish I had kept them closed. The hurt lingering in his light brown eyes has me feeling like a monster. "Patrick..."

"Tell me why! Ain't nothing but a heartache..." Lindsey sings off-key as she enters the hallway. Patrick pushes away from me and folds his arms as he casually leans against the opposite side. Lindsey notices us and pulls an earbud out. "God, why on earth did Backstreet Boys ever break up? So glad they're back together again."

"Yeah, so awesome," Patrick answers, his gaze remaining on me. But I can't even breathe, much less answer a question. I realize I'm shaking as I lift my hand to where he grazed my neck.

"No one likes sarcasm, Trick. Tell me why!" She belts out as she puts the earbud back in and bounces into her bedroom, shutting the door. I deflate against the wall as I look warily at Patrick.

"Patrick, look—" He holds up a finger, cutting me off. Lindsey's door swings back open.

"Trick, just for your 411 the Backstreet Boys came back after twenty years and had a number-one hit. Your taste in music is worse than mine. No one can rock it out to Motown. Kelsey, do you find a guy that loves Motown the least bit sexy?"

"Uh…"

"From now on, we will blast Backstreet Boys before every show to get us pumped up!"

Patrick groans. "Super. Don't forget the Spice Girls."

"Who also rock." Lindsey beams as she looks between us. "What are you two doing anyway?"

"Nothing." Patrick barely glances at me before pushing off the wall, sauntering down the hallway. "Absolutely nothing."

The front door closes with a quiet click, but to me, it's as loud as a gunshot. I've hurt him—I know I have, but I have my reasons. I can't be truthful with him right now, so he'll have to understand and respect my wishes. Someday he'll forgive me.

"Why does it look like someone just told Patrick that Luke Skywalker lost the battle against Darth Vader?" Lindsey folds her arms over her chest and glares at me.

"I don't know." I shrug innocently.

"Why are you so mean to him, Kelsey? Trick is the nicest guy I have ever met. Yeah, he's a little goofy and loves Star Wars a little too much, he has terrible taste in music, but he'd be there for you in a pinch if you needed him. In fact—"

"We slept together!" I blurt and then cover my face with my hands. Shit, fuck, dammit, I did not want to tell her that. *What was I thinking?*

"What?!" Lindsey screeches as she looks down the hallway to the front door where Patrick exited. "Does he know this? Of course, he knows, he was a participant! I can't *believe* he didn't tell me. Why didn't he tell me? We tell each other everything! When did this happen? Was it here? After date night? Why the hell am I always the last to know?"

"The last to know what?" Nick steps into the hallway from the living room. Oh great, exactly what I need right now. My brother cannot find out about us. Not only could it change the dynamics of his friendship with Patrick, but he'll tell my sisters, and then I'll never hear the end of it. I glare at Lindsey, who has thankfully decided to zip her lips. I tell them the surprise I was actually saving for the end of the trip.

"The last to know that I got the two of you dinner reservations at The Forge tonight. It's a nice place, so dress up. Have fun, kids!" I turn on my heel to go back to my room and grab a towel.

"The Forge?" Nick asks incredulously. "It's impossible to get last-minute reservations there."

"Well, I called in a favor to a friend of mine in New York who has some connections as a thank-you for entrusting me with Olive and letting me stay here, so enjoy...uh, but you have to pay. It's a little too pricey for my unemployed budget."

"Figures." Nick smiles at Lindsey, who looks like she swallowed an ice cube. "Guess that answers my question about what to do for dinner."

"I'm kind of tired." Lindsey narrows her eyes at me. "Maybe Kelsey and Patrick should take our reservation."

"What? No, absolutely not." I slash my hand in the air. "Besides, I just said, not exactly in my budget."

"We'll pay."

"I'm not paying for my sister and Patrick to eat at a five-star restaurant." Nick looks at Lindsey like she lost her marbles. "Sorry, Kels."

"I might be offended by that if this were a different cir-cumstance, but please go…eat. This may be the last time you two get alone time for a while. I'm only here for another few weeks. Take advantage of me!"

"Please, Lindsey? I've been wanting to go there." He bends down and kisses her neck.

She points her two fingers at her eyes and then to me to let me know she's on to me. "Okay, fine, let's get fancy."

"Yes!" Nick continues to kiss her as he backs her into their bedroom and slams the door shut. "Thanks, Kels," he yells as an afterthought through the closed door.

Whatever, I don't care as long as it got me out of having to explain what was going on between Patrick and me. I grab my book, my towel, the baby monitor, and head out to the back pool to hide while Olive naps. I call my friend, praying to the gods I can squeeze them in for dinner tonight.

Chapter 15

Patrick

Comfort Out of a Can

I WALK INTO the kitchen after scouting some locations for *Lindsey Loves Love* to find Kelsey trying to open a can while Olive kicks excitedly in her highchair. "What are you making?"

Kelsey looks over her shoulder at me. "Oh hey, making some SpaghettiOs."

I make a noise of disgust in the back of my throat. "Is that your dinner?"

"I'm hungry, and it's not like I can go out to dinner with Olive in tow. Unlike my mom and my sister Mary Katherine, I'm a terrible cook."

"Stop, I can't let you eat pasta out of a can made for kindergartners. I'll order something in from Uber Eats."

"Honestly, you don't have to do that. I don't mind SpaghettiOs. It's like comfort food for me."

"I'm not letting you eat comfort out of a can." I pull up the app on my phone. "What do you feel like?"

"Really?" She hesitates before setting the can opener down on the counter. "You can never go wrong with Mexican or Cuban."

"Now we're talking. Lovie and I ate at this great spot the other night. I'll see if they deliver."

"Okay, thanks." She scrunches her nose as she looks down into the can before throwing it in the trash. She walks over to Olive with a bowl of cubed fruit and chicken. Olive squeals in delight, which makes me smile. "Look, Patrick, about earlier, I'm sorry if I hurt your feelings…"

"It's water under the bridge." I dismiss her apology as I call in the food order. I was disappointed by what she said earlier, but I need to put my feelings aside so I can figure out where she's going Wednesday night with her mysterious phone-caller. Putting my plan in action, I turn to her as I put my credit card back in my wallet. "Lovie and I were going to check out another restaurant Wednesday night. Want to join us?"

Kelsey stills as she washes a bowl in the kitchen sink. "Oh…uh, I'd love to, but I have plans."

"Oh, too bad. Plans with your cousin who lives here?"

"Yep, exactly."

"Why haven't we met him yet? Weird that Nick hasn't even mentioned him. Will Nick be joining you?"

"What is this, the Spanish Inquisition?" she huffs as she dries her hands on a dishtowel.

I hold my hands up and then grab a blueberry off Olive's tray and pop it in my mouth. "No need to be touchy, I was just asking." I wink, which makes her scowl. I've got her right where I want her. Enough on edge that she might spill her secret. "Maybe once we put Olive to bed we can watch a movie. There's this new spy thriller I want to see. You said you like thrillers, right?"

"I'm not really in the mood." She wipes down the counter with the towel. "What do you mean, *we* put Olive to bed?"

"I've helped with her bedtime routine before," I say as Kelsey eyes me suspiciously, sitting down across from Olive. "So, tell me about your cousin. Maybe we can all meet up after."

"We can't."

"Come on, Kelsey, I know you're hiding something."

"Gah! Okay, I told Lindsey we had sex!"

Her outburst makes Olive's face crumple into tears.

Not exactly the secret I wanted spilled. I feel you, Olive, I want to cry too.

"Why would you do that?" I stand up and pace as she frets over Olive. "Shit, she's probably telling Nick as we speak. I'm a dead man."

Nick will want to kill me for sleeping with his sister. Lindsey will want to for not telling her the morning after it happened. They'll collaborate, stuff me in a suitcase and throw me in the Atlantic Ocean. They'll make up some elaborate story that I've run off to be a cast member at Star Wars Land and changed my name to Chewbacca. No one would ever question it or come looking for me. Dammit, they know me too well.

"Uh Patrick, you're about to light the floor on fire with your pacing. What's the big deal?" Kelsey asks over her shoulder as she picks up Olive.

"What's the *big deal*? You don't know those two like I do."

She smirks. "Pretty sure I know my brother, and Lindsey was—"

"Neurotic? Did she scream and wail? Did she try to hold you down for answers?"

"What are you talking about?" She has the audacity to laugh as she bounces Olive in her arms. "She was surprised, but we didn't get a chance to talk about it because Nick came home."

"Please tell me he didn't find out."

"No, that's when I surprised them with a night out."

I grunt, stressed over what Lindsey plans to do with this information. Blackmail me for sure. She'll keep this info tucked away until we're eighty, and then Bam! She'll pull out her *you never told me you slept with Kelsey* card, and I'll have to commit to some lame retirement community contest with her, like polka dancing.

"I don't see what the big deal is..." She looks up suddenly, her beautiful blue eyes flash. "I mean, I don't want to complicate things for Lindsey, but it's not like we're currently sleeping together."

I flinch as her words hit their mark.

"Are you embarrassed of me?"

"What? No, no, no. That's not why I'm freaking out. Your brother is..." a freaking killing machine, ex-Jason Bourne, who could snap my neck like a twig. But I can't tell Kelsey that. It's top secret, and none of Nick's family know that he used to be a secret agent. "Scary," I finish as the doorbell rings.

Kelsey jumps up to get it. "Thank god, things were getting weird," she grumbles as she hands Olive to me. "Watch her. I'll get the food."

I pick up a piece of chicken as I make the airplane noise

guiding it to her mouth. She bangs her chubby fists on my chest and laughs. "Your mommy and daddy are going to kill Uncle Trick. What do you think I should do?"

"Bah bah ma."

"Nah, I can't run away. I'd never leave you with your crazy mom."

"Baba dada!"

"Avoid your dad? Good plan. Think I can avoid your mom too?"

Olive starts to fuss. "Yeah, I didn't think so either." I grab her pacifier and stick it in her mouth. She smashes her sticky hands to my face, so I lift her and blow a raspberry on her belly, which makes her burst into giggles. I lower her and notice Kelsey leaning in the kitchen doorway, smiling. She brings the bags of food over and puts them on the kitchen island.

"You're so good with her."

I grin as Olive yanks my glasses. "She's a good baby."

"Do you want kids of your own?"

Here we go. The dreaded question I get asked by every woman I've ever dated, not to mention by my family and friends at every holiday event. *Patrick, why aren't you settling down and having kids yet? Patrick, you'd make the best dad. Patrick, you're so good with kids, I'm surprised you don't have a van full! Patrick, you're not getting any younger. People think single men over thirty-five that aren't gay are peculiar.* That one was from my aunt Marsha.

"I like kids. I adore Olive, but I'm not sure I want them for myself. I'm kind of a nomad…a free spirit who loves to travel. I don't know, I don't feel that need that others might when it comes to kids."

Kelsey looks at me for a beat, lifting Olive out of my arms as I wrangle my glasses from her. "You might want them if you met the right woman."

"Maybe, maybe not. If she wanted kids, then I would be happy to give her what her heart desires. I would do anything for the right woman. But given a choice right now? I'm happy just the way things are."

Kelsey's lips tip up into a smile as she assesses me. "And what is the right woman?"

"A woman who sees all my faults but loves me anyway. Someone who craves adventure and wants to see the world with me but has her own passions she wants to pursue. A woman who challenges me but also knows when I need space. Someone I find undeniably attractive in body and spirit. Someone I respect enough to let in my heart…"

She chews her bottom lip as I fold my arms over my chest, assessing her. It's strange because people usually look at me with pity after saying kids aren't in my near future or that I haven't found the 'right' woman, but not Kelsey. She's looking at me with something akin to awe…either that or I have something all over my face.

"You uh…" She points to my glasses. "Mashed blueberry."

I quickly take off my glasses and wipe them on my shirt, feeling like the biggest idiot. I professed my perfect woman to her with mashed blueberry on my glasses. Fucking great.

"Let's take this into the family room where Olive can toddle around while we eat," I mutter as I scoop the bags up and grab two beers from the fridge. After Kelsey puts Olive in her walker, we sit down on the couch as I search to see what's on TV. "*The Mandalorian* is on. Oh wait, you haven't watched any of them yet. Can't watch them out of order." I put on a *Discovery Channel* show about the Alaskan Wilderness and dig into my food.

I feel Kelsey looking at me. I turn my head slightly and she smiles at me.

"What?"

"Can I ask you something?"

I lean back in my chair and drink my beer. "Shoot."

"Why do you like *Star Wars* so much? I mean, why the obsession?"

"It's not an obsession, Kels, it's a...connection. I feel connected to the movies. I was orphaned when I was eight. My parents died in a car crash."

"Oh Patrick, I'm so sorry, I didn't know."

I shrug. "It was a long time ago. My dad's cousin and his wife adopted me, but I always felt like an outsider in their family. They weren't mean, they just...didn't care. I always felt in the way. I was like an extra sofa in their already-cramped living room. I struggled with fitting in at school. I had to wear hand-me-downs of my cousins that were too small. I had glasses and bad haircuts and loved sci-fi. My dad had an old collection of *Star Wars* movies and watching them made me feel connected to him. It was the good guys taking out the bad guys."

I take a bite of food, unable to bring myself to look at her expression. I can't believe I'm telling her all this. The only person I've ever confessed this to was Lovie, but Kelsey's silence spurs me on.

"In college, I met Lovie. She was my girlfriend's room-mate. My first girlfriend, so you can imagine how awkward I was…but Lovie, she didn't see my gawkiness. She was such a pain in the ass." I chuckle, remembering my first time meeting her. "She was this high-strung boisterous little pixie bomb. She was going to be my friend come hell or high water."

"She has that way about her." Kelsey laughs.

"Yeah, she does." I smirk as I wipe the condensation off my beer. "She's my Princess Leia, and Nick's my Han Solo, and they accept me as I am."

I look up to see Kelsey wiping under her eyes. "I'm sorry I've been so awful to you," she whispers.

"Hey, why are you crying?"

She sniffs as she quickly rubs her nose with a napkin. "I'm not…this is spicy." She stands up and walks down the hall to her bedroom. I look at Olive, who's slobbering on one of the toys attached to the walker.

"Did I say something wrong?" I ask Olive, who gurgles in response as drool drips down her chin.

Kelsey walks back in holding a scrapbook journal and sits down beside me. She hands me the book.

"What's this?"

"Just open it." She nervously rubs her palms on her jeans. "You shared something personal with me, so I'm sharing something back."

Kelsey pretends not to watch as I open her journal, keep-ing her focus between her food and the little cutie gumming her toy. I thumb through the pages littered with one-word phrases, short stories, and photographs of exotic-looking places, white sand beaches, and sun-drenched mountaintops. Postcards of Italy, Spain, The Netherlands, Austria, and Greece adorn the pages.

"Have you traveled to these places? They're spectacular."

"No, Nick gave me those, but I'd like to...someday. Take a boat and sail off into the sunset and see where life takes me. Write about my journeys...maybe write a book, adopt a cat to keep me company. Send these postcards once I get there."

"It sounds—"

"Crazy and stupid, I know. Or as my parents like to say, 'reckless and irresponsible'."

"I was going to say, thrilling." Our gazes lock as I close the book. "It's beautiful. I didn't know you could sail."

"Yes, my dad taught me when I was six. I started competing in regattas the following summer."

"Why a cat? A dog would be a better companion. I mean, I don't know much about cats except for Lindsey's, and he's an asshole."

Kelsey laughs. "Well, a cat would be easier to take on long journeys than a dog, but I do love dogs. Maybe someday." She looks vulnerable as she leans into my space and gently takes the book from my hands, placing it on her lap. "It's just a dream. It's silly."

"It's not silly, Kels. Dreams are never silly. We wouldn't have hope without dreams."

"Most people's dreams don't come true."

"But sometimes they do."

I can't help myself as I twine a piece of her strawberry-blonde hair around my finger. The texture is silky as it slips easily between my fingertips. Her breath hitches as I lean in, counting the dusting of freckles on the bridge of her nose. Her eyes, the color of moonstones, widen before fluttering closed as I swoop in and capture her lips with mine. Her fingers thread through my hair as the book slips off her lap, hitting the floor with a loud thud. My tongue gently sweeps across her velvet-soft lips, begging for access to the sweetness inside. She parts them, my tongue tangling with hers as I greedily grab her hips and shift her onto my lap. She moans as she deepens the kiss, and I want to feel her against my skin. Scratch that, I *need* to feel her. She's silky soft and warm where my fingers spread across her back. My thumbs find the satin edge of her bra when Olive starts to cry.

"Olive." She pants as she pushes me away. "I should get…I need to get…"

"Olive." I frown as she launches off my lap. She turns to pick Olive up out of the walker, swinging her on her hip.

"I need to get her ready for bed and get her a bottle." Her eyes dart around the room.

"Why are you so flustered?"

"I'm not…flustered! I'm irritated!"

"By what?"

"I completely lost all track of space and time. Olive could have been hurt. Nick and Lindsey could have walked in on us!" She picks up Olive's pacifier. "I…never mind, you don't understand."

"What don't I understand?"

"You're a distraction, Patrick. One I don't need right now."

I get up and walk to her calmly like I'm trying to talk her

off the ledge. I kind of like that our kiss has her unraveling like a ball of twine. "Why don't you go give her a bath, and I'll make her a bottle."

"Okay, yeah, good idea." Kelsey rushes out of the room before I can kiss her again.

Leaning against the wall, I rake my fingers through my hair, exhaling the pent-up tension. *Jesus, what the hell are you doing?* She's made it clear this could never work, so why do you keep pushing her? Because that distraction she's talking about was totally worth it, and I know she feels it too.

Chapter 16

Patrick

The Stakeout

I LOWER THE magazine I picked up from the coffee table as I covertly watch Kelsey in the kitchen. She hasn't mentioned the kiss from the other night, and neither have I, but I can't stop thinking about it. I wonder if it's put her on edge as well. She opens the fridge, pulls a bottle of water out, and slips a granola bar into her purse. Why is she taking a snack if she's going to dinner? She doesn't notice me sprawled out in the living room chair until I clear my throat, causing her to jump as she walks by me.

She puts a hand over her chest. "Jesus, you scared me. Why are you lurking in here?"

"I'm not lurking, I'm reading a magazine."

She peers at the cover, and now I wish I hadn't mentioned it.

"*You Go Girl* magazine?" She smirks.

Dammit, Lovie, this is all her fault for leaving stupid shit like this lying around. Why couldn't it be something cool and manly like *GQ* or *Rolling Stone* or some auto mechanics magazine?

I clear my throat. "It's important to know..." I flip the

magazine over to the front cover, "uh, how to wax your…oh wow, okay. No need to go there." I throw the magazine onto the coffee table as Kelsey laughs.

"You're going to wax off your pubes in the shape of a heart for Valentine's Day this year? You go, girl! Are you going to vajazzle it too?" Her lips curl beautifully into a sly grin as she picks up the magazine and thumbs through it.

My ears feel like they are on fire. "What? No. I don't even know what a Vajazzle is, nor do I want to." *Jesus, get off the subject, you idiot.* "Where are you headed tonight? You're dressed nice." She looks fantastic in a red sheath dress. A pang of jealousy makes my skin itch for whoever she's meeting.

"Nowhere special. I'm meeting my cousin."

"Dressed like that?"

"Is there something wrong with the way I'm dressed?" She folds her arms over her chest and glares at me.

"I didn't mean it like…I mean…you look gorgeous." I trip over my words as she wraps a thin sweater around herself. "Is he picking you up? What time will you be back?"

"Patrick, is there a problem? I feel like my dad is questioning me. Don't you have something better to go do than harass me?"

I huff indignance at being called out. "I'm not trying to be invasive. I'm curious. I want to make sure you're safe. There are some dangerous parts of Miami."

"Patrick, I assure you, I can handle myself. And you know what they say about curiosity." She arches an eyebrow as she pulls the handle of the front door. "It killed the cat." The door shuts with a loud bang.

"Lovie! Let's go! Cranky Cat is on the move!" I bellow down the hall. "Where are you? Come on!"

Lindsey comes out of the bathroom in pajamas, brushing her teeth. "Who's Cranky Cat?"

"Our code name for Kelsey. What the hell are you doing? Why are you brushing your teeth at seven p.m.? We've got a stakeout to go on!" I go to the front window and see Kelsey looking at her phone. "Quick, go get into the car! Where's Olive?"

"Nick is out with her. Look, I understand Mission Cranky Cat is important to you, but I'm tired, and I wanted to watch Gordon Ramsey. Besides, Nick will be home soon. I feel like I've barely seen him."

"I swear it's like trying to hustle the Golden Girls out the door," I mutter as I throw her bag at her. "Lovie, if you don't get your ass in the car, I'm going to suggest that live insect place on the website for the fans to vote for."

Lindsey swallows and grimaces from the toothpaste. "You wouldn't."

"Try me."

"Some best friend you are," she gripes as she rinses her mouth, ties a bathrobe around herself, and stalks toward the garage. "I can't believe you've talked me into going on a stakeout to spy on Kelsey because you don't have the balls to ask her yourself what she's doing."

"I've tried," I squeal as I push her out to the minivan in the garage.

"Wow, let's bring it down a notch and not sound like a prepubescent thirteen-year-old. Isn't she going to see us roll on out of here in the mom-mobile?"

"She thinks we're going to dinner." I start the car and slowly pull out of the garage.

"Look, there she goes in that Honda," Lindsey yells. "You're going to lose her. Mrs. Bixby can drive faster than this!"

"Eat your heart out, Mrs. Bixby." I peel out of the driveway, except I've put too much gas and horsepower, causing the tires to spin and squeal on the new asphalt. The car fishtails on the road as I try to regain control.

"Well, that was incognito, Ace Ventura. Why don't we roll down the windows and shout to Kelsey that we're spying on her?"

"Sorry, I got a little excited." My eyes return to the road. "We're not spying per se...we're making sure she's not in any danger."

"Potayto, potahto."

I shoot down a side street and catch up to the blue hatchback.

"Follow that Uber!"

"Yeah, I'm on it. No need to make me lose hearing in my right ear."

"Can't you at least go above fifty?" she gripes. "Sheesh, eighty-year-old Mario Andretti drives faster than this."

"Lovie, what the hell do you expect me to do? The speed limit is forty. We're in a residential neighborhood. I can't tail the Uber driver, that would be obvious."

"Well, you can't hang so far back that you'll get stuck at a red light and lose her. I knew I should have driven." She drums her fingers on her knee.

"Please, you can barely see over the steering wheel." I

snort as I look over at her.

"Nice one," she sneers back at me. "The short jokes are *so* original. How about you pay attention to the road?"

I follow the little blue Honda but keep at least one car between us. They zig-zag through the city into a seedy neighborhood as dusk turns into evening. Lindsey rolls up her window. "Where are we? Are you sure about this? I'm not so sure about this." Her voice quivers as we pass by a drug deal going down out in the open. "I better get the Miami heat out."

"We're still in South Beach. What the hell are you talking about?" My gaze flits from the road to Lindsey and back again. She reaches down and pulls something out of her diaper bag.

"Oh my God, Lovie! Is that a gun?" I swerve the car as I stare down at the little pink and white Glock 42. "Where the hell did you get that, and why the hell is it in Olive's diaper bag?"

"It's totally fine. It's mine, isn't it cute? Nick bought it for me. Pink like the pink wire. Don't worry. He taught me how to use it."

"Why does that not make me feel *at all* at ease?" I start to sweat. "I can't *believe* Nick thought it was a good idea to give you a gun. Point that thing at the floor. Jesus, this is going downhill quickly. Is the safety on?"

"How the hell should I know?"

"Lovie! Jesus!"

"Calm the fuck down, Trick, of course it's on." She giggles. "Nick made me take a written and verbal exam on this thing. Not to mention I had to take one to get my gun license."

"They'll sell them to anyone these days," I grumble as I slow the car down. I look in the rearview. "Look, Kelsey's getting out of the car. Where are we?" I didn't notice that we had turned down a private lane with all the gun commotion. I switch my headlights off and pull to the side, so she doesn't see us.

Kelsey pays the driver and walks toward a dock ramp leading down to a gorgeous large yacht.

"I can't believe she's alone right now." I look over at Lindsey, who is unusually quiet. She has a pair of binoculars glued to her eyes as she chews on Twizzlers. "Where the hell did you get those?"

"You can't go on a stakeout and not have snacks. Hello? It's like spy 101 common knowledge."

"I was talking about the binoculars." I side-eye her. "I think I'm going to have to go in and get closer."

"Hmm...she's talking to some security guy and showing her license. Oh my god, Trick, what if this is like that Liam Neeson movie where his daughter gets taken and then drugged and sold into the black market? What if Kelsey is about to be kidnapped and shot up with drugs, so out of her mind she can't remember who she is as she dances in lingerie for wealthy foreign businessmen?"

"You are not helping my anxiety at the moment. At all!" I yank the binoculars from her grip and try to locate Kelsey with them. "I don't see...oh wait, she's talking to some guy. Is that Kiernan? I don't remember seeing him at the wedding. She's hugging him."

"I don't remember meeting a cousin named Kiernan."

Lindsey chews off a bite of her Twizzler, elbowing me hard in the arm.

"*Really?*"

"What? Oh, you want some? I only have one left." She holds up a limp piece of licorice. She doesn't look like she wants to share it, so I pluck it from her fingers out of spite.

"Thanks." I scan the crowd on the yacht. "There are other people…it looks like a cocktail party." I lower the binoculars. "I need to get on that boat."

"No way, that's a bad idea. There's probably security detail everywhere. I'm hungry. Did you bring any snacks?" She shoves the rest of her Twizzler in her mouth.

"Didn't you just tell me you brought a bunch of food since that's spy 101?"

"You ate my last Twizzler. Who knew you were going to finish off the bag?" she gripes.

"How can you think about food right now? You put the image of her drugged and kidnapped in my head."

"Sorry, I'm pregnant. I could kill for a veggie burrito or a steak and bean with extra guac." She groans as she rifles through her bag. "This is torture. Now I can't stop thinking about burritos."

We sit in silence for a few minutes. Lindsey starts drumming her fingers on the console. "Oh my god, this is sooo boring."

"Lovie, just chill."

"I have to pee."

"Of course you do," I gripe. "Can't you hold it, I dunno, for five minutes?" I reach into the back and grab my hooded cape.

Lindsey snorts when she eyes what I'm holding. "Please tell me you didn't bring your lightsaber as well."

"I figure the cape will make me more incognito—"

"Or like a superhero?"

I ignore her taunt because she's right; it does make me feel like I'm about to save the world. "Look, I need to get closer. Give me your gun."

"But you don't know how to use it. Nick will kill me if—"

"Lovie, it's supposed to make me look badass. I'm not going to use it."

She reluctantly hands over the pink gun. Well, maybe not badass carrying a pink Glock, but I feel better having it. "Wait, take this too." She hands over a black handheld device.

"Is this a taser? Did Nick give you this? I'm seriously starting to question his judgment." I hand the taser back to her. "You should keep this with you, but don't use it unless you feel threatened. Nod if you understand me."

She nods. "Fine, but hurry, I still have to pee."

"Stay in the car. Don't leave unless you have to use the taser. Lock the doors."

"But—"

"I promise to get you a burrito in ten minutes, okay?" I slide out of the mom-mobile. "Worst stakeout partner in the history of ever," I mumble to myself.

"I heard that! And you don't look badass, you loo—" she yells before I shut the door on her. I raise the hood on my cape and crouch down, running along the edge of the lawn, blending in with the thick hedges that line the property.

The house that this yacht belongs to is a sprawling stucco castle. They have to have security prowling around. I almost wish I had taken the taser in case I get tackled. It was the ideal choice for a weapon, but I don't actually know how to use it, and with my luck, I'd end up tasering myself. At least with the gun, I know the safety is on. I pull out the Glock just in case. If all else fails, I can clock a guy in the head with it, right? They make it look easy in the movies.

I stop and lift the binoculars. There's one security guy at the front of the ramp and another on the deck. Kelsey is drinking champagne as she talks to a smartly dressed woman along with the man she hugged earlier—the supposed cousin, Kiernan. I pull out my phone and take a few pictures, but I'm too far to get a clear image. A thousand different scenarios of what could be happening race through my brain. She shakes the woman's hand, smiling as she laughs at something 'Kiernan' says. The older woman steps back inside the yacht while Kelsey hugs her cousin.

Frustration churns deep in my gut as I watch them rejoin the party inside. I know now that she isn't in immediate danger, but curiosity still plagues me. What exactly is she up to? There's no doubt in my mind she's hiding something.

I'm about to move back toward the car when I hear a commotion to my left. I lift the binoculars. "Oh god, oh no."

Lindsey, in her bathrobe, is flailing one arm wildly at the security guy blocking the ramp to the yacht while a new security guard stands behind her. Dammit, I told her to wait in the car. What are we going to tell Kelsey if she discovers us out here? I take one more look back at the yacht to make sure the party is still going strong inside. I run across the perfectly manicured lawn to the boat ramp.

"Lovie! What are you doing?" I bark at her.

"There you are! See Alberto? I told you he was here!"

I approach her as I look at Alberto warily.

"I can't believe you'd leave me in the car alone. You know I'm scared of the dark!" She tries to edge past Alberto.

"Uh ma'am, I've already told you, this is a private party," Alberto says gruffly as he blocks Lindsey from the ramp.

"Is he the entertainment?" the other security guard asks Alberto. They eye up my black cloak. "Did they hire a magician? I didn't get that on the itinerary."

"Lovie, we should go." I nod and smile nervously at the two security guards.

"But we have a job to do, remember? You're the magician, and I'm your assistant?" Her eyebrows are up to her hairline as she jerks her head toward the security guards. She looks like she's bobbing her head to some bad nineties tune.

I glance wildly between the two security guards. "Okay, gentlemen, I'm so sorry. The truth is, I am the entertainment for this evening. She's my assistant. I lost her at the party. I'm so glad you found her, but I don't think she's feeling well, so I should get her home."

"I caught her peeing in one of the bushes back by the road," the security officer behind her says. I look him over and thank the stars she didn't use the taser on him.

"Uh, could you excuse us for one moment?" I will throttle her if we make it out of this unscathed. "What are you doing?" I whisper harshly as I pull her off to the side.

"Saving your butt. I'm in character, don't ruin it!" she

hisses back, throwing her arms about.

"Uh, ma'am? Is everything okay?" Alberto barks as he steps forward, trying to block our little squabble from the guests on the boat.

"Look, Alberto, my piece-of-shit magician boyfriend decided he wants to skip out on tonight's job, but I said no way, we need the money. He told me in the car while he mingled with the party guests. For an hour! That's why I had to pee so bad. I'm so sorry. I just wanted some food and to go home and binge-watch Gordon Ramsey. Is that too much to ask?"

I look on in disbelief as the two security guards exchange looks.

"That's really low, mister."

"But...but...can't anyone hear how crazy that sounds?"

Alberto turns to his partner. "Well, they should go up inside. I don't want the boss to be upset that we turned away the entertainment."

"Yeah, this guy isn't skipping out on the job on our watch."

Oh god, oh no. "I—"

"Great idea, Alberto, thank you so much." Lindsey tugs my arm. "Come on, Magical Mike, you heard the man. Let's get to work."

Alberto lets us walk past him up the ramp to the yacht.

"What the hell are you doing, Lovie?!" I hiss. "Kelsey can't see us! Our cover will be blown!"

"Trust me, we'll do a few magic tricks and poof! Disappear like a rabbit in your hat. She won't even know we're here. Do you think they'll have a cheese plate?"

"But I don't *know* any magic tricks!"

"Perhaps you shouldn't strut around at night in dark capes pretending to be a jedi."

"If we ever get out of this intact, I'm going to kill you."

The security guy at the door speaks to his wrist and opens the door for us, nodding as we walk into the crowded room. I see a woman in a red dress and almost dive behind a couch, but luckily, it's not Kelsey. Thank goodness it's crowded in here, giving us lots of coverage to hide.

"Lovie, we need to get out of here *now* before we get caught!" I hiss over my shoulder, but she's no longer behind me. I spin around desperately, looking for my short little bathrobe-wearing lunatic. I spot her chatting amicably with a waiter as she stuffs a napkin full of hors d'oeuvres into her robe pocket. "Lovie, what are you doing? We've got to go!" I grab her sleeve as I scan the crowd nervously.

"Okay, give me a sec. Tony is going to go grab me a cheese plate. My blood sugar is low."

A man walks by us and eyes my cape curiously. "Lovie, for fuck's sake, now is not the time to think about food! We have to figure out how to get off the boat."

"Patrick, relax. It's fine. We'll walk off the same way we came on."

"So, you're the entertainment? Fantastic!" A meaty hand grasps my shoulder. I turn to an older gentleman dressed in a tuxedo. He's holding a highball of whiskey. He eyes Lindsey's bathrobe, his brow furrowing. "They told me they were sending acrobats, but let's see what you've got."

"Oh shit," Lindsey breathes before shoving a stuffed mushroom in her mouth. I'm starting to sweat profusely.

"Oh, er, I think there's been a mis—"

"You two can set up in the main salon, or would you rather be on the top deck? Let me get my chief stew to get you situated."

"Main salon," Lindsey says at the same time I say, "Top deck."

The man chuckles. "Okay, well, I'll let you two duke it out. Please let the staff know when you're ready. We're certainly looking forward to this." He waggles his eyebrows at Lindsey. "Can't wait to see the outfit under the robe."

I see a flash of red, and without thinking, I crouch down. The man looks at me quizzically. "Uh, okay then, I'll leave you two to it. I'll send Danielle over now."

Lindsey laughs nervously. "Cheerio!"

"Get down! I think I saw Kelsey," I harshly whisper as I tug her robe.

Lindsey cranes her neck. "I don't see her. So, I think we should go up top because—"

"Are you *crazy*? We are not staying here! We're getting the hell off this boat, pronto! We don't know any magic tricks…"

"We could be acrobats," she says hopefully as she starts doing stretches. "I did gymnastics in grade school."

"What are you *doing*?" I watch, horrified, as she tries to put her ankle behind her neck. Several people around us notice and give us a wide berth.

"Duh, I'm stretching. Although I'm not as limber as I used to be."

I shake my head. "This is not an audition for Cirque du Soleil. I can't even do a cartwheel, much less a split. You are pregnant in a bathrobe, and oh, I don't know, maybe the little fun fact that we are on a stakeout and Cranky Cat *can't* see us!"

"But that man in the tuxedo seemed so nice. I feel bad leaving him in the lurch."

I want to bang my head against the wall. "Is the pregnancy sucking oxygen from your brain? The real 'acrobats' are going to show up any minute! We need to leave!"

Lindsey's eyes widen. "Oh, well, that would be embarrassing."

"You *think*?"

"How do you think they'll take it when they find out they've been replaced by us?" She chews her thumbnail as she scans the crowd.

I growl in exasperation, "Come on." I tug her back to where we entered. "I'm going to blame this on pregnancy hormones. I have to, or else I'll kill you—"

"Wait!" She digs in her heels. "What about my food?"

"I do not need to end up in the bottom of this ocean with a cinderblock tied to my ankle courtesy of Alberto because you needed a *cheese plate*!"

"Geez, you're grumpy on stakeouts," she grumbles behind me as I lead the way toward the door. I hold my hand up to shield my face in case Kelsey looks our way. I nod to the security guy at the door.

"Uh, we left some props in our car. We'll be right back."

We're halfway down the plank when we hear a commotion behind us. "Ma'am! Hello? I have your plate of food!"

"Oh yes! Tony, you're the best. Thank you so much!"

Alberto holds up a hand. "Where do you think you two

are going?"

"Oh, we forgot some props in the car. We'll be right back." Sweat collects on my brow as my heartrate kicks up a notch.

"Right back," Lindsey says around a mouthful of cheese.

A flash of bouncing light catches my eye over Alberto's shoulder. A couple dressed in sparkly sequined leotards approach the plank. Alberto's radio squawks, and I swear I hear the word 'imposter'.

"Lovie, run!" I scream hysterically as I pull her gun out of the back waistband of my jeans, just in case.

Lindsey bolts, and I don't think twice as I dart past a bewildered Alberto and the two acrobats. In my haste, I stumble over a small rock and get tangled up in my cape, which sends me flying to the ground. My fingers clench the trigger of the gun, and it goes off with a loud bang. Surprise and fear have me scrabbling to my feet as I hear several partygoers scream, the security team bellowing after us.

"Lovie! Start the van! You're driving!" My voice breaks as I scream in pure panic looking over my shoulder. I reach the passenger side and fling the door open. "Go, go!" I barely manage to swing myself in before she peels out. "What the fuck, Lovie? The safety was *not* on!"

"Did you shoot someone?" Her eyes are saucered as I look back to see if anyone is following us. "Holy shit, that was so close. Did you see the acrobats? I almost peed in my pants and dropped my cheese plate. Thank god I peed earlier, or we'd have a much bigger problem on our hands."

I punch in our home address as I will my speeding heart to slow down. Lindsey shoves some kind of appetizer into her mouth from the plate sitting in her lap.

"Did you hear them say imposter over the radio? I for sure thought we were toast."

Lindsey snorts. "He didn't say imposter, he said we need more pasta. Probably a server was talking over the radio."

"Well, regardless, how were we going to explain our way out of it with the acrobats? That was close, too close." I run my fingers through my hair and sink back into my chair as the pulsing adrenalin slows to sludge in my bloodstream. "Didn't I tell you to stay in the car? You almost got us arrested because you wanted a charcuterie board from the yacht!"

"I was hungry," she whines around a mouthful of crackers. "I was about to pass out, and I had to pee like a whale. My blood sugar was at like zero. Oh, and by the way, you shouldn't be yelling at me. You owe me big time."

"For what?" I turn to her, completely exasperated. "For almost getting us arrested because you were peeing on private property? For pretending we were the entertainment for the evening? Or for almost shooting myself with your gun because the safety was *not* on?"

Lindsey rolls her eyes as she shoves a toast point with cheese in her mouth. "Someone's a little tetchy. If it wasn't for me, you wouldn't have gotten on that boat."

"I didn't *need* to get on the boat," I say irritably.

"I thought that was the whole purpose of Mission Cranky Cat!"

I shake my head. "How does Nick do it? How does he endure? Aren't you worried he's going to snuff you out in the middle of the night?"

She huffs. "Nope, he loves me. I cut the pink wire, remember?"

I roll my eyes.

"Well, did you find anything out?" She offers me a cheese cracker as a peace offering which I grudgingly accept.

"She met with an older, well-dressed woman and her supposed cousin, Kiernan."

"That's it? I missed Gordon Ramsey for *that*?"

"You got a nice charcuterie board out of the deal," I say dryly.

She pops some grapes into her mouth as she looks over at me. "Tony does make an excellent cheese plate."

I run my hands over my face as I fast-track the night's events through my brain. "I'm glad we didn't get arrested. No more Cranky Cat missions, that was too close."

"One thing is for sure, we can't tell Nick about any of this."

"Agreed. This will be our little secret."

"Speaking of secrets…" She punches me in the arm.

"Ow, what was that for?"

"I can't *believe* you slept with Kelsey and didn't tell me!"

"I can't believe it's taken you this long to bring it up."

"When did you guys…How did that happen? Why didn't you tell me? It must not have gone well, she doesn't seem to really like you. You two are the least likely pair I thought would hook up. I mean, she's the exact opposite you normally date."

"Well, maybe the whole 'opposites attract' thing is true. She needs time to get used to the idea of me."

Lindsey snorts. "You're definitely going to need some

wand skills to tame that one. She's feisty."

I eye her warily. "Yeah, reminds me of someone I know."

"I agree, she's exactly like her brother."

I chuckle as I shake my head. "We hooked up at your wedding. We both had a lot to drink that night. She left before I woke up," I admit. Lindsey blanches. "I'm sorry I didn't tell you, but I was worried it would upset you. Life kind of went on after that and that was it. I moved on with Candy—"

"Glad you saw the light with that one." She looks over, worry creasing her brow. "Kelsey seems like she likes to keep everyone at arm's length. When you fall, you fall hard. I don't want you to get hurt."

I huff out a laugh. "I'm a big boy, Lovie. I'll be fine. Even though she doesn't seem to like me much, there's something about her I'm drawn to. It's like the more she tells me to go away, the more I want to settle in and stay."

"That's what I'm worried about."

"Don't worry about me, Lovie."

"You're my twin from another mother, Trick, of course I'm going to worry." She looks at me affectionately. "How can she say no to you? You're like a sweet gangly stray puppy dog." She ruffles my hair. "Ooh, yes! Burrito stand."

"Not exactly the image I'm going for," I grumble as she pulls the car over. "Are you sure it's a good idea to get a burrito from a stand? Remember what happened the last time we ate from a taco stand?"

"Luckily, I won't be trying to impress any cute life-guards. If I need to puke, I'll throw up on Nick." She winks as she gets out of the car.

I laugh and shake my head as I watch her walk up to the stand in her pajamas and bathrobe without a care in the world. I tap open my phone and look at the pictures I took tonight. They're grainy and not that good, but I can still identify the people. Kelsey obviously knew her cousin tonight on the boat, but who was the older woman? Why would Kelsey be at a fancy party like that anyway?

I know I should drop it and let Kelsey handle her own life, but the thought of anything bad happening to her makes my stomach clench. And if she is up to her neck in trouble, we need to get Nick involved.

Lindsey sighs as she bites into her burrito after getting back in the van. "Best damn veggie burrito ever."

We drive home and pull the van into the garage next to Nick's car. "Okay, what's our game plan?"

"No game plan. We went out for food. Keep it simple." Lindsey holds up her half-eaten burrito. I nod and tuck the gun back in her diaper bag. "I think you need to retake your test on that."

We walk in through the back door and find Nick standing in the kitchen. "Where have you two been?"

"Oh, hey, handsome!" Lindsey reaches up to kiss his cheek. "We went out to grab something to eat. How's Olive?"

"She's fine, I'm about to give her a bath." Nick holds her to him. "Craving burritos again?"

"Yes! If this continues, I'm going to give birth to a burrito."

"Where's Kels?"

"Oh, out with your cousin, I think," I say as I carefully

lay the diaper bag on the kitchen table.

His brow creases. "Huh…where's your food?" He eyes my empty hands.

"Oh, um, I ate it already." My stomach erupts with a loud growl. Lindsey gives me a look, but it's not like I can control my hunger noises. "Uh." I laugh, slapping a hand over my stomach. "I meant I ate earlier. Must be going through a growth spurt. Hungry again."

Nick arches an eyebrow and looks at me dubiously. "A growth spurt? At thirty-three?"

"I wish I could have a growth spurt," Lindsey says sourly.

"You're perfect just the way you are, babe." Nick slings an arm around her and bends to kiss her. "Even if you're a pain in my—"

"Hey, I'm home." Kelsey walks into the kitchen and shrugs out of her sweater.

"You're home early." I cross my arms and lean against the kitchen island. She must have left right after us. That was close…*really* close.

"Oh yeah, the weirdest thing happened. I was with Kiernan—"

"Our cousin Kiernan?" Nick arches an eyebrow.

"Yes…our cousin Kiernan."

"Huh, I talked to him the other day. He didn't mention you guys were going to dinner."

"Oh really? I don't know…"

I make a noise of disbelief and quickly slap my hand on my stomach. "Hungry. I'm growing."

Kelsey gives me a strange look before continuing. "Anyway, we were at dinner, and there was a gunshot outside, so they cleared the restaurant. Said it was a domestic fight. Kind of crazy, but I was tired anyway, so Kiernan drove me home."

"He didn't want to come in and say hi?" Nick looks at her incredulously. "Why would they clear a restaurant if there were gunshots outside of it?"

"I don't know. I was following what the security guards were saying."

"Security guards at a restaurant? Where did you go?" Nick eyes her suspiciously, and I'm one hundred percent on board with his line of questioning because her story is totally bogus. If I can't crack her, Nick can.

"I already told you, I went to dinner with Kiernan. Stop being all 'Dad' on me. I'm older than you, Little Dick, and I can come and go as I please, so chill out. I'm going to change into some PJs." She exits the kitchen.

So much for Little Dick being able to crack her. I stare at Lindsey intently as we have a silent conversation.

Can you believe she just lied?

She did, didn't she. Okay, you were right, something is up.

I told you so.

Should we tell Nick?

No! Worst idea in the history of Lindsey's ideas.

I might have told him something was up.

Lovie!

Nick sighs as he looks from Lindsey to me. "What the hell are you two doing right now?"

"Nothing!"

"We have something to tell you!" Lindsey shouts over me. God, she sucks at being a sidekick.

Nick exhales and looks up at the ceiling. "I have a bad feeling. Why do I have a bad feeling? Did you two have something to do with why Kelsey is home early and why her story is total crap?"

I try to copy Nick's infamous glare to tell Lindsey to keep it zipped. "Of course not, sidekick. We were out getting a burrito."

"Lindsey?" Nick looks over at her for confirmation. She avoids us by warming a bottle of milk for Olive. "Lindsey..."

"What? We went for burritos. That's it."

"Well, what did you want to tell me?"

"Um...that they were really good."

"Uh-huh." He straightens up and looks at her closely. "Why do you have cracker crumbs all down the front of your robe, and why did you go get burritos in your pajamas?"

Lindsey gulps. "Oh, haha, that. I was hungry...so hungry I couldn't wait to get dressed."

"So you ate a sleeve of crackers on your way to get burritos?"

I jump in because I know Lovie is seconds away from cracking under pressure. "Her stomach was upset, so I told her to eat those first."

Nick looks from me to her and runs a hand through his hair. "I'm not sure what you two are up to, but whatever it is, leave me out of it and try not to get arrested. I'll give this to Olive." He grabs the bottle and strolls out of the kitchen.

"Whew, that was close." Lindsey deflates against the counter. "I hate lying to him."

"You're the one who didn't want to tell him."

"Well, I've had a change of tune. Why don't we want to

clue Nick in again?" she asks.

"Because I need more evidence to know what Kelsey is up to before we go running to the big guns. Haven't you watched any spy movies? You collect your evidence first before taking it to your supervisor. You would never make it as a detective," I say grumpily as I grab a bottle of water from the fridge before going to take a shower.

"I saved your butt twice tonight, thank you very much!" Lindsey yells after me. "And I can cut the pink wire!"

Chapter 17

Kelsey

Midnight Swim

I'M IN MY bed reading, unable to concentrate on the words on my e-reader. I'm pretty sure I've read the same sentence three times over. I'm restless but not sure what to do with myself. I'm on a high from my meeting tonight, and I want to shout it to the world, but I can't. If I told Nick, he'd tell my sisters or my parents, and I don't want to unnecessarily hurt my dad's feelings. He worked hard to get me the weekly Cookie's Cleaning Corner column at *The Ithaca Herald*. I can't tell my parents until I'm sure *The Miami Times* job is mine. I can't say anything to Lindsey because she would accidentally spill it to Nick. But I need to burn off this exhilarating energy. To celebrate that I've got a chance of a lifetime! I want to run and jump in the ocean and holler to the stars in the sky. Tonight I was thrown a lifeline, a second chance!

Kiernan's friend Marco set up the meeting for me tonight on the yacht. I met with the editor in chief of *The Miami Times*, and she invited me to set up an interview at the paper the week after next. I excitedly kick my legs in my sheets. I'm so glad I decided to go. I almost didn't. Fear had squeezed my courage to a pulp. All my self-doubts rose to the surface, telling me I didn't deserve it, that I wasn't a good writer, that I wasn't worthy. But at the last minute, I went anyway. What's the worst that could happen, I don't get the interview? Elizabeth Greyton was lovely, poised, and intimidating as hell. She told me she saw potential when she read my resume that Marco had pushed in front of her and wanted to talk to me more in-depth. She wanted me!

I jump out of bed and grab a towel. I want to dance in the moonlight and splash in the sea. I feel like walking on clouds to celebrate, and who better to do it with than a friend? I see the light under Patrick's door and softly knock before changing my mind. His footsteps shadow underneath the door before it slightly cracks open. Concern washes over his features as he opens the door wider.

"Hey, you okay?"

"Yes." I gulp a swallow. "No. I'm not sure. I have some energy to burn. Want to go for a midnight swim with me?" He hesitates, and my heart sinks. I know I don't deserve his kindness or his friendship. "I could use a friend right now."

He nods once as he walks back into the room and puts his book down on the nightstand. "Yeah, sure. Just give me a minute."

"I'll meet you out by the pool." I slowly retreat from his room and stealthily make my way through the family room and out to the back porch. I hesitate as I turn on the pool lights, wondering if Patrick would want to brave the ocean with me instead, but the pool looks so inviting and tranquil as the lights turn the ordinary water into a magical aqua lagoon. The air is tangy with salt blowing off the ocean, the sky midnight black. I drop my towel and slowly step into the water at the shallow end. The sun baking down on the pool all day has left the water warm, but I welcome it like a soothing hug. I breaststroke down to the deep end and wait.

Patrick steps out onto the patio, and I can't help but ogle his long, lean body. He's built like a swimmer with just the right amount of muscle. His broad shoulders taper down into a narrow waist, the moonlight glancing off his rigid abdominal muscles. His skin is smooth and taut as he bends to place his towel on the chaise lounge. If I were an artist, I'd sketch him for hours.

"Come on in, it's nice."

He smiles as he slowly walks down the stairs into the shallow part of the pool. I cling to the edge of the deep end, waiting for him to join me. Without a word, he dives in, and with two quick strokes, he's at the end of the pool.

He breaks the water and shakes his head as he leans on the warm terracotta tile ledge. "You're right, that's nice."

"Yeah." I study his silhouette in the dark. My foot brushes his, and I instantly pull it back.

He studies me for a moment as the lapping water casts eerie shadows over his face. "So, what's going on? Why the midnight swim?"

"I just needed...you," I say boldly, telling myself to block out everything else going on in my life right now. To live in the moment, happy and carefree. This moment of a warm saltwater pool in the dark, alone with Patrick. It magically transports me back to that night we stared at each other with the same longing in his hotel room a year ago.

He licks his pouty lips, and it makes me want to lean in

and bite them. His eyes are like pools of amber and gold as they cautiously roam from my eyes to my lips. I want to tell him about the interview, but something holds me back. Not yet, the little voice in my head whispers.

"I've been lying to you," I confess. He blinks as he holds perfectly still. "I've been lying when I said that night meant nothing to me. It scares me how much I've thought about that night. How much I've thought about you. It terrifies me that I can't put that night in my past and move forward."

The air stirs around us, the breeze like a kiss against my fevered skin.

"Say something," my husky plea breaks the silent spell night has cast on us as my foot brushes his leg again. Instead of pulling away, I brazenly glide it up his calf as we cling to the edge. Something unnamed and electric buzzes in the air, urging me to bring him closer as I feel his breath skate over mine. Beads of water drip down his muscular freckled shoulders, my tongue itching to lick them off his skin. His golden-brown eyes darken as they stay locked on my own. I fight the urge to lean in and wrap myself around him.

"I've known you were lying. I've just been waiting for you to realize it." His voice is barely above a growl as he gently grips my calf and pulls me flush with his rock-hard body. I suck in a breath, simultaneously scared and incredibly turned-on by the feral look in his eyes.

I let go of the edge, and for a moment, my heart drums to a beat of longing against my chest as we stare into each other's eyes. I want this to happen. God, I need this to happen. I reflexively squeeze my thighs around him. Without a word or a warning, his lips capture mine as my fingers push into his wet hair. It's not a gentle kiss. It's a mixture of regret, need, and pleasure. His tongue slides with mine as I cling to him. With one hand he holds us to the ledge while the other squeezes my ass. I can feel his hardness as he grinds against me, causing a spark of pleasure to zip from my toes up to my breasts.

Patrick breaks the kiss and peels down the edge of my bikini top. His lips feel cool against my hot skin as he sucks my nipple. I feel like a lit firecracker about to burst into the inky sky.

"Patrick," I sigh as he does the same to my other breast. He groans as I palm his hard dick through his swim trunks. "Do you want me?" My head falls back as he kisses his way up my neck.

"You have no idea," he says, his voice hoarse as he returns that luscious mouth to my breast. I arch into him and cry out as he tugs my nipple with his teeth. "But not in the pool."

I pull up the cups of my swimsuit and place my hands on the warm stone ledge as I push myself up. In one languid movement, he lifts himself out and sits next to me, water sluicing down his muscles. Reaching, he holds my face tenderly as his lips find mine again. I shiver as the evening breeze cools against my wet skin. He pulls me up and grabs a towel, wrapping it around us.

"I'm not ready to go inside yet." Making love to Patrick under the stars appeals to me.

Patrick nods and lays our towels down on the cushioned double chaise lounge. He turns to me, pulling me flush to him. I shiver in anticipation as his lips crush mine. He unties my bikini top and lets it drop to the ground. I push on his shoulders, indicating that I want him to lie down. I straddle his lap as he sucks on my breast, knowing how much it turns me on. I arch into him, needing more.

"Do you have protection?" I whisper.

"Shit, not out here."

I nod as I nip his lips. "Will you run away if I run inside and grab a condom?"

He smirks. "Will you?"

"Fair point."

"Look in the bathroom in my Dopp kit."

"I'm so sorry this is such a mood killer. Don't move," I say. "Think about sexy stuff, so you stay in the mood."

He eyes me and raises his eyebrows, smiling. "No problem there."

I dash inside, careful not to make too much noise. It would be exactly my luck to have Nick and Lindsey walk out on us. I grab a condom and run back out, panting as I throw myself down next to him. He looks at me bemusedly as I press the condom foil on his stomach, trying to catch my breath.

"Jesus, I think I need to start running again," I pant. "This is so not sexy."

"Kels, look at me." Patrick rolls me toward him. "You are the sexiest woman I have ever laid eyes on."

"But I'm panting…out of breath, oh my god, why can't I get it under control?"

"I'm pretending you're so in lust with me it leaves you breathless."

I giggle as I land soft kisses over his chest and down his

ribcage, trying like hell to regain my composure. "I am in lust with you," I mumble as I continue to kiss him as he peels his swim trunks off and throws them to the side. He sucks in a breath as I wrap my hands around his hard shaft. I lick the salty tip and then slide it into my mouth. His hands tangle in my hair as he groans.

"Feel the force…Jesus, Kels…Jedi…Yoda…wookies…"

"Are you quoting…*Star Wars* while I go down on you?"

"Shit, sorry. I was trying not to blow my load. It feels so fucking good. Come here." He places his hand behind my neck and guides me to his lips. His fingers stroke down my waist and hook into my bikini bottoms.

"Patrick, wait," I say. His hands still as I lean up. "Are you worried?"

"About what?"

"What if…what if it's not as good as we remember it? What if we've built that night up so much in our heads? What if we're like a dud firecracker? The kind that starts with a bang and then fizzles out."

Patrick laughs. "Kelsey, it's going to be even better. I promise."

He dips a finger into me, and I cry out as I grind against him. I feel myself building as he quickens his pace. I want to unravel in his arms with an intensity I've never felt before. "Yes!" I pant as he brings me closer to the edge. He removes his finger, and I want to cry out.

"Take off your bottoms," he says huskily as he rolls the condom on. I do as he says and straddle him, guiding him slowly into me, letting my body adjust to his size. I slowly start to move as he leans up and sucks on my nipple. I drive my fingers into his silky hair as I pick up my pace, right back where I was.

"Don't stop, Patrick," I murmur, arching my back in ecstasy. He lies back down, grabbing my hips as he controls the rhythm and speed. I feel an overwhelming pressure pushing me forward to release and let go. My hips move on their own as I give over to the sensations. "Oh my god," I whimper as the desire in me builds so fast I can barely hang on as I explode around him. The dark sky above evaporates into white-hot stars as I ride out my orgasm.

He quickly flips over my spent body as he kneels and bends my leg up so he can get a deeper angle. "You feel so fucking good, Kelsey, so wet and warm I could bury myself in you forever." He pumps into me over and over, relentless in his rhythm, his thumb swirling circles right where I need him to.

"Patrick, I'm going to come again." I arch my neck as my body shudders under his.

"Come for me, Kels," he grunts as he thrusts harder. I cry out as I come undone for a second time, my walls clenching around him as he pushes me past my limit. He follows right behind me, growling my name as he drives into me.

Patrick leans over me, supporting himself on his elbows, my leg still wrapped around him.

I smile up at him. "Even better than before."

"Even better than before." He bends to kiss my nose.

Chapter 18

Patrick

Minions vs. Pineapple Pizza

I WAKE UP the following morning and stretch as I turn my head and smile. I run my fingers down Kelsey's tanned arm she's thrown over my chest, her body snuggled into mine. I'm on cloud nine that she stayed through the night. She hums in pleasure as I run my fingers up and down her satiny skin. "I'll go get us some coffee."

"Mmm, yes...coffee."

I slowly get up and throw on some sweatpants. I run a hand through my hair and saunter down the hall feeling like a million bucks. Kelsey is the real deal and last night cemented that our chemistry is sizzling. I didn't realize until this moment that she is what I've been searching for in every woman I've ever been with.

I go straight for the pot of hot coffee as I whistle a happy tune.

"So, you're sleeping with my sister."

I jump and nearly drop the mug I'm grabbing out of the cabinet. "What? No! What are you talking about?"

Nick folds his arms over his chest as he sits at the table and gives me the scariest *I'm going to fucking kill you* look. "I heard you two last night."

"Okay, look, I didn't want you to find out this way, but yes, Kelsey and I are together." Nick's nostrils flare like a bull, but I press on because if I'm gonna die, I'm gonna die a fully confessed man. "We slept together at your wedding and again last night."

He remains still as he sits there, eerily silent. So, I swallow past the thickness in my throat as I plunge on.

"I'm sorry you heard us last night. That's got to be some sick shit for a brother to hear his sister having sex, probably lots of therapy sessions from here on out, but look, I don't want things to change between us…can you stop staring at me like that? I care for her. A lot. And even if you disapprove, it doesn't matter because we're adults, and we're going to do what we want." *Jesus, where the hell is Lovie when I need her most?*

Nick clears his throat and takes a sip of his coffee. At least he's finally moving, and I won't have to call an ambulance to electric paddle shock him to start his heart.

"I didn't hear you having sex last night. I heard you swimming." His jaw clenches. "I was trying to be funny, but that failed more than I ever could have imagined."

Well shit.

"Lindsey know about this?" he asks.

"Yes." I suddenly find my coffee cup super interesting. "Look, I'm sorry this is how you found out, but you really need to work on your opening one-liners."

"It doesn't matter. You're right, you and Kelsey are both adults." He gets up, and I flinch as he reaches out his hand, smirking at my reaction. I reluctantly accept the newspaper he's holding out to me, feeling stupid for thinking he was going to put me in a chokehold. "But, if you hurt her, then you and I will have a problem." He pauses at the kitchen entrance. "Oh, and Patrick? Please don't ever tell me again that you and my sister had sex. Years of therapy won't even begin to erase that from my fucking brain."

"You got it, sidekick."

Nick grunts as he leaves the kitchen. I deflate against the counter. He could have snapped my neck like a twig, but he surprisingly took it quite well. I fill two coffee cups and pause. I don't know how Kelsey likes her coffee. Honestly, there's a lot I don't know about her that I'd like to discover. I try to think back to the morning after we got here if she had put anything in her coffee, but so much has happened since then, my brain can't keep up.

I keep hers black like mine. I open the cracked door with my shoulder. She sits up, pulling the white duvet up over her chest. Her hair is mussed, and she looks thoroughly edible. I kick the door shut and join her in bed.

"Hi." I hand her the coffee.

"Hi." She smiles back tentatively as she takes a small sip.

"I wasn't sure how you took your coffee…"

"Usually with cream, but this is perfect, thanks," she murmurs into her cup.

"Tell me something else about you that I don't know."

Her lips curve up as she places her cup on her nightstand. "Like what?"

"Like, what's your favorite kind of food?"

"Chinese."

"Seriously?"

"Yours too?" She turns on her side and her smile widens.

I can't help grimacing. "No, never. I can't stand it."

"What? How is that even possible? I have never met a person who doesn't like Chinese." She looks at me like I'm a puzzle she's trying to put together. "What's your favorite food? Star Wars boba?"

"Boba is not a food." I grin. "Pizza, thin-crust is by far, the best thing ever invented. Give it to me with ham and pineapple or loaded down with pepperoni, and I'm in heaven…what?"

"Pizza with fruit on it? That's disgusting. What's wrong with you?"

I huff out a laugh. "What's wrong with *me*?"

"Yes! Chinese is chicken and veggies stir-fried with amazing brown sauce and noodles. Crab rangoon with creamy—"

"Melted cheese with sauce. Sweet pineapple with spicy meat."

She rolls her eyes. "Okay, okay, what's your go-to movie…besides the obvious."

"Anything Marvel."

"I didn't realize I just slept with a twelve-year-old," she teases as she pokes my abs. "Which Marvel character is your favorite?"

"Ironman, hands down."

"Hmm, he's okay."

"Why, who would you pick?"

"I'm more of an Aquaman fan myself."

"That's not even Marvel, that's DC comics, the Justice League."

"You're cute when you go all nerdy on me. Is there really

a big difference?"

I place my hand over my heart. "Yes, there's a difference. Huge! DC is more about superpowers, while Marvel characters are regular guys fighting the world. Let me guess, you like Aquaman because Jason Momoa plays him."

She grins like a Cheshire cat and pinches my nipple. I laugh and bat her hand away.

"What's your favorite movie? Wait, let me guess..." I stare at her for a beat, but my mind is blank. "Uh, honestly, I have no clue. Oh, wait!" I snap my fingers as the first female spy movie comes to mind. "That movie with Jennifer Lawrence where she's trying to fight her way out of something."

Kelsey snorts. "*Hunger Games*? Kind of a random guess. No, I love Christmas and Valentine Hallmark movies."

"What? That's not even a real movie! That's made-for-TV crap."

"It is too real! They fall in love over baking cookies or ice skating and then someone dies and they get reunited."

"Someone dies?"

"I mean they were old..."

"This sounds awful."

"So good."

"It kind of scares me that you think an old person dying off in a Hallmark movie is so good...Okay, okay, let's try this another way." I tease. "Monster Jam or Comic-Con?"

"Pfft, no brainer, Monster Jam."

"What? Seriously? You were just saying how you wanted to get in Jason Momoa's pants."

"I did not." She laughs. "But given a choice, I'd rather

take my nephew to watch trucks racing in mud than geek out over comic books at Comic-Con."

"You're killing me, Kels. Country or rock?"

"Neither. Pop. What about you?"

"I like Motown."

"That's kind of old-school, but that's cool." She scrunches her nose adorably.

"My dad used to love it and play it a lot. It reminds me of him."

Her eyes soften as she leans in and kisses me. "I'm sorry. Sweet or salty?" she whispers against my lips.

"Sweet." I run my fingers along her smooth skin.

"Hmm, I prefer salty. Disney or Universal?"

"Like you even have to ask..." My fingers halt. "Wait, you'd choose *Universal?*"

"I mean, those little minions are so adorable. What? I love yellow blobs in overalls..."

"I can't even look at you right now."

She laughs. "Beach or mountains?"

"Mountains."

She side-eyes me. "Okay, we're going to have to agree to disagree on all of this."

"Clearly." I nip her shoulder, which makes her shiver. "Does it worry you?"

"Does what worry me?"

"That we have nothing in common?"

"No...it's not like we're...does it worry you?"

I smooth out the little wrinkle on her brow. "No, you can't help it that you have horrible taste in everything."

She pinches my bicep and then kisses it.

"Your brother knows about us."

"Hmm, let's hope he doesn't tell the others. How did he take it?" She picks up her coffee cup and takes a sip.

"Pretty well considering...wait, who are the others?"

"My sisters. How did he find out?"

"Well, it was an unfortunate accident on his part."

She freezes. "Did he see us last night?"

"No, nothing like that. He stumbled upon it." I grin down at her as I take her coffee from her hands. "But he didn't try to kill me, so you know, that's a plus." I lean down and kiss her lips.

"Mmm...I'm glad you made it back here in one piece." Her fingers trail down my chest, softly grazing my skin, turning me on like a light switch.

"So am I. We may not agree on much, but there are other ways to find out what you like," I mumble as I kiss my way down her breasts and stomach.

Her fingers thread through my hair. "I definitely like that." She hums in pleasure as I work my way down her body.

Chapter 19

Patrick

Any Way You Want It, Captain Ron

I LOOK AT my watch, noting that we're almost out of time as Lindsey sits in the editing booth finishing up her voiceovers for her last piece. I haven't seen much of Kelsey in the past few days since I've been focusing all my time and energy on the show. I'm nervous that if I push her faster than she wants to go, she'll clam up on me again. I'm still curious about the night on the yacht, but it's taken a backseat to the show and our budding relationship.

I press the button to talk to Lindsey in the recording booth. "Let's do the end piece, Lovie, and then I think we should be done."

She nods as she adjusts the headphones over her ears and flips to the page our writer Leslie gave her. I grin as I think about how far this show has come since we started. The fact that we have a professional sound and lighting guy, a writer, two cameramen...it blows my mind. Gone are the days of my portable lights and video equipment.

"Join me next week when we'll be taking an airboat to a little ol' shack out in the middle of the Glades to try...wait, what?" Lindsey looks up from the script, her eyes widening with dread, shaking her head. "No, no, no. Nope. I'm not eating alligator. It's not safe for the baby, Trick."

I press the button to talk to her. "I already checked with Shannon. As long as it's completely cooked through, it's safe." My face hurts, I'm grinning so hard.

"Shannon? What does she know?"

"Uh, she's an OBGYN and your doctor. I'd say she's an expert."

"But—"

"A viewer requested it, Lovie. It will be fun! Don't be a party-pooper. JD and Nick will be tagging along too."

"I'm not happy about this."

"You never are." I laugh as I signal her to start again. She finishes her lines and takes off her headphones before charging out of the booth.

"When are we going on this little 'field trip' you've so cleverly planned behind my back?"

"Tomorrow. Adventure Animals will be tagging along to do a piece on their end."

"What? So I have to eat alligator in front of all their crew members?"

"Uh...yeah." I say goodbye to the studio engineer. "I've heard it tastes like chicken. I can't wait!" I rub my hands together excitedly while Lindsey groans, punching me in the arm.

"YOU WANT ME to get on *that*?" Lindsey's gaze travels from the airboat to the burly guy with beady eyes, whose face is covered in a bushy red beard. He's patiently waiting as he holds his hand out to her. "It looks like a piece of tin with an alligator painted on the side. Will it hold all of our weight?"

"Get on, Princess." He holds out his hand.

"But I—"

I gently shove her forward. "Come on, you're holding up the rest of us."

Lindsey stumbles and grabs the man's hand. He hoists her unceremoniously onto the small craft. "Why is there a fan and a cage on the back?"

"Because if you fell into the blade, you'd be chopped up like beets in a juicer," the bearded captain says gruffly.

"Well, that's a pleasant image…"

Our videographer Gary gets on after Lindsey, and then I climb on behind him. The rest of our crew boards another airboat behind us. Nick, JD, and their crew are taking separate boats.

The bushy-bearded man stretches and rubs his pale hairy belly as he steps onto the boat. He hikes a leg on Gary's seat and looks dubiously at his crew…which is us. He spits a wad of chewing tobacco into the murky water. "My name is Captain Ron, and I will be giving you the Alligator Alley tour today before heading over to Al's."

"This isn't even a boat. It's like a platform with a chair and a big fan that will chop you to a pulp." Lindsey squeals in my ear. "Oh my god, did you ever see that movie called *Captain Ron* with Kurt Russell?"

I huff out a laugh. "I don't think this Ron is a pirate.

Look, he doesn't even have an earring."

"Alright, listen up, and that means you, Chatty Patty." He spits another wad of tobacco and hands us each a pair of headphones for ear protection. "We're gonna see some hogs, some gators, and some birds. Sometimes even some water snakes. I gots some rules that you need to obey. No hands or feet in the water. If you have glasses, I suggest putting them on. Keep your mouth shut, or you'll get extra protein in your teeth." He smiles a gap-toothed grin at Lindsey, causing her to shudder. "But the number-one rule is, don't fall in. The alligators can smell fear a mile away."

Captain Ron pulls his Alligator Alley hat down low, dons a pair of mirrored aviators, and pops a can in an Alligator Alley koozie before settling into his seat above us.

"Ten bucks says that's a Bud Light he's drinking," I whisper to Lindsey.

Her eyes bug out as she eyeballs the koozie. "Is that even legal? No way, he can't drink on the job." She shifts nervously in her seat. "I wish Nick were on this boat." Lindsey raises her hand. "Um, Captain Ron, where are the seatbelts for this thing?"

Captain Ron snorts. "This ain't a Mercedes, ma'am. This is an airboat. You hold on."

"Right." She breathes in through her nose, her nostrils flaring. "I'm going to kill you for this, Trick."

I motion to Lindsey that I can't hear her as Captain Ron starts up the airboat. She rolls her eyes and grips the railing next to her as Ron hollers an Alligator Alley 'yeehaw' as he fishtails over the water.

Twenty minutes in, Ron kindly slows the boat down and

shuts it off as we approach a mangrove of trees. "There are usually some gates hangin' out in here." He spits a wad overboard. "Just remember, don't stick yer hand in the water, it will bite it clean off."

"It will not," I whisper to Lindsey. "He's trying to scare you."

"He's doing an A-plus job. He's so charming," Lindsey deadpans as she looks over her shoulder. "Where are the other guys?"

I pull out my phone and see a new message from Nick. "There was some kind of emergency, and they went straight to the farm. We're headed to Alligator Al's."

"Ah, the fine establishment for our show," she says smugly. "Of all the incredible restaurants in Miami to choose from, we're out here in the middle of fucking nowhere Everglades to eat at Alligator Al's."

"Good eats," Ron says as he not so subtly picks his nose with a dirty finger.

"To be sure," Lindsey mumbles as she leans into me. "Five bucks says he's referring to his boogies."

I bark out a laugh as my eye catches movement. "Hey, I think I see one." I point to the head of an alligator cresting the water.

"Yep, that's a gator," Ron says in a bored tone as he sits back and looks up at the canopy covering the captain's chair as he settles back for a nap.

Gary is filming Lindsey as she stands to get a better look.

"Careful, don't fall in," I chide.

"You'd probably enjoy that for the ratings," she gripes. "Oh my god, that thing is huge! It's like twelve feet long!"

"That's Big Gus." Ron begrudgingly gets up and hands me a bag of cheese puffs. "Throw him some of these, he likes 'em."

"Uh, aren't you not supposed to feed the wildlife?" I ask suspiciously. Ron grunts and resumes his nap, so I hand the bag to Lindsey.

"I don't want to get in trouble," she hisses.

"Fine." I grab the bag back, take a handful and lob some into the water. A bluish-purple bird lands on the boat deck, waiting for a cheese puff.

"Oh, he's cute! His coloring is so pretty!" She takes the bag back from me and throws him a puff which the bird gobbles up and then flies off. "Oh, look, there are more!" She throws some puffs onto the lily pads around us. The birds pluck at the cheese puffs as Lindsey happily looks on.

Swift movement in the water has me swiveling in my seat, but Lindsey remains focused on the birds. Big Gus rolls towards the cheese puffs, his jaws snapping out of the water. Lindsey screams, tossing the bag overboard. Orange balls innocently bob in the water like a dozen fishing bobbers.

"Lindsey, grab the bag!" I shout.

"Are you fucking crazy? I'm not putting my hand in there!"

Captain Ron lumbers down from his perch and surveys the situation. "I said give him a cheese puff, not the whole goddamn bag. That was my lunch," he grumbles as he leans over Lindsey, his beer belly and sweaty pits right in her face. Repulsed by Ron's sweaty body odor, she tries to make herself as small as possible. I look back to see if Gary is filming all of this, and he gives me a thumbs-up.

Ron starts cussing and pitching his body forward as if something were tugging on him, which causes Lindsey to scream hysterically that the gator is eating Ron alive. She slides away from his bulk as I quickly leap over the front seat to see if I can help him, but Ron stands up a few seconds later with his hand intact, holding the bag. He stands back as he gloats. "Had you going there for a sec, didn't I, Princess?"

Lindsey looks flushed and, frankly, murderous as Gary and I barely contain our laughter. "Good one, Captain Ron, you sure got her."

"Yeah, good one, Captain Ron, you're a regular Chris Farley." Lindsey sits back in her seat. "Can we please move on to the next torturous destination?"

Ron glides the airboat up to a shack on stilts ten minutes later. I look around the marshy surroundings and note that there are no other buildings in sight as far as the eye can see. A faded old sign reads Alligator Al's.

"*This* is it?" Lindsey shoves the headphones off her ears and winces when she tries to run a hand through her ratty hair. "Please tell me we brought Linda's case or that she somehow is miraculously already here waiting for me. Linda? Linda!"

"It's me, Dean, Greg, and Gary today. No case."

"Super. Of course, bring Dean for lighting and Greg for sound. Who cares about Linda? Why on earth would we need her to fix my hair after an *airboat ride*? But yes, sound decision on bringing Dean. Let's get the best lighting for this dump." She waves her hand at the shack like she's Vanna White.

"Is she always this cranky?" Ron cracks a smile as he

yanks Lindsey up onto the rickety dock he's tied the airboat to. The other airboat with Dean and Greg pulls up behind us.

I ignore Ron as I catch up to Lindsey as she reaches the door. "Hey, don't forget we need to do an intro."

Lindsey pauses in the open doorway as she surveys the restaurant's interior. "You have got to be fucking kidding me. This is a joke, right? It's like an old gritty Captain D's meets a Hell's Angels biker bar out in the middle of a swamp. They even have rope netting and stuffed alligators... everywhere. Ooh, and a cheesy neon sign that flashes good eats. I guess Captain Ron wasn't talking about his boogies."

"It's so great!" I push past her into Alligator Al's shack. "Wow! Look at that twelve-footer hanging from the ceiling!" I marvel at the giant stuffed alligator.

"That poor guy didn't even have a chance at life, maybe a cheese puff or two, and now he's stuffed hanging over a bunch of swamp hillbillies as they eat his cousins."

"Which is exactly what we'll be doing!" I rub my hands together like an evil scientist. I love eating weird adventurous food, while my sourpuss partner, who stands with her arms crossed as she inspects the restaurant, would rather starve to death.

"I thought Nick and JD were supposed to be joining us for lunch?" she asks grumpily.

"They had to rush over to the alligator Rescue Center, remember? Apparently, one of the volunteers lost a shoe and a gator ate it. So now they have to perform surgery."

"How the hell do you lose a shoe at an alligator park? That's like losing a shoe on the side of the highway."

"I don't know, but I'd rather be here eating fried gator than having to remove a shoe from one."

She picks up a greasy plastic menu. "Ugh, fried, sauteed, grilled, hush-puppied, pickled and kabobbed, 'have your gator any way you want it.' They even can make gator burgers, chili, and pizza. That sounds revolting." She wrinkles her nose in disgust. "Linguini with a white gator sauce? Oh, they've gone too far."

"I say we order it all."

"Don't you find it a little bit creepy that we're eating the gators a couple of miles down from where they're trying to save them?"

"I don't really think about it. Gators are like squirrels, they're everywhere down here." I clap my hands together. "Alright, Gary got you pulling up to the dock. Let me grab everyone to get set up in here, and I'll have you walk in and act like this is the most fabulous fucking place in the world." I smile as I steer her toward the door.

"God, you're starting to sound like my ex-asshole producer."

"You mean your husband?"

"Yup, that's the one...I'm sure he was in on this plan," she grumbles as she puts the menu back down and wipes her hands on her shorts before I shove her outside.

"Welcome to Al's." A tall man with a potbelly covered by a greasy apron comes out from the back. His voice is gravelly and rusty, his bald head shining like Mr. Clean under the fluorescent lights. "You the foodie?"

"Hi, I'm Patrick Healy. You must be Al." I reach out my hand to shake, but he just stares at it as he wipes his hands on a dirty dishtowel. Pleasant fellow. I drop my hand and give him a winning smile. "I'm Lindsey's producer. Thank you for shutting down for us to be here today."

"I didn't."

"Oh, of course, of course, we must have missed the lunch crowd." I quickly note that it's twelve pm on my watch. "So let's get started, shall we?" I motion to a table. "Can we film right here?"

"Wherever you want, Mr. Big Shot." He folds his arms over his barrel chest. "What do you want to eat?"

"Wow, Lovie, this is like first-class service! We're getting Big Al himself to cook."

Al growls and I move Lindsey a little in front of me. Surely, he won't harm her? She's like a cute innocent little bunny rabbit. Big Al probably eats them…or feeds them to the gators.

"I'm the *only* cook. How do you want your gator?"

"Can we do like a sampler platter where we try a bit of everything?" Lindsey asks innocently.

"What do I look like, a sous chef at fucking Denny's?"

"Well, ye—"

I clamp a hand over Lovie's mouth and laugh nervously. "Why don't you just surprise us with your best?"

Al grunts and lumbers back into what I'm assuming is the kitchen area.

"Do you think he has to go hunt down an alligator like that Australian dude?" Lindsey asks as she fumbles with the door.

"Uh, are you referring to Crocodile Dundee or Steve Irwin?"

"Does it matter?"

"I guess not. He looks like he could, but I'm guessing it's going to be frozen."

Lindsey jumps at what sounds like an ax chopping into wood from back in the kitchen.

"Mmm, what a treat, to hear your own meal being chopped up. Thanks for subjecting me to this fabulous...I can't even call it a dining establishment. It's a shack on stilts."

We step out into the hot Florida sunshine and gaze out upon the never-ending landscape of willow reeds, marsh, and water. I motion for Gary, Dean, and Greg to come inside to film Lindsey walking in.

"Lovie, stop being such a snob, it's going to be fun! Trust me. There's a reason a viewer suggested it. They must really love it. Besides, Al's cooking skills are going to make you tell everyone to come to Alligator Al's in the middle-of-nowhere Everglades." I slide my arm around her neck and pull her into a side-hug. "At least it's not turtle."

She elbows me in the ribs. "Do you think Captain Ron will be able to get us back home?"

I look over at the man in question as he eats something fried out of a greasy red and white cardboard boat, cracking open his second beer. "God, I hope so."

Chapter 20

Kelsey

Free the Gator

"WOW, YOU GUYS were gone all day. I thought it was supposed to be lunch and then back by the afternoon?" I lift Olive out of her highchair and turn toward Patrick and Lindsey, who just came in from the garage. "Oh, um…wow Lindsey, your hair…" I try not to stare, but it looks like a family of squirrels built a nest in it for a long winter. I paste on a bright smile. "How did it go?"

"Ron and Al and gators and hair and cheese puffs…shower," Lindsey mutters as she shuffles to her bedroom.

"Is she okay?"

"She'll be fine. She had a long day."

"Yeah, you got some sun." I brush my fingertips across his forehead. "Was it fun?"

"Fun? Well, Lovie probably won't talk to me for a couple of weeks, but sure. Is Nick home?"

"He got home about an hour ago but left again to pick up dinner for all of us. He should be back soon."

"Okay, I'm going to take a shower and then I'll tell you all about our day, but first I need to show you how much I missed you today."

"Can't wait." I lean into him as he sweetly kisses my lips. I crinkle my nose and push him back. "You might want to take a shower first. You smell like a bait shop."

He laughs and then walks out of the kitchen. I sigh and wonder if this is what life would be like with Patrick. Him coming home with funny stories and adventure. Me with a baby on my hip, wondering what he's been doing all day…and questioning why I don't have adventurous stories of my own to tell.

I shake my head. *Geez, Kelsey, get a grip.* That's not what's happening here. I don't want anything serious right now, and I'm not sure I ever want to have kids. But a life with Patrick is so easy to envision if I let my mind go there. I would be living my dream job as a journalist for a paper like *The Miami Times.* Traveling overseas and covering stories of war and terrorists, jumping from city to city as I run down my next cover story. I'd see Patrick when I had time in between jobs, or maybe we'd end up in the same cities while he's out filming for Lindsey's show.

My heart sinks. Why does what once sounded like a fantastic adventure now seem so hollow and lonely to me?

Olive bangs a wooden spoon breaking the trance my daydream had me under. I shake my head because I'm fretting over nothing. Patrick and I are temporary—just a little fun while in Miami. Nick comes blasting through the garage door as he shakes the rain off like a wet dog.

"Jesus, the skies suddenly opened up!" I hand him a dishtowel. "Thanks. I see Patrick and Lindsey are back."

"Yeah, they're taking a shower. Not together, obviously."

Nick side-eyes me as he unpacks the food.

"You okay?"

I rub my forehead. "Yes...no. I don't know."

"Oh my god, I'm starving!" Lindsey pads into the kitchen, freshly showered as she hugs Nick. "Tell me you got me something normal and I'll love you forever."

"Shouldn't you love me forever regardless?"

"Yeah, yeah, yeah." Lindsey pokes her head into the bag. "Oh my god, you've sealed the deal. I am yours forever."

I laugh as she pulls a burrito out of the bag. "Aren't you tired of burritos yet?"

"Nope. Never."

"I take it Alligator Al's didn't fill you up?" Nick smirks.

"I don't want to talk about Alligator Al's ever again. I hope it burns down in an intentionally set grease fire. I will have nightmares from the stuffed alligator hanging over my head as I had to sample Al's famous cidered gator and BBQ." Lindsey shivers as she kisses Olive, taking her out of the highchair.

"God, I wish I could have seen it." Nick laughs.

"You're in luck. Patrick made sure Gary got everything on film. He's almost as bad as you now when it comes to doing retakes."

Nick sits down beside Lindsey and kisses her. I busy myself at the sink, feeling like I'm intruding on their private moment. I want what my brother has. I wish I was ready, that I knew how to let love in again. I feel stuck in this void of sadness, desperately trying to find my way out of the dark. Why is it so hard to get my shit together? Just as I'm about to excuse myself and creep back into the shadows of my room, Patrick walks into the kitchen.

"Why aren't you eating?" He quirks an eyebrow as he looks in the bag on the counter. He hands me a packet of tacos as he collects his dinner. He sits down next to Nick, not caring that he's interrupting because he's Uncle Trick; he's family. And even though I'm Nick's sister, I've never felt more like an outsider looking in.

"Thanks...for dinner. So tell me about this tennis shoe."

"You were lucky to be at Al's."

"Doubtful," Lindsey snorts.

Patrick looks up, catching my eye. "Come sit down with us, Kels." I grab my food and a drink and quickly sit next to him, thankful he threw me a line. He leans in and kisses my cheek. I'm self-conscious at the open display of affection in front of Nick and Lindsey, but they seem nonplussed.

I clear my throat. "So what happened?"

"A gator at one of the farms ate a tennis shoe after a worker got stuck in some mud and lost it. The gator was too fast for her to retrieve it without losing her arm."

"Oh my god."

"I almost lost my arm today from Big Gus," Lindsey says around a mouthful of burrito.

Nick assesses her to see if she's hurt as Patrick snorts and waves for him to continue. "Anyway, JD had to stick his arm down the alligator's mouth to retrieve the shoe. He couldn't get it, so we had to transport the gator to his clinic for surgery."

"He stuck his arm in an awake alligator? You couldn't pay me enough." I cringe.

"Want to know what Lindsey wanted to do at Alligator

Al's?"

"Patrick!" Lindsey glares at him across the table. "Remember we said we weren't going to bring that up ever again?"

Nick sits back and scrubs his hands down his face. "Oh, God, what happened?"

"She asked the owner if she could free the alligator hanging on the wall."

"What do you mean free it?" Nick looks to Lindsey, who averts her eyes.

"She wanted to release it back into nature so it could swim in the water."

"Babe, you do realize—"

"I couldn't take it, Nick. All those beady little eyes staring at me. It was so creepy!"

"Lindsey, they're stuffed. Those beady little eyes are glass, nothing is staring at you. You aren't reviving them by throwing them back in the water."

I try not to giggle as Lindsey gives Nick an eat-shit-and-die glare. "Thanks for mansplaining it for me, Nick. It was just a suggestion. I wasn't going to actually *do* it. I was having serious Tucker the Turtle flashbacks, and Al was such a jerk."

"Oh Jesus, here we go again." He rubs her back gently. "Babe, maybe you should look into becoming a vegetarian."

"I think it's safe to say we won't be returning to Big Al's again," Patrick says. I grin. "Especially when Big Al served her BBQ in a gator head that looked curiously authentic."

"I will vomit up this burrito if you keep talking about it," Lindsey gripes.

"Don't worry, we got that reaction on camera too."

We all laugh as Patrick launches into another story about Captain Ron and Big Gus. I look around the table, smiling so hard my face hurts. I realize that my mood went from feeling utterly lost to complete happiness with the snap of a finger. And I owe it to the guy sitting next to me, bringing me to tears with his storytelling.

Maybe letting people into my life is worth the risk. I know Todd crushed me, but he didn't kill me. Perhaps Patrick is that little light bobbing in the darkness coming to find me.

Chapter 21

Kelsey

A Sunday Kind of Love

I KNOCK SOFTLY on his door before poking my head in. He looks up from his laptop and smiles.

"Hey."

"Sorry for interrupting."

He shuts his laptop. "You're not. What's up?"

"I was wondering if you were free today? Lindsey and Nick took Olive to the beach, but if you're busy, it's cool, I under—"

"Let's do it!" He hops off the bed and runs a hand through his hair. "What would you like to do?"

"Let's go to Universal!" I squeal. His face falls and it's all I can do not to burst out laughing. "I'm kidding. Wouldn't want you to go postal on a minion because I like him better than your Chewbaca."

"You're hilarious." Patrick pulls his phone off the nightstand. "Let me make some calls, I have an idea."

"Okay. What can I do?"

"Hang tight." He kisses my lips hastily as he shuffles me out the door. "Sorry for this, but I can't surprise you if you're standing here listening."

He shuts the door in my face and I huff out a laugh. I haven't felt this giddy in years over an outing. I head to my room and pack a swimsuit, a dress, and my makeup bag, just in case.

THE SUN IS high in the bright blue sky as the sailboat skims over the water out to sea. The ocean is the most beautiful aqua blue. I breathe in the sea salt as the wind whips around me, and I couldn't feel more at home. I turn and study Patrick, who is looking out at the horizon, his handsome profile shadowed in the shade of the sail.

"Hey, Patrick?"

"Yeah?"

"I don't know who you know, but this is amazing."

He pulls me to his side and kisses my temple. "I'm sorry they wouldn't let us take it out on our own."

"Ha! I'd be too nervous to try and sail your friend's boat. Honestly, I've never sailed something this big, so I'm happy to sit back and relax. This is a seventy-five-foot Oyster sailing yacht. You don't mess around with a boat this beautiful. Someday I'd love to have a boat of my own like this. Not this big, of course, something I could manage by myself, but I'd love to be able to go out on the water whenever it calls to me," I say.

"You know a lot about boats." He looks impressed.

"I'm into sailboats like you're into *Star Wars*. Do you

know how to sail?"

"No, but I think I need to learn. I love being on the water like this. It's so peaceful."

I timidly smile as I take his hand and thread my fingers with his. "I could teach you."

"Are you saying that so you can get in my pants later?"

"Totally." My grin widens as I return my attention to the water. "So, whose boat is this anyway?"

"A friend of JD's. I called in a favor."

"That's a really nice favor." I take in the sleek lines and the teak wood. We're comfortably lounging on cushioned chaise loungers on the upper deck as a crew member fills our champagne glasses.

"It all started with a lizard named Spike."

"You got us this boat for the day because of a lizard?"

Patrick smiles easily. "And it helps that he likes me."

I stare at him curiously. There are so many layers to Patrick that I don't know, and I worry because time is running out for us. If I don't get offered the job from *The Times*, then I have to return to New York at the end of next week. "Everyone likes you, don't they?"

He shrugs and looks away.

"It's because you're a genuinely nice guy, Patrick. Own it. You're also incredibly hot." He side-eyes me and I waggle my eyebrows. "If we didn't have a whole crew of people on the boat, I'd take advantage of you for sure."

"Who says I'd let you?" He smirks. I arch an eyebrow causing him to laugh. "I'd totally let you."

"I know." I set my champagne glass down on the table and slide into his lap, placing my hands on his sharp jawline.

I gently press my lips to his. "Thank you for making this day incredible. No one has ever done something like this for me before."

"You're welcome." His brown sugar eyes dilate as his Adam's apple bobs. I press my lips lightly to his again and he groans in protest as I sit back. I like having this effect on him.

"I'm so sorry to interrupt, but would you like an afternoon snack? Dinner will be served at six so that you can view the sunset," the boat stewardess says.

I slide off of Patrick and smile so big my face hurts. "We have this until dinner?"

"Surprise." He winks before turning his attention to her. "We'd love a snack, and I'd love a beer. Are you good with champagne?"

"Yes, I'm good, thank you."

We're quiet for a moment as I sink back into the comfy cushion. I swing my legs up and put my feet in his lap like we're an old married couple. He slips my sandal off and starts to knead the bottom of my foot. "Oh, that's heaven right there." I moan.

"I wanted to rub your foot the first time I met you…"

I arch an eyebrow and giggle. "That's kind of creepy, Patrick."

He smiles goofily, his warm brown eyes dancing as he squeezes my foot. "If you'd let me finish. Your feet were hurting after we went out to the back patio. I wanted to offer to rub your feet, but I didn't want you to think I was a creeper, which apparently, you do, so I was correct in that assumption."

I laugh. "Oh my god, that night…did we seriously try and reenact the *Dirty Dancing* scene?"

"We did. I blame Bridget for convincing you you could do it."

"We did it."

"No." He shakes his head, chuckling. "No, we most definitely did not. We were a *Dirty Dancing* fail."

"We were? I had no idea. I thought we rocked it! Everyone was cheering and clapping."

"Cheering that we got off the dance floor."

"Remember that old lady who you stripped half her dress of bead? I was dying."

"Yes. Aunt Mildew now refers to me at all family events as The Pervert."

I giggle and then quickly sober. "I'm sorry, Patrick."

"What for?"

"For leaving you the next morning and not calling or leaving a note. I…I was scared."

He concentrates on his knuckles as they lightly skim over the arch of my foot. "Why were you scared?"

"Because I liked you…a lot. I got spooked." I need to tell him about Todd and the interview, but something holds me back. I'm not ready for him to know my past mistakes, especially not today. "Tell me something about you I don't know."

Mercifully he smiles and lets me off the hook. "I wanted to be a musician when I was a kid."

"Really? I love that! What instrument can you play?"

"Uh, none."

I can't help but laugh. "How did you expect to be a

musician if you can't play an instrument? Are you a good singer?"

"Ah no, totally off-key." He shrugs. "I was twelve. It's not like I tried to break into the music industry. I knew it was a hopeless pipe dream."

"How did you choose to be a part of *Lindsey Love Loves*?"

"It kind of happened organically. I was thinking about film school—"

"Because you loved *Star Wars* movies so much?"

He smirks. "Because I thought how cool would it be to be a film producer?"

I arch my eyebrow at him.

"Okay, fine, because I loved *Star Wars* and the Marvel movies so much. Anyway, freshman year, Lindsey asked if I wanted to go off campus with her to some little hole-in-the-wall place she drove by one day."

"Was it good?"

"No, it was terrible, but Lindsey's reaction to the food and service was hysterical. I told her she should do this weekly and start a food blog. She looked at me and smirked and said only if I'd help her. The rest is history."

"You and Lindsey are close, huh?"

He shifts nervously in his seat. "Does that bother you?"

"Why would that bother me?"

"I had an ex-girlfriend who was jealous of our friendship. Lovie is like a sister to me."

"Well, she *is* a sister to me through marriage, so I'm positively not threatened by it."

Patrick looks relieved as the stewardess sets down an array of fruits and cheeses and hands Patrick his beer. He excuses himself to use the bathroom while I sit back with a smile on my face as I soak up the afternoon sunshine. I haven't felt this relaxed in a long time. I haven't thought about the heaviness of my future once today. Patrick makes me feel like I'm in a bubble of happiness whenever I'm around him. I know we should talk about what's happening between us, but I don't want that bubble to burst yet.

PATRICK HOLDS MY hand as he helps me up from the table. The sunset is incredible as streaks of melon orange and pinks saturate the sky. The stark-white sails above us glow pink like the inside of a seashell. The warm ocean breeze whips around us as I put my hand in his. "Dinner was amazing."

"It was, but the company was even more so."

"Bet you say that to all the girls, charmer." I smile as he holds me in his arms.

"I do." He grins as I grip his shirt and give him a gentle shake as he dips me. "Want to dance with me?"

Under the stars as we float across the ocean on a sailing yacht? "Hell yes." I blush as I duck my head. "I mean, yes, yeah, I'd love to."

His smile grows wider as he plays a song from his phone that he hooked to a wireless speaker on our table. He shared some of his favorite Motown songs during dinner, which endeared me to him even more. I love that Patrick isn't embarrassed by his sensitive, quirky side. Most guys would try to hide it, but not Patrick. He owns it. A woman starts crooning about a Sunday love as I sway in Patrick's arms.

"Who is this?"

"Etta James. It's called 'A Sunday Kind of Love'."

I listen to the lyrics as my gaze lingers on Patrick's lips. "What does she mean she wants a Sunday kind of love?"

His mouth tilts up into a smile. "It means she wants more than just one night. She wants the relationship to continue through Sunday, maybe beyond." He brushes a strand of hair off my cheek. "Not just one night of fun. A love that lasts."

I look up into his soulful brown eyes. "Is that what you want? A Sunday kind of love?"

"Doesn't everybody?"

I ignore the thrumming beat of my heart and the sudden flutter in my stomach. I close my eyes as my lips find his.

Chapter 22

Kelsey

The Middle Sister

I WALK INTO the kitchen to find Nick grabbing a bottle of water from the fridge while holding Olive in his other arm. I smile because it's funny seeing Nick with a baby, *his baby*, in his arms. When did we become such *adults*?

"Hey stranger, do you have some free time? Maybe we could grab lunch. I feel like I haven't seen much of my little brother."

"Ahh, I'd love to, Kels, but I'm on my way over to the clinic."

"Okay, maybe tomorrow?" I cringe at how pathetically hopeful I sound. He turns around and stares at me for a beat.

"Why don't you come with me?"

"Oh, I can't, I'm watching Olive. Patrick and Lindsey are shooting an episode right now. I wouldn't want to get in your way."

Nick flashes me a rare smile. "It will be fine. I have a meeting at two, but let's grab something from that deli down the street and head over to the clinic. I haven't seen enough of Olive or you."

"Great! Let me grab her diaper bag and stroller and meet

you in the garage."

Nick and I head over to the deli first, order some sand-wiches, and then stop at a park to eat and push Olive in a swing.

"You doing okay, Kels? I mean, Bridget told me you aren't thrilled about working for the paper in New York."

I chew my turkey sandwich and watch the blur of kids run like crazy around the playground. "It's a job, I guess." I'm itching to tell him about the interview at *The Times*, but I'm worried he'll tell Bridget, who will most definitely tell MK, and from there, it goes straight to the head honcho, Mom. I'll never hear the end of how Dad stuck out his neck for me to get the Cookie's Cleaning Corner assignment.

I look at Nick and wonder how he's so put-together after everything he's been through.

"Nick, have you ever…I mean, did you ever struggle with…" I silently berate myself for opening up to him. I like to keep my feelings tucked close to my heart, not wear them on my sleeve. Maybe he'll let it go. Nick doesn't enjoy talking about his feelings, either.

"With what?"

Great, now he decides to care. "Life," I say miserably as I take a drink of my soda, avoiding his penetrating stare.

"What do you mean?"

"I guess I feel like everyone has their shit together, except for me. It's depressing. When will it be my turn?"

"You have to work for it, Kels. It doesn't just fall in your lap."

"It did for you."

Nick snorts. "How do you figure?"

I wave my hand over him. "You're an executive producer living the dream with a beautiful, successful wife, an adorable baby—"

"It wasn't always like that. I had to jump a lot of hurdles to get to where I am." He sighs as he gives Olive some turkey. "Do you know why I have to go into the clinic today? I have to babysit grown adults. One of our 'veterinarian' actors stole drugs out of the safe. I have to figure out if they truly have a drug problem or if it was done as a stunt led by the idiotic co-creator Adventure Animals hired. He wants to get JD confronting them on film, but I think it's a terrible idea because it puts a blemish on his reputation and the clinic. It's a nightmare, Kels, trust me. Not everything is as pretty as it's painted out to be." He shakes his head. "Anyway, you'll find your groove, it just takes time."

"I feel like we're all running a sprint, and I'm stuck at the start having knocked down a hurdle, trying to get up with my dignity still intact. Meanwhile, our sisters are at the finish line holding their medals up, waiting for me."

"You do realize that we love you just the way you are, don't you? I mean, yes, we tease each other relentlessly, but when it comes down to it, we're all there for you, Kels. Some of us may be at the finish line, but we're cheering like hell for you to pick yourself back up and join us. You'll get there, I promise."

"And what if I don't?"

"Then we'll come get you and help you get across. You've always been the most stubborn out of all of us—"

"No way, Arden is way more stubborn than me."

"Okay, fine, but you are a close second. It's okay to ask

for help. We love you, Kels. Remember when you used to interview all of us when we were kids?"

"Yeah, I'd get so mad when you guys would try to be silly and wouldn't give me factual answers."

"You'd write up your own newspaper and paste our pictures next to our interviews. Mom and Dad were so tickled by it that they went to Kinkos and made copies to send to Gramps and Grandma. You were always destined to be a writer. Don't let that dream go."

I give him a watery smile. "Thanks, little brother."

"So, what's going on with Patrick?" he asks. I raise an eyebrow, but he rushes on. "Not that I want details, but are you two dating?"

"I don't know what we're doing. I think right now we're having fun and enjoying each other's company."

Nick nods. "I get that, but tread lightly. Patrick is…a romantic. He falls fast and gets his heart broken easily."

"Don't worry, we both know it's a temporary thing," I say, feigning nonchalance. "We have an understanding." I swallow past the guilt eroding the lining of my stomach. Even though my mouth just spoke those words, my heart is beating a different story. I'm falling for Patrick, and I'm at a total loss as to where to go from here. "It's all good Nick, I promise."

Nick looks at me for a beat and grunts as he cleans up his trash. "You sure about that?"

EXHAUSTED AFTER SPENDING the afternoon at the veterinary clinic with Nick, we return home and notice another van in the driveway. "I wonder who that is."

"I don't know, but we're about to find out." Nick pulls the car into the garage next to Lindsey's minivan. "You go on in, I'll get Olive out."

I freeze as soon as I open the door that leads into the kitchen. Confetti is thrown in the air around me. In fact, it's all over the floor.

"Kelsey!" A chorus of voices surrounds me as my sisters hug me.

"Wow! What are you all doing here?" I try to pump some enthusiasm into my tone, but I can't muster up any excitement. I'm not a fan of surprises. Having my sisters here puts a damper on things. They're too loud, too pushy and invasive. Kind of like when you're on your honeymoon and your parents are staying in the room right next to you.

Bridget bounces on her toes. "We decided to come down and surprise you guys!"

"Isn't it great?" Lindsey's voice cracks and her cheeks pink as Arden shoves a wineglass in her hand. "Where are Nick and Olive?"

"Right here…what the hell?"

"Surprise!" Bridget shrieks as she throws confetti in Nick's face. MK leans against the island and laughs.

"We all had some time off and thought it would be fun to surprise you guys for the weekend. No kids or husbands, we wanted to come and have a girls' weekend."

"Yeah, let loose, beach and booze it up," Arden says as she hugs a stunned Nick.

"Oh…wow, okay…where are you staying?" Nick asks as his eyes dart to Lindsey.

"Here! Isn't that great, Nick? All of your sisters are here." Lindsey's laugh holds a note of panic as she stares longingly at her wine. "All of them."

"Don't worry! We'll sleep in Kelsey's room and the couch. No big deal. Here give me Olive, I need some baby snuggles." Arden smiles as she relieves Nick.

"Oh my god, this house is so amazing! I'm so glad it has a pool!" Bridget chatters excitedly as she exits the kitchen.

"Yeah, great…where's Patrick?" Nick looks around. He seems even less enthused than Lindsey.

"I think he's hiding. We already put our stuff in Kelsey's room."

I don't blame him. My sisters can be a lot to take. I'm kind of feeling sucker-punched myself that they are here. I love my them dearly, but I've just found my footing with Nick, Lindsey, and Patrick. I was looking forward to being alone with Patrick and seeing how his day went, telling him about my afternoon at the clinic watching them film. I have my interview on Monday, and then I was planning to spend my last few days with him before I had to return to New York. The last thing I want to do is booze it up all weekend with my sisters.

"I'll go check on him." Their loud chatter is already grating on my nerves. "Why don't you guys figure out where you want to go for dinner."

"On it!" MK pulls out her phone and starts tapping away.

I gently knock on Patrick's door. "Hey, it's Kelsey. Can I

come in?"

No answer. I hope he's okay. Maybe he's taking a nap. I don't want to disturb him, but I also need an escape from my sisters' sudden invasion. Snuggling in bed with him sounds way more enticing than going back into the kitchen. I twist the knob and gently push the door open.

"Patrick?" I whisper as I duck into his darkened room. The bathroom door opens and he walks out, naked, as he rubs a towel over his hair. I'm momentarily speechless as I take in his beautiful, well-proportioned limbs and…other extremities.

"Uh…" I gurgle, unable to move away from the door.

He looks up and smiles. "Hey."

I quickly snap back into consciousness and slam the door. "What are you doing?" I hiss.

"Taking a shower?" Thankfully, he wraps the towel around his waist.

"What if one of my sisters came in?"

"Guess they would have gotten an eyeful," he says. "What's the big deal?"

"What's the big deal?" I scoff. "You're naked! I don't want them to see you naked."

He gives me a devilish smile. "You staking your claim on me, Kels?"

"What? No! That's absurd. I'm merely pointing out—" I gasp as he tugs me into his warm, slightly damp arms. He smells like ocean and mint.

"Pointing out that I'm yours and no one else can look or touch?" He tips my chin up and kisses me gently. I run my fingers into his wet hair. The kiss turns hungry, his towel dropping to the floor. His hands move under my shirt, his fingers gliding over my peaked nipples. I can feel his hardness press into me. "I've been thinking about you all day," he says in a low voice as he tries to pull my shirt off.

"Patrick, wait." I laugh as I tug my shirt back down. "My sisters are in the kitchen."

"Just a quickie? They won't even notice you're missing. Look, I'm already hard."

I laugh as my hand clasps around him. He hisses out a breath as I pump him slowly, feeling the satin over his steel. His hooded eyes have me wanting to bend to my knees and take him in my mouth. "Your Jedi stick is pretty hard."

"It's about to shoot lasers off, it's so hard."

"Hey Patrick, we were going to head out...oh!" Bridget freezes in the doorway. "Oh my god, you're naked...oh wow, and Kelsey is holding your...oh god...naked." Bridget's eyes are about to pop out of her head as they roam down Patrick's body. I quickly drop my hand and turn toward her, shielding Patrick from her roving eyes as much as I can. Patrick doesn't even pretend to be modest, his towel still on the floor.

"Bridget!"

"Huh...what?"

"Get the hell out!"

"Oh, yes, I'm so sorry!" Flustered, she bangs the door shut, but it pops back open with force. "Gah! Sorry, so sorry. Still naked...uh, come meet us in the kitchen when you get sexed...I mean dressed! Shit!" The door gently closes. "Get dressed, that's what I meant to say... Jesus, Mother Mary, and Joseph he is so fine," she mutters.

I turn around and thunk my forehead against his chest. "I'm so sorry."

His chest vibrates as he chuckles. "It's okay."

"I guess a quickie will have to wait."

"Hmm…if you don't mind, I think I'm going to pass on dinner tonight."

"I completely understand." I look bleakly into his golden-brown eyes. "Unfortunately, I have to go."

"Naturally. It would be weird if you didn't."

"I know, but their visit was unexpected." I sigh as I wrap my arms around his waist. "I love my sisters, but I kind of wanted to spend time with you."

He kisses me. "Maybe you can sneak in here later."

I pinch his butt. "I'll make it happen."

"Good."

"I'm going to have to fight Bridget off with a stick. Apparently, she thinks you're fine," I croon as he picks up his towel and snaps it at my butt.

I leave him to get dressed and wonder what the hell I'm doing. I've never been this needy or wanting to spend all my time with a guy before Patrick. But I can't help myself. He makes me feel desirable, giddy, and scared, all tightly rolled into a little knot that sits guiltily in the pit of my stomach.

Even though I have feelings for him, I know with certainty that I will choose my career first this time.

Chapter 23

Kelsey

Chum in the Water

"CHEERS!" MY SISTERS and I chorus, clinking our drinks together as we sit out on the patio of a restaurant facing the ocean.

"So, Kels, how has it been so far?" Arden asks after taking a sip.

"It's been good." I dip a chip into some guacamole and shove it into my mouth. The last thing I want to do is talk about myself.

"Are you excited to start your new job as Miss Cookie?" MK peruses her menu.

"Um...sure, I guess," I say around a mouthful of food.

"What about you and Patrick?"

I kick Bridget under the table and narrow my eyes at her, but it's too late. The other two pick up on *you and Patrick* like a shark smelling chum in the water. "What about Patrick?"

"Is something going on?"

"We..."

"They've hooked up! I saw him naked!" Bridget exclaims giddily. I'd like to go drown her in the ocean. She shrinks

185

back into her seat when she notices my expression. "Oops, sorry, Kels."

MK and Arden exchange glances. "Really? This is so romantic! How did it start?" Arden asks.

"I'm ninety-nine percent positive they hooked up at the wedding. Kelsey didn't return to our roo—"

"Oh my god, will you shut up?" I turn to Bridget, utterly exasperated with her.

"Oh yes, sorry, you tell it."

"Gee, thanks," I grumble. "So…we may have hooked up at Nick's wedding."

"What? How come I didn't know about this?" Arden slides a look at MK, who shrugs.

"I thought you guys were so cute on the dance floor." MK smiles.

"Oh my god, remember when he slipped on the floor and grabbed onto Lindsey's great-aunt? Holy shit, that was hilarious. He stripped half the beads off her dress." Arden snorts.

I chuckle, remembering the scene vividly. "I've never laughed so hard."

"He's super cute. I think you've managed to grab a good one."

"I haven't grabbed anything, Bridget." I shift uncomfortably in my seat.

"That's not what he said," she murmurs as the waitress arrives with our food.

I'm grateful for the brief respite. "I'm leaving at the end of next week. I'll be back in New York, and he'll be…wherever Lindsey's show takes him."

"Oh, that's so romantic! Long-distance lovers." Bridget sighs next to me.

"Long-distance isn't easy. Remember when John and I tried to be long-distance when he was in med school? It was rough." MK's brow creases with worry.

"Which is why I'm not planning on a long-distance relationship."

"Wait, I'm confused…" Arden takes a bite of her salad, chewing thoughtfully. "So, you're not coming back to New York?"

"I am," I say flatly. "Patrick and I are having fun, that's all." Bridget snorts. "What?" I take a sip of my margarita, irritated with my sisters.

"When I walked in on you guys, it looked like more than just having fun."

"Well, then you need to get your eyes checked," I gripe.

"Wait, you walked in on them? When?"

"About an hour ago."

The three of them exchange looks.

"Ugh, can we move on from this subject already?"

MK smiles. "Of course! We care about you, Kels, and don't want another…"

"Another what?" I stab my fork into my steak testily. "Another Todd situation? Well, don't worry, Patrick and I won't be getting engaged anytime soon. I have everything under control."

"No offense, but he's not your usual type." Bridget wriggles in her seat next to me. "What's he like in bed?"

"First of all, I don't have a type." I glare across the table at Arden as she snorts. "*Second* of all, I will never share a shred of what he's like in bed, so please don't ever ask that again."

Bridget pouts. "You're no fun."

"Why are you giving me that look, Arden?"

"Because you're kidding yourself when you say you don't have a type. Remember David Pruitt in high school?"

"Sandy-blond hair, WWE muscles, dumber than a box of rocks?" MK laughs.

"Hey, he wasn't dumb..."

"Oh please, don't you remember when he thought the school bake sale meant the school was handing out pot brownies for everyone? He thought he was high all day. He was such an idiot."

"Okay, yeah, he was."

"Remember Mike, the bartender?" MK looks at me pointedly. "Sandy-blond hair, WWE muscles, dumber than—"

"Remember Seth, the lifeguard? Sandy-blond—" Bridget cuts in.

"Okay, we get it! I like dumb blond jocks. Todd wasn't like that though, he was smart, short, athletic, and had dark hair..."

"He was also a complete douchebag."

I nod. "True...Patrick isn't, though. He's smart and sensitive, and..." My sisters exchange another telling look. "What?"

MK shrugs. "Nothing...please be careful, Kels. It sounds like you're more into him than you're letting on. We like Patrick—"

"A lot, so don't go breaking his heart," Arden finishes.

I'm reminded of the Backstreet Boys' song Lindsey was screeching the other day and how terrible I felt when I hurt Patrick's feelings.

I hold up my hands in surrender. "No hearts being broken by anyone. I told you, we're both on the same page. So, what are we going to do tomorrow?"

I tune my sisters out as they prattle on about going shopping versus going to the beach. I'm finding myself rattled by the conversation about Patrick. I do have everything under control, don't I? So why do I feel all edgy? Patrick and I haven't discussed what will happen when I leave next week. Will we try long-distance? Will we go our separate ways and remain friends? What worries me the most right now is that I'm itching to leave my sisters and go back home to snuggle with him on the couch while we watch some dumb Alaska in the wild show. Falling in love with Patrick was not in my plan.

And why do my sisters think I'm the one who could crush Patrick? In truth, it's the opposite. Patrick could break this newly mended heart wide open.

Chapter 24

Patrick

To Be or Not to Be, That Is the Question

I OPEN THE French doors leading out to the patio and pool. I scan the area to make sure there aren't any Elliot sisters around. They seem to pop out around every corner. I don't know how Nick managed to grow up with them. It explains a lot about his personality. I'd be a surly asshole too if I were called Little Dick.

Kelsey is sitting at the teak wood table with her feet propped on a chair and the baby monitor on the table. She's reading, which strikes me as odd since she's admitted she's not much of a reader.

The more I learn about Kelsey, the more I realize we don't have much in common. But that hasn't stopped me from discovering her likes and dislikes. I love being around her. I want to know more each day we grow closer. And the sex, of course, is out of this world. Whenever we're in the same room together, I'm drawn to her. She's been crawling into my bed every night, and trying to have quiet sex has brought on a whole new level of excitement. I made her lose the bet last night that I couldn't make her scream my name. Having to face a grumpy Nick this morning over coffee wasn't ideal, but it was totally worth it.

Even if we are polar opposites, I like Kelsey. A lot. If I were honest, I'd tell her I was falling in love with her. In the back of my head I'm wondering if we'll continue what we've started once she moves back to New York.

"Whatcha reading?" I walk up behind her and pull out a chair. She jumps and quickly tucks the book behind her back.

"You scared me," she says. I hand her a Corona with a lime wedge. "Ooh, thanks!"

"Where are your sisters?"

"Well, after they kept pushing chardonnay on Lindsey last night and asking why she wasn't drinking, she finally broke down and told them the news. So they took her shopping at a baby boutique. I said I'd stay behind and watch Olive since Nick is at JD's clinic."

"Hmm." I take a long pull on my beer as she squeezes the lime into hers. "So what kind of book does one need to hide behind their back? Is it something totally kinky?" I waggle my eyebrows which causes her to blush.

"No, of course not. It's a stupid thriller. Honestly, it's not that good."

"Really? Because you seemed pretty engrossed in it since you didn't even hear me approach."

"It's just a book. So, where have you been?"

"I had to go to the editing studio. Can I see it?"

"See what?"

"Come on, Kels, your book. If it's no big deal, then who cares? Maybe I've read it. Unlike you, I enjoy getting lost in a book."

She rolls her eyes and tries to ignore me, but when she leans forward to put her beer on the table my lightning-fast reflexes snatch the book from her chair.

"Hey! That's private!"

I hold the book up and smirk, but I have a thousand questions running through my head. A little kernel of love bursts in my heart like a shooting star streaking across the night sky. "*The Last of the Jedi Warrior?*"

Kelsey takes a deep breath, her cheeks stained a pretty pink. "It's just some fanfiction book the guy at the bookstore said I'd enjoy. Maybe I wanted to see what all the fuss was about."

"And?" I prod. "What do you think?"

"It's okay if you're into space and stuff." She reaches for the book and looks at the cover.

"Why were you trying to hide it?"

"I don't know," she says and places the book on the table. "I didn't want you to think I was stalking you."

"Hmm…" I lean into her and kiss her lips. "As long as it's not creepy stalking, I'm okay with it."

Worry creases her brow as she pulls back from me. "Look, Patrick, there's stuff you should know, stuff I've wanted to tell you about my past relationships…about why I need to keep things simple between us." She doesn't make eye contact with me as she runs a finger along the front of the book.

"So, tell me."

"I had a bad breakup right before Nick's wedding. I'm sure Lindsey has told you that I was engaged." I nod when she looks up for confirmation. She sits back in her seat, nursing her beer. "When I was a kid, for as long as I could remember I wanted to be a journalist. I remember watching Katie Couric and saying to myself, that's going to be me someday. I used to walk around with a pencil behind my ear and a ratty notebook interviewing anyone who would pause long enough to answer my questions. I was relentless, just ask my siblings.

"My dad even bought me a tape recorder with a microphone, he got such a kick that I was so passionate about it. I was the chief editor for my high school paper and then went on to write for my college paper. I loved journalism and I never veered off course. When I graduated college I interned at *The New York Post*. I met Todd through some friends and one thing led to another.

"Life couldn't have been more perfect. I was living in New York City, happily engaged to a doctor, and I was offered a job writing a weekly column at *The New York Times*. I thought my life was right on track."

She sets her beer down and stares out across the pool. "Then Todd got offered to be a partner at a general family practice in Ithaca. I should have been elated for him, but I wasn't. How would we make it work if I was in the city and he was two hours away? I could commute home on the weekends, but he wasn't keen on that idea. I asked the paper if I could work from home, but that wasn't an option. He gave me an ultimatum, either move to Ithaca and be his wife or stay in the city and be single. I felt like I was stuck. I loved him, but I didn't want to give up my chance of working at my dream job. I see now that his ultimatum wasn't love. Asking me to give up my career that was important to me so that he could advance his."

"So what happened?" I get up and pull two more beers from the patio fridge and hand her one.

"Thanks. So, I did what I thought was a selfless thing. Because when you're in love, you will do anything for that person, right? I gave up my dream so he could have his. We bought a cute little cottage on the lake, and I convinced myself I was happy as I spent my days redecorating it."

"But you weren't."

"I was so fucking miserable. I pretended for a while that I wasn't. When I told Todd how unhappy I was, he somehow twisted it around that it was my fault, that I wasn't trying hard enough. He wanted me to work for the local paper, but the only job available was ad placement sales. I tried to find happiness and work on my relationship. I wrote for magazines, submitting short stories here and there. I'd surprise him at the clinic with lunch, or I'd have a four-course meal waiting for him when he got home, with me as dessert."

She looks up, catching me wince.

"Sorry, my point is, I tried. Anyway, on one of my little jaunts to the office with a basket of fried chicken and fruit, I found him banging his practice manager in his office. The fucker didn't even have the decency to lock his door."

"Oh Jesus, Kelsey, I'm sorry."

"I lost my career, my dreams, and my identity when I said yes to Todd. I gave up everything. You win some, you lose some, right?" She tries to sound nonchalant, but I know she's hurting. "When I met you at the wedding, I needed to feel wanted and desired. You were so damn hot and funny." She smiles ruefully. "And I wanted a night of hot no-strings-attached sex. I want a chance with you, Patrick, but I just…god, my life is such a mess. I'm scared to get involved with someone and make the same mistake again."

"I'd never hurt you like that."

"I know…but what's the point? Our lives are going in two opposite directions. We live in separate states. You constantly travel for the show and I'm stuck writing a stupid weekly column about Lysol when I return to New York. It would be crazy to start something."

We stew in silence for a minute, her words like a knife pierced to my heart. "I tried to move on from that night," I say eventually. "I dated other women, but they never measured up to you." I lean forward and stare into her bottomless blues. "I couldn't forget you, Kels. I know it will be hard, but we can make this work if we make an effort. We can figure it out."

"I haven't dated anyone since that night. I haven't wanted anyone the way I want you."

"I'm not giving up on us." I wrap my hand around her neck and bring her lips to mine, surprised and encouraged by her confession. I stroke her lips tenderly, savoring the shape and the texture of them. I need to clear the air of everything if we hope to make this work. I have to ask her about the secret she's been hiding and about the yacht. "Kelsey, the other week—"

"Aw! You guys are so adorable."

Kelsey grimaces as she pushes back from me. I sit back and smile at Bridget, but I'm annoyed by the interruption.

"Don't stop on my account." She pulls a chair out across from us and takes a sip from Kelsey's beer.

"Did you guys have fun?" Kelsey asks, grabbing her beer back.

"A blast. Lindsey went to take a nap. I don't think she's used to three sisters throwing baby clothes at her." Bridget laughs. "Oh! We called Kiernan, and he's agreed to come over tonight for dinner!"

"Wait...what? Why?" Kelsey sits up on full alert.

"Um, because he's our cousin and we're in the same city? I haven't seen him since the wedding."

"He's coming here...tonight...for dinner?"

"Yes, ding-dong, I've said that already."

Kelsey fidgets in her seat. "Will Nick be here for dinner too?"

"Uh, I assume so..." Bridget gives me a baffled expression.

"Didn't you have dinner with your cousin the other week?" I ask Kelsey, my Spidey senses going on full alert. Why is she suddenly agitated?

"Um, yeah." Kelsey grabs her book and mumbles something about a shower before she practically runs back into the house.

"What the heck is wrong with her?"

"I don't know, but I'm excited to meet the infamous cousin Kiernan."

"I mean, he's nice, but there's nothing that exciting about him. He's a CPA. Whatever you do, don't get him talking about taxes. It will make your ears bleed." Bridget picks up Kelsey's beer.

"Good to know. Was he at the wedding? I don't remember meeting him."

"Yeah, I felt so bad for him. He got food poisoning the night before, so he wasn't very social at the wedding."

I smile at Bridget, but my mind is working a million miles a minute. Why is Kelsey so worried about Kiernan coming to dinner? What is she hiding, and why?

Chapter 25

Patrick

Intentions

I TRY SENDING Lindsey another text. She's not answering her phone and she won't come out of the bedroom. Shopping with the Elliot sisters must have been pretty traumatizing for her. I need to inform her of the latest development. I've even sent her an SOS Cranky Cat text, but I've gotten nothing back from her. She's the worst co-conspirator partner ever. I need to sit down with Kelsey and get to the bottom of it, but she's currently on an errand with Bridget. I can't seem to get more than five minutes alone with her before we're interrupted by one of her sisters.

Aromatic smells waft out of the kitchen as I walk down the hall into the kitchen. MK and Arden are chopping vegetables on the island as they talk. MK looks up and smiles at me as I enter.

"Do you guys need help?"

"Hi, Patrick! I hope you like chicken and steak kabobs. Nick said he'd grill them up for us."

"Sure, I love all kinds of food."

"That's great. You're the best, Patrick, so easygoing..." MK smiles and gestures to a chair at the island with her knife. "Have a seat and join us."

Arden drops her knife and pulls a beer from the fridge, placing it in front of me. "Yeah, sit with us."

"Uh, sure. Thanks." I glance down at my phone for the five hundredth time—nothing from Lindsey. I look up and smile as they covertly watch me. I don't really want to chit-chat with MK and Arden because of the more pressing matter of Kiernan coming to dinner, but I don't want to be rude. "So tell me about Kiernan. Is he some big-shot tax guy here in Miami?" I picture the tall, dark-haired man standing next to Kelsey on the yacht, his hand on her back. "A guy fighting off the ladies with his debonair good looks and swagger?"

MK snorts. "Kiernan? Not exactly."

"What? Why is that funny?" I smile as the two sisters look at each other and giggle.

"Kiernan is passionate about taxes, that's for sure, but he's not a big shot. Picture a short James Corden with glasses who loves to wear Hawaiian shirts."

Hmm, that doesn't match up with the guy I saw on the yacht. Knowing these two, they're probably pulling my leg, and Johnny Depp's twin brother will be walking through the door.

"Do you know when Kelsey will be back?"

"She should be back soon. I only needed a few ingredients and some wine."

"Aw, isn't that so cute, MK? He misses his honey."

"So cute."

"I guess Bridget told you about us." I rub a hand across my jaw.

"I think half of Miami knows about you two." MK smirks. "You're not exactly quiet."

I blanche as I pick up my beer and take a large gulp. Guess our "quiet game" hasn't been so quiet.

"So, Patrick, now that we're on the topic, what are your intentions with our sister?" Arden pauses and looks at me, her knife held in midair. The beer I just swallowed goes down the wrong pipe causing me to choke. Arden comes around the island, but I hold up a hand. I don't need her to accidentally stab me to death.

"I'm good." I wheeze.

"I think what my sister is trying to say is that Kelsey has been through a lot. She doesn't need someone messing around with her heart."

"I don't intend—"

"And she doesn't need drama."

"I agree—"

"Do you plan on marrying her?"

"What?" I swallow as I desperately look around the kitchen for help. Where the hell is Lindsey or Nick when I need them?

"Oh my god, she's not pregnant, is she?" Arden raises her eyebrows.

"Wait a minute, pregnant?" I panic, breaking out in a sweat as my eyes bounce between the two sisters. "I don't think so. Why, did she say something?"

"Do you not *want* kids?" MK's eyes narrow as she chops an onion with a loud thwack.

"You should be on the same page about these kinds of things," Arden says.

"I mean, we just want to know your intentions." MK smiles sweetly.

"Yeah, what are your intentions?" Arden echoes.

"Would you move to New York for her?"

"Yes, that's important, good one, MK. How do we know you're trustworthy? Would you ever date someone on your production team?"

My brain immediately pings to Gary, Dean, Greg, and fifty-year-old Linda, and I cringe.

"How old are you? How come you've never settled down?"

"Do you have a problem with commitment?"

"Ooh, Yes!" MK turns to Arden with her knife. "I didn't even think of that possibility. Are you in therapy?"

I would give anything at this moment to be able to melt into the floor to get the hell away from these two staring me down as they slice and chop, pummeling me with questions I don't want to answer. My eyes hurt from ping-ponging between them.

I take a swig of my beer, but it does nothing for the dry mouth I suddenly have developed. "I uh…"

"Hey, we're back!" Bridget breezes in from the garage door.

"Thank fuck," I mutter as I wipe the sweat from my brow.

"We were just having a fun little chat with Patrick." Arden smiles. "Getting to know Kelsey's sweetie."

Bridget wraps an arm around my neck and hugs me closer to her. "Isn't he adorbs?"

Kelsey comes in slogging six grocery bags. "Thanks for

the help, Bridge," she grumbles as she sets the bags down on the kitchen table. Her eyebrows rise when she sees me. She walks over and puts her cool hand on my forehead. "What's wrong with you? You look sick."

"Yeah, you know, now that you mention it, I think I need to go lie down."

"You don't have a fever, but you feel a little clammy."

"Yeah, um…I…" I stand up, trying to get out of the kitchen before I have a full-blown panic attack.

Kelsey looks at her sisters suspiciously. "What were you guys talking about? What have you done to Patrick?"

The doorbell rings, and I jump on it. Anything to get out of this claustrophobic kitchen. "I'll get that."

"No, you sit. I'll get it." Kelsey tries to push me back into my seat.

"No, I insist." We struggle for a second before Bridget breezes past us.

"You guys are weird. It's probably Kiernan."

Kelsey gives me a frustrated growl as she turns and starts unpacking the bags. Nick and Lindsey walk into the kitchen, and I about blow my gasket. "Where have you *been*?"

"Uh, taking a nap, why?" Lindsey shifts Olive to her other hip.

"I've been texting you for an hour! When is that thing not glued to your hand?"

"I silenced my ringer. Geez, are you okay? You're kind of scaring me with your intensity right now."

"Kiernan!" Arden crows as a short guy with light brown hair, wearing a red Hawaiian print shirt and shorts, walks in behind Bridget. Their description was to a T. My brain short-circuits because that's not the man Kelsey stood next to on the boat.

"That's not cousin Kiernan," I mutter to Lindsey as MK hugs him. "You know what this means, right?"

Lindsey turns to me, eyes wide. "Oh god, don't tell me Cranky Cat is back on."

I nod. "Cranky Cat is back on."

Chapter 26

Kelsey

Cousin Kiernan

I'M DESPERATELY TRYING to get Kiernan alone so that I can tell him I used him as a cover the night I went on the yacht, but no one will give me a chance. Especially Patrick. He's commandeered Kiernan's attention for some weird reason, glued to his side like they're long-lost bosom buddies. I want to walk over and kick him in the shin and tell him to share. JD also showed up to join the party, and the four of them have been hanging out by the grill like they are guarding the Queen's tiara. Does it *really* take four guys to watch meat cook?

I make my way over to them, bringing four fresh beers and a winning smile. "Hey, I hate to break up this little party, but can I borrow Kiernan for a sec?"

Nick, Kiernan, and JD smile, but Patrick looks at me suspiciously. He's acting so strange, and it's making me feel uneasy and tense. Something happened during the time I left him out on the patio to the time I got back from the store, I'm just not sure what. I want to pull him away from the party and talk about it, but I currently have a more pressing problem I need to deal with. I tug Kiernan off to the side under the covered patio behind a potted banana plant.

"Kelsey, I'm so glad you finally made it to Miami! I hope Marco was—"

"Yeah, yeah, great to see you too, um, so listen…I might have told an eensy-weensy—"

"Hey Kiernan, I heard you are an accountant! That's fascinating!" Lindsey appears out of thin air, making my confession die on my tongue. "I want to hear all about it!" She looks at me and waggles her eyebrows.

Who the hell finds accounting exciting except for accountants?

"Oh, well, it's not that exciting." Kiernan blushes as he fumbles his drink.

See?! Even Kiernan realizes the topic is a total dud. I want to take Lindsey by the shoulders and steer her in the opposite direction, but I know that might look rude while he starts in on the exciting life of being an accountant during the upcoming tax season.

"Excuse me, Kiernan," I rudely interrupt. "Um, Lindsey, where's Olive? I hope she's not crawling around by the pool. Maybe you should go check." I crane my neck, emphasizing that she needs to make sure Olive is okay.

"Oh, don't worry, MK has her." She turns her attention back to my cousin. "So, Kiernan, talk to me about taxes. I want to know it all." She winks at me as I look at her skeptically. Why is she so suddenly interested in taxes? Suspicion wraps around me like a tight, suffocating scarf. Does she know I didn't have dinner with him last week? Is that why she and Patrick are acting so weird tonight? I shake my head. There's no possible way they could know. She was in her pajamas that night when I got home. Could Patrick have followed me? He was asking me a lot of strange questions that night.

I chew on my thumbnail as I contemplate the possibilities. Is that why they're trying to stop me from talking to Kiernan? Do they know I'm trying to get my story straight with him? It's farfetched, and I'm acting paranoid. How could they possibly know?

Lindsey nods as Kiernan drones on, pretending he's the most thrilling storyteller, interjecting a teasing laugh when she can. James Patterson, he is not. This conversation makes me want to stab my eyeballs with the kabob skewers, it's so dull.

"So in short, with a straight-line depreciation, you would be permitted to write off twenty percent of the cost each year—the accelerated method generally lets you deduct twenty percent of the business cost the first year, thirty-two percent the second, nineteen-point-two percent the third..."

"Uh-huh...wow, yeah, that's so great. Makes perfect sense." Lindsey's glazed eyes are staring at a spot over his shoulder. Nick walks by with the platter of kabobs, setting it on the outdoor table.

"Let's eat, everyone," he shouts.

"Oh, thank god," Lindsey mumbles, and then as if realizing her blunder, she smiles wide. "Because I am *starving!*"

We follow Lindsey over to the table as everyone takes their seats. I try to squeeze in next to Kiernan, but Arden beats me to it. Dammit, I needed one last-ditch effort to let him in on my secret. I end up sitting between Bridget and JD, across from Patrick. We all pass the dishes around and fill up our plates as chatter permeates the air. Sangria is passed around the table as dusk envelops us, the twinkling lights and citronella candles casting a warm glow over the table.

I start to relax in my teak chair as JD launches into a story about the infamous Spike the iguana who attacked Patrick. His owner returned today to be on the show. She was thrilled Patrick wasn't in the exam room this time. We all laugh as JD describes the look of horror on Dawn's face when Patrick tried to throw him off his head. He still has a shadow of a mark on his forehead.

"Yeah, well, there won't be any future reunions between Spike and me. It's safe to say I'd rather eat weird things than work in the veterinary field."

"Oh, I know a great place if you want to eat weird things." Kiernan smiles.

"What? No, don't tell him!" Lindsey pleads from the other end of the table.

"Yes!" Patrick rubs his hands together. "Give me the info when she's not paying attention." He winks at Lindsey. "So, Kiernan, tell us about the restaurant you and Kelsey went to last week. I heard there was a shooting?"

Oh shit.

Kiernan looks at me blankly. "Uh, I'm not sure—"

"Kiernan, ha!" I shout, cutting him off. I'm tempted to kick him hard under the table, but I don't think I can reach him. I'd probably end up kicking Patrick, who definitely deserves a swift one to the nuts. "Remember? It was that Vietnamese restaurant and the waiter was so forgetful? And then we had to stay in the restaurant because there was a domestic shooting outside?"

"What? That's awful!" MK pipes up, but it doesn't save the situation. Kiernan looks completely mystified, like he just woke up from a coma.

"I don't remember—"

"Yeah, remember you had pho and I had Cha Ca?" I smile nervously, trying to will Kiernan to play along with my eyes, but he tilts his head like an adorable little pug. At this point, I should throw the towel in and tell everyone the truth, but I feel manic and wild. I've brought the lie this far...if I can just convince him.

"I thought you went to a Mexican restaurant?" Nick inserts from the end of the table. Shit, did I tell him Mexican? I can't remember. My palms feel sweaty as everyone looks at me baffled.

I give Nick a sickly-sweet smile that I hope makes him feel unsettled. "No, silly, what gave you that idea?"

Kiernan pushes his glasses up on his nose. "Last week? I—"

"Kiernan! Tell us about accounting!" I exclaim, and Lindsey groans loudly from her end. "Do you have any celebrity clients?"

"Oh, well—"

"Oh my God, that reminds me!" Bridget exclaims. "We saw Jennifer Lopez's yacht, and I swear she was on it, right, Arden?"

"Yes, it had to be her or her doppelgänger. I wonder if she has a decoy to throw the paparazzi off."

"Some of them do," JD agrees as he winks at Arden.

"Kiernan, JD, have you guys had any celebrities come

into the office?" Bridget squeezes my leg under the table, and I want to cry in relief. Thank god for my sisters for always having my back. They don't know why I'm lying, and I'm sure I'll get a full shakedown later, but for right now, I'm relieved. They are throwing me a life vest and I'm grabbing it with both hands. JD, who loves the attention, prattles on about celebrity clients, as the awkwardness from a few moments ago is quickly forgotten.

I look up from my plate, my eyes colliding with Patrick's golden-brown gaze. I'm afraid he can read me with his Jedi mind tricks. I give him a tremulous smile, but he doesn't return it. I'm not sure how he knows that I'm lying about that night. I should just tell him I have an interview at *The Miami Times*, but I'm scared and superstitious it will ruin everything. What if he reads too much into it? What if he wants to take things further with what is happening between us and moves to Miami to be with me?

Would that be so bad, Kelsey?

I have feelings for Patrick, there's no doubt, but I'm afraid. I don't want to get into another relationship after my last one crashed and burned. I certainly don't want to give up on my dream job again. I'm terrified that I'll fall in love with Patrick and forget everything I learned from Todd. This is fate offering me another chance, and nothing is going to screw it up. Not even Patrick Healy.

Chapter 27

Patrick

The Truth

LINDSEY WALKS INTO the quiet kitchen as I sip my coffee. Kelsey left about twenty minutes ago to take her sisters to the airport, and Nick is out running with Olive. "Oh my god, Trick, do you hear that?"

I put the paper down and look up at her. "I don't hear anything."

"Exactly, blissful peace and quiet. I love the Elliot sisters, but sheesh, they are a lot to take. They tried to convince me that I needed them in the delivery room for this baby. Can you imagine?"

Their verbal barrage of questions from yesterday floods my brain. "That would be awful."

"Last night was weird, wasn't it?" She grabs a water and some fruit and sits across from me. "Don't you think it was weird? Kiernan was nice but strange. Yeah, it was definitely weird."

I sigh as I fold the paper. So much for a quiet minute. I lean back in my chair and take a sip of my coffee.

"Oh, I'm sorry, Your Grace, am I disturbing you?"

I smirk and shake my head. "Would it matter? I think

you managed to use the word weird at least three times, maybe four."

"You'd think you'd be a little more appreciative." Her spoon clatters dramatically in her bowl.

"For what?" I pick up the paper and try to tune her out. Impossible when she slams her hand down on the paper pinning it to the table.

"Hello? For interrupting Kiernan and Kelsey? Remember when you shoved me into their little powwow?"

"Shh."

Lindsey waves her hand. "No one is here. I had to stand there for like forty minutes and listen to him droll on about taxes. I thought my ears were going to bleed."

I chuckle. "It was more like five minutes. I knew she was trying to get him alone to collaborate her story."

"Yeah, she was annoyed I interrupted." Lindsey tilts her head, pondering. "But don't you think it was kind of mean to put her in the hot seat last night? You supposedly love her, so why would you do that?"

"Because I don't like being lied to. It was abundantly clear that she didn't have dinner with Kiernan, so what is she hiding?" I remove her hand from the paper. "I'm not in love."

Lindsey narrows her eyes and clucks her tongue. "Uh-huh. Maybe she has her reasons for lying and she's not ready to share them yet." I'm about to protest, but she holds her hands up. "Look, I know how you're feeling. Remember when Nick lied to me? About *a lot* of stuff."

"Yeah, totally different. He was lying to protect your life from the Russian mob."

"God, it sounds so crazy when you say it out loud like that," she muses as she spoons fruit into her mouth. "We've come so far."

"Your point is…"

"Right, sorry. My point is, maybe she's protecting you from something." Her green eyes widen as she points the spoon at me. "Maybe she's a spy too."

"Where the hell have you been these last few weeks?" I say, completely exasperated. "Lindsey Love, welcome to Mission Cranky Cat. Glad you finally decided to join us."

She rolls her eyes. "OK, first of all, it's weird that you're talking like we're part of some FBI sting operation. Second, we never came up with the theory about the Russian mob, only that she was working with the FBI." She slowly drags the spoon out of her mouth. "Oh my god, I just thought of something. What if the Russian Mafia has come to exact their revenge on Nick? This has always been my biggest fear since he left The Syndicate. He and Olive are out on the mean streets of Miami as we speak!"

"Lovie, calm down. You're seriously overreacting right now and letting your imagination run wild," I snap. "I'm not sure why Kelsey lied, but I'm going to get to the bottom of it. Nick would never let anything happen to you or Olive. Nod your head if you understand me," I say, and her wide eyes lock onto mine. She nods as she tries to control her breathing.

Nick comes in from the garage, sweaty, as he lifts Olive's stroller up the steps. "Hey guys, it's going to be a hot one today."

Lindsey runs to him and wraps her arms around his

waist. "Oh my god, I'm so glad you guys are okay."

Nick kisses her head as she buries her face into his t-shirt. He gives me a questioning look over her head as he holds her to him. I shake my head and mouth *hormones*. Nick nods in understanding.

"I bought you some Peanut M&Ms," he says quietly as he rubs her back.

"Any breakfast burritos in that stroller?"

"Of course. Stopped at that little stand we found the other day."

"Oh god, I knew marrying you was the right thing to do."

"The right thing to do?"

"Yeah, after you knocked me up. You stink, by the way."

"I'm one lucky guy." He smirks as he peels his damp t-shirt off and throws it in the laundry room off the kitchen.

"Damn right you are." Lindsey smiles as she lifts Olive out and snuggles her. Nick hands her the burrito. "Oh god, I love you."

"I should hope so since it's *the right thing to do*," he murmurs as he bends to kiss her. "I'm going to go hit the shower. You okay?"

She nods. Satisfied, he walks to the bedroom. Lindsey turns to me and gives me the evil eye.

"What now?" I ask.

"Nick needs to know what's going on."

"How can I tell him when I don't even know?"

"I don't know, but this Crazy Cat business needs to stop, Trick. Whatever this thing that's going on between you two...you need to trust her."

"Uh, weren't you the one telling me minutes ago you thought she was part of Nick's old Syndicate group or possibly working for the FBI?" I shake my head. "I don't know what she's involved in, but it's hard to trust someone who's lying to you, Lovie."

"I think you're just going to have to let this go and trust her. She's an adult. She can handle herself, but if it's really bothering you, then definitely talk to her about it."

"I'm pissed she can't trust me enough to tell me," I yell, exasperated with this conversation and with myself.

"Pick up your ego, Trick, I just tripped over it," she laments, her expressive eyes flashing irritation to pity in a heartbeat, making my gut churn. "It's her decision if and when she needs to share it with you. As much as it pains me to say this, maybe she isn't the right one for you," Lindsey says sadly. She places her spoon and bowl in the dishwasher. "You deserve to have an open, honest relationship." And she walks out of the kitchen with Olive on her hip.

I slump against the counter.

She's right, I know she's right, but I can't make Kelsey open up to me. And there within lies the problem. Aren't we supposed to be transparent with each other? Dammit, I hate it when Lovie is right. I need Kelsey to communicate with me and I need to do the same in return, or we need to go our separate ways.

Chapter 28

Patrick

The Sweaty Pig

I PRESS THE button to connect me to the recording booth. "Okay, take a break, Lovie. We have twenty minutes left of studio time. Maybe we can redo that opening for Al's. Perhaps you could be a little more upbeat?"

"Hardly. That place was a live-bait hellhole."

"Okay, well, our viewers apparently love live-bait hell-holes, so let's make it a good experience for them." I smile and give her a thumbs-up as she pulls off her headphones, grumbling about where I can stick Alligator Al's you-know-what. She fishes her phone out of her bag and checks her messages as she bites into a granola bar. I sit down in a chair next to Bob, who is helping us produce the voiceovers, and stretch. It's been a long morning and I'm feeling down about Kelsey. I haven't been able to talk to her since her sisters left, and my time with her is almost up. I don't want us to part on a sour note. Heck, I don't want us to part ways at all, but I know the future for us doesn't exactly look like sunshine and rainbows and happily-ever-afters.

Lindsey bursts through the recording door, her face alight with worry. "Trick! Kelsey's in trouble!"

"What? How do you know?"

"Come on! We have to go!" She chucks the granola bar into the trash and motions for me to hurry up.

I shake my head. "No, Lindsey, you were right. I shouldn't get involved. Call Nick."

"When have you ever listened to my advice before?" She yanks my arm, practically pulling it out of its socket, forcing me to the door. "I left Nick a message. He's not answering. Come on. I'm worried. She left a message fifteen minutes ago. That's a long time when you're in trouble."

"Bob! We'll be back," I shout through the door as I rub my arm. I check my watch. Dammit, our recording time is almost up. "Never mind, I'll call you tomorrow." Bob gives me a lazy wave as I hustle out after Lindsey to the parking lot. "Where is she?"

"She's at *The Miami Times*."

"The paper?" I unlock the minivan with the keyless remote.

"Yes, her voicemail said something about secrets, and oh my god, she sounded like she was crying, Trick," Lindsey wails as we get into the minivan.

"Okay, okay, calm down. We'll go down there. Have you tried calling her?"

"Twice, but I'll try again." Lindsey pulls up Kelsey's contact and shakes her head after a minute. "Nothing. It goes straight to voicemail."

Worry has me gunning the van out of the parking lot. I quickly punch in the paper's address as Lindsey plays the voicemail on her speakerphone.

"Hey Linds, it's Kelsey. I need help." The message garbles as she says something else. "Fifteen minutes…secret…help. I have…interview…Elizabeth Greyton…story…sweaty pig…new identity. I will die…help." She ends with a cry of anguish.

I step on the gas. "What the hell is that about? It sounds like she's underwater."

"I don't know, Trick, but maybe you were right all along. Maybe she's gotten herself into some bad shit."

"Well, then why the hell is she at *The Miami Times*? Shouldn't she be at the police station or the FBI?"

"I don't know. Her message kept cutting out." Lindsey chews on her thumbnail as I concentrate on not ramming into the person in front of me who keeps slamming on their breaks. "Oh my god, what if…what if she is going to the paper to tell her story, and then she's going into witness protection? Maybe some sweaty pig of a guy is trying to kidnap her! What secret is she talking about? Drive faster!"

I clench my jaw as I maneuver around the sedan in front of me. "That message was very choppy. We can't jump to conclusions, Lovie. Try calling her again."

"Voicemail."

I grip the steering wheel tight. "Dammit, how long does it take to get to *The Miami Times*!" Panic starts to claw at my chest as I bang my hand on the steering wheel. The horn honks, causing Lindsey to jump in her seat and the guy in front of me to flip me the bird. "Sorry."

"Okay, let's go over Mission Cranky Cat and try to piece together what we know." Lindsey looks at me, and I nod my approval. "Okay, so far we know she's met a strange man on a fancy yacht. The sweaty pig. Clearly, it was a Liam Neeson moment."

"We don't know that. She came back in one piece."

"She's a spy. She made a deal on the yacht, and now they are after her after finding out her true identity. She is now on the run from mister sweaty pig and has to go into witness protection. Maybe cousin Kiernan really does work for the FBI! He was wearing that terrible Hawaiian shirt, and he doesn't even have a tan! You can't live in Miami and be pasty white."

I side-eye her as I turn left. "Okay, getting off-track. Pretty sure Kiernan is just an accountant with bad fashion sense and pasty skin who works at his desk all day. But who was the tall dark-haired guy she met on the yacht?"

"Sweaty pig!"

"Wait, why are we calling him sweaty pig?"

"Because that was in her message! I don't know, Trick, I have a bad feeling about this."

I screech to a halt in front of *The Miami Times*. "Go find parking. What was the woman's name she mentioned again?"

Lindsey unbuckles. "Elizabeth Greyton. Hurry, hurry!"

"Call Nick while I search for her. Don't worry, Lovie, I've got this." I run into the busy main lobby and skid to a halt in front of the white marble information desk.

"May I help you, sir?" A man wearing a sweater vest and bowtie looks up at me.

"Uh, yes," I pant. "Where can I find Elizabeth Greyton's office?"

The man looks at a directory. "Sixth floor. The elevators are down that hall." He points to the left and then turns his attention to someone behind me. I race down the hall and jam my finger into the button while I pace. The bronze elevator to my right dings as the doors slide open, and I almost run into a poor woman trying to get off first.

"Excuse me, I'm so sorry." I hastily step on and press the sixth-floor button. I press the close-door button as I see someone approaching. "Sorry! Emergency!"

The elevator trundles up. I rub my hands together and try to think. I'll calmly walk into Ms. Greyton's office and whisk Kelsey out of there. Simple as that. She doesn't *have* to tell her story to any reporters. We'll get Nick's old group to help figure out how to keep her safe. Nick will do anything to keep his sister safe, and so will I. The elevator opens to a small lobby decorated in grays and lavender. I approach the woman sitting behind a large desk answering multiple phone lines.

Reluctantly, she looks up at me and frowns. Her dark brown hair is smoothed back into a severe bun, pulling her face taut. She doesn't look like the type to bend the rules and let me in the back offices unannounced. "May I help you?"

"Yes, I need to find Elizabeth Greyton's office."

"Do you have an appointment?"

"No. Look, this is an emergency. My friend is in there—"

"Hold, please." I can't tell if she's talking to me or someone in her headset. "Have a seat."

"But…"

She looks at the dual monitors in front of her, completely ignoring me. I sit down in the seat she indicated, pull out my phone, and try calling Kelsey but it goes straight to voicemail. I try Nick next—no answer. Where the heck is everyone when you need them? Minutes crawl by. I pop out of my seat, anxious and frustrated over being ignored by the surly receptionist. I'm going to have to take matters into my own hands. That's what Nick would do. I get up and head for the closest door.

"Sir? Sir, you can't go through there!" she clamors as I push open the heavy door. I rush into the maze of cubicles, stopping when a guy typing on his keyboard looks up at me curiously.

"Excuse me, can you point me in the direction of Elizabeth Greyton's office, please?" I ask.

"Uh, back corner."

"Great, thanks." I jog down the labyrinth of desks, bumping into a woman carrying copy paper. "Excuse me, sorry!" I call out over my shoulder. I find Ms. Greyton's office, take a deep breath, and push the handle down.

Chapter 29

Kelsey

Jedis Wearing Tinfoil Hats

THE DOOR TO Elizabeth's office bangs open as I'm talking about my brief stint at *The New York Times*. We both look up, completely surprised by the loud intrusion. My jaw almost drops to the ground when I see Patrick standing there.

"Oh my God, Patrick, is everything okay?" I stand up, completely dumbfounded.

"Kelsey, whatever you think you need to do, just stop." He holds his hands out in front of him like I'm a skittish animal he's cornering. "You don't have to tell your story, and you don't have to go into a witness protection program. We can help you! Nick can help you. He *knows* people!"

Silence envelops the room as I stare at Patrick. I'm struggling to wrap my head around the words that just came out of his mouth, waiting for him to shout that the aliens are coming before passing out tinfoil hats for us to wear. But he just stands there, his eyes pleading. I want to laugh and say, good one, Space Boy. Is this an April Fool's prank? But it can't be, it's only February. I take a chance and look at Elizabeth, who appears as gobsmacked as I am.

"Excuse me, young man, but you're interrupting—"

"Oh, I know what I'm interrupting," Patrick bites out as he steps farther into the room. "Journalists and their need to get the story. Well, you're not getting it from Ms. Elliot." He holds his hand out to me.

"Patrick!" I hiss. "Go away!"

"Ms. Elliot, do you know this man?" Elizabeth takes off her reading glasses and gives me a stern look.

I want to melt into the floor and die. I want to be swallowed up by the ocean and resurface in some far-off land where no one knows my name. I want to kill Patrick for interrupting my interview and ruining my chance to work at an upstanding paper.

"I uh…no? I think this is a bad joke," I fumble as I look anywhere other than Patrick. Two security guards come up behind Patrick, bending his arm against his back.

"Come on, buddy. You're coming with us."

"Kelsey, you don't have to do this! We'll protect you!" Patrick yells as they wrangle him out. The whole office watches as the security guards drag him away. I'm beyond humiliated. Elizabeth clears her throat, bringing my attention back to her. I have a hard time meeting her gaze. I can still hear Patrick hollering my name.

"He's not stable. He's my brother's friend. He thinks he's a jedi out of *Star Wars*, you know, Luke Skywalker…" The words die on my tongue as Elizabeth lifts an eyebrow. "I guess this concludes my interview," I say awkwardly as I bend to gather my purse.

Elizabeth leans forward and tents her hands in front of her on her desk. "I'm not sure what that was all about, Ms.

Elliot, but I think you need to get some affairs in order before we would consider hiring you here at *The Times*."

I nod, trying to quell the tears that threaten to dribble down my cheeks.

"I think you have a great future in journalism, but unfortunately, not with us. I hope you understand."

"I completely understand." I bend and wipe my cheek. "Ms. Greyton, for my own peace of mind…would I have gotten the job if we hadn't been interrupted?"

"It was certainly a possibility." She sighs as she takes in my tearstained cheeks. "Look, call me in six months, that should give you enough time to get your personal life in order. If we have a position open, I'll consider it."

I swallow, knowing I'll never be able to show my face in front of this woman again. "Thank you so much for your time, and I can't apologize enough for the interruption."

"Thank you, Ms. Elliot." She pulls some papers out of a folder, spreading them across her desk. She unfolds her glasses and begins reading, effectively dismissing me. I take one last, long look at my closed file perched on the corner of her desk, and my heart breaks. With the snap of a finger my whole dream went up in smoke.

I HAVE THE Uber drop me off about a half mile from home. I need to clear my head before I confront Patrick. I slip off my heels and walk barefoot along the beach. I sit and watch the waves crash as I cry, mourning the loss of my potential future. I have no choice now but to return to Ithaca and start the Miss Cookie column.

The afternoon's events replay in my head. How did Patrick even know I was there? And how dare he barge in on my interview like that! And what on earth was he talking about, *witness protection*?

Standing up, I dust the sand off as I head back to the house. I pick up my speed until I'm practically jogging. I walk into the kitchen to find Nick leaning against the counter. "Are Lindsey and Patrick home?" I ask.

"No, I'm not sure where they are. Hey, you okay?" Nick's vibrant blue eyes, a shade darker than mine, scan my splotchy, wet cheeks.

I burst into tears and tell him everything.

Chapter 30

Patrick

A Heart of Ice

NICK FOLDS HIS arms across his chest with a stern look on his face as Lindsey and I enter the kitchen.

"Is Kelsey here?" Lindsey asks. "Where have you been? I've been trying to get a hold of you for the last hour!"

"My phone died. It's in the bedroom charging."

"Where's Olive?"

"She's napping," Nick says quietly. Too quiet.

"Where's Kelsey?" I glance around the kitchen, looking for her purse.

"Not here." Behind his calm is a thunder ready to rage, the tension crackling in the air between us.

"We need to talk. Out to the pool deck, now," Nick orders.

Lindsey shoots me a nervous look as we follow him out.

He rounds on us as soon as the door slides shut. "What the fuck were you two thinking? What on earth…no, I can't even begin to wonder." He paces in front of us. "Why would you go to Kelsey's job interview?"

I swallow guiltily as I quickly take a seat at the table before he decides to waterboard me in the pool.

"Nick, I know it sounds bad, but we thought she was in trouble. Lovie got a voicemail that sounded like she needed help."

"What message?" All three of us turn. Kelsey stands by the patio doors holding a sweater and her purse. Her eyes are puffy, her face splotchy as if she's been crying for days. I want to leap over this table and hold her. Tell her how sorry I am, but the coolness in her gaze tells me to stay put.

"The one about secrets and dying, and you needed a new identity. It was all garbled. We thought you were in trouble! I'm so sorry, Kels!" Lindsey cries out.

"The message I left right before my interview?" she shrills. "I left you a message asking if I could borrow your secret deodorant because I ran out and I had an interview that I was running late for, and I didn't want to arrive like a sweaty pig. If I did, I'd have to get a new identity because who would hire a stinky journalist!"

"Oh god...I'm sorry, we jumped to conclusions—"

"We?" I huff as I look over at Lindsey. Jesus, how did this go so wrong?

"Yes, *we*. Okay, maybe I put scenarios into Patrick's head, but ever since Nick and the Russians—"

"Lindsey!" Nick barks as he rounds on her.

"Nick"—Kelsey rolls her eyes at her brother—"everyone knows you were working for the CIA or something like that."

"What do you mean *everyone* knows?" he asks incredulously, looking completely thunderstruck.

"Mom, Dad, MK, Arden, Bridget...all of us. Don't worry, your secret is safe with us."

"Mom and Dad know?"

"What? Did you not think we were all smart enough to figure it out? God knows we're nosy enough." Kelsey grimaces. "I mean, you were always traveling, always secretive. All of a sudden, you have this amazing career. We put two and two together."

Lindsey snorts as she sits down next to me. "Your whole family should work for the CIA."

"Kelsey, I'm so sorry. I was scared and worried you were hurt…" I get up out of my chair, but she holds her hand up, halting me. "You have to believe me, that message sounded like you were in trouble, and Nick wasn't answering his phone. After the yacht incident—"

"Yacht incident?" Nick scowls. "What yacht incident?"

"How did you two know about…did you *follow* me that night?"

"We were concerned for your safety," Lindsey pipes up, trying to help my case, but by the look in Kelsey's eyes, this was the final nail in the coffin. I can't say I blame her. Now that I know the truth, my actions were deplorable.

"Unbelievable."

"Kelsey…" I plead, wanting to hold her and explain everything. To make her see my side of things, but I feel her slipping through my fingers. "I was trying to protect you."

"Patrick, I don't need protecting! I'm a grown woman, capable of taking care of myself." She breathes deeply, straightening her shoulders. "I have to go, my Uber is here. Nick, I'll text you later."

"Kelsey, wait! Where are you going?" I rush to her, but she takes a step back, out of my reach.

"No, Patrick, I can't." Her voice wobbles, and something inside me cracks. "You've ruined everything. There's nothing left for me here." She quickly wipes a tear from her cheek as she picks up her bag. Without a backward glance, she walks away.

"Kelsey, don't do this." I sink to my knees as the door slams.

If she had stabbed me right in the heart with an actual knife, I wouldn't have noticed the difference. The pain is blinding. Spreading through my veins, it crystalizes into ice, leaving me feeling like a frozen wasteland.

I don't know how many minutes pass before I feel Lindsey's arms circle around me.

Nick shakes his head. "I don't understand why you didn't come to me."

"I didn't have all the facts. I didn't want to get you involved until I knew what was going on. I'm sorry, Nick. I truly am. It was all a misunderstanding," I say numbly.

"I told you not to break her heart." He glowers.

I look away, the guilt eating me up inside. I should have left it alone. "I messed up, sidekick."

What Nick doesn't see is that mine is broken too.

Chapter 31

Patrick

Tell Me What You Want

"PATRICK, COME *ONNN*, please? For me?" Lindsey flops across my bed. "I'm not going to ask you again."

"Good."

"No, come on, I lied. Please come to the wrap party tonight? Pleeease don't make me go by myself."

"What are you talking about? You have Nick." I neatly fold some shirts I pull out of my drawer and place them in my suitcase. "Besides, you need someone to stay home with Olive."

"I got a sitter. So, you have to go, or else it will just be you and Rosa from Sitters' Club hanging out on the couch watching *Jeopardy*."

"Rosa sounds like the perfect date for me."

"Rosa is eighty, according to the company website."

"Lovie, I have to pack. I don't feel like socializing."

"Look, I know you've been beating yourself up since Kelsey left last week, but—"

"Lovie, she left without letting me explain. Poof...she disappeared into thin air."

"Well, actually, she took an Uber and got on an airplane..."

I throw a t-shirt at her. "You know what I mean."

Lindsey rolls over onto her back and hugs my pillow to her chest. "I'm sorry she hurt you, Trick, I truly am, but that's why you need to get out. Live our last night in Miami like a crazy single bachelor. Tomorrow you can go back to being the sad sack that's been moping around here like his dog just died."

I pick up my *Star Wars* t-shirt and feel another punch to the gut. The trip to Hollywood Studios was one of the best days I had in Florida, but it was also when I first suspected Kelsey was sneaking off to do something dangerous. I'm such an idiot. I throw the t-shirt in the trash, feeling Lindsey's eyes blaze into me.

"Hey, Lindsey, I got a text from the agency. Rosa's on her way, you ready?" Nick sticks his head into my room. "Oh, hey bud, you coming?"

"No."

"*Yes*, he is." I catch Lindsey silently pleading with Nick.

"Yeah, you're coming. Come on man, you're my side-kick. I need you." Nick steps into the room and slings an arm around my neck. He's warmed up to me since Kelsey left. He knows I would never intentionally hurt his sister. He pulls me down like he's about to give me a noogie.

"Don't mess up the hair," I yell and shove away from him. "Fine, you two win. But when I say it's time to play 'Careless Whisper', we're out."

"'Careless Whisper' by Wham?" Nick looks confused. "Why?"

"Because that's Patrick's song he plays when he wants to call it a night."

"Just for the record, I *did not* choose 'Careless Whisper'. She did."

"How did I not know this?" Nick smirks at me then turns to Lindsey. "Do you have a song?"

I snort. "Who do you think came up with this idea?"

"'Wannabe' by Spice Girls," Lindsey says, snapping her fingers.

"It started in college at a karaoke bar. It should have ended there too." I throw another shirt in my suitcase.

"You guys have awful taste in music." Nick picks up the t-shirt I threw on the ground.

"Okay, Trick, I promise to be your wingwoman at this party, and when you request 'Careless Whisper', we'll leave."

"I'm going to regret this."

Lindsey giddily claps her hands with a triumphant smile on her face. "Yes! I promise you won't."

I'M ALREADY REGRETTING it as soon as I walk into the club with flashing strobe lights and loud pulsing music. "Are we seriously having the wrap party at a club?" I shout into Lindsey's ear. I can't even talk in here without screaming.

Lindsey shakes her head and motions for me to follow through a door in the back. We come out in the back alley of the club. Silence slams into me like a welcome friend as I rub the headache away. Nick walks about twenty feet and stands at a green wooden door set into a brick wall with no handle and texts someone on his phone.

"You guys, this is ridiculous. Why are we standing in an alley outside a club waiting to walk through a door that doesn't even have a handle?"

"I've got serious spy vibes, don't you, Trick?" Lindsey performs an excited little jig.

"No, just annoyed vibes. I can't believe I got dragged out for this. This is creepy." I look up and down the deserted alleyway and shove my hands in my pocket. "Is this one of your Syndicate friends?"

"You guys are so impatient," Nick says as he knocks on the door four times.

The door gets shoved open by JD. "Hey, friends, welcome."

We walk into a beautiful walled-in backyard with a pool surrounded by lit palm trees. Waiters walk around with drinks and canapes. There's a band warming up in the corner and a full bar set up on the patio. Twinkling lights are everywhere as people mill about, drinking their cocktails.

"What is this place?" I ask in wonder.

"This, my friend, is The Green Door. It's a private venue attached to The Green Door restaurant. You can only get in by invite and a secret knock on the green door." He winks at us. "Isn't it amazing? My friend Katrina Elkson owns it. She rents out the space for private parties."

"Katrina Elkson, *the actress*?" Lindsey confirms.

"The one and only. Her brother runs it with her. Sadly, she's on location right now—"

"Ohmygod, is that Sonja from *Miami Heat*?" Lindsey veers off in her direction.

"Unfortunately." JD grimaces as he takes a sip of his cocktail. "Come on, let's get you guys some drinks. Patrick, glad you could make it." JD slaps me on the back as he steers us to the bar. "I've heard you've been a little blue. Wait until you meet Genevieve." He waggles his eyebrows.

"Tell me you didn't bring a snake to the party…" I quickly scan his body for a reptile.

"What? No, she's one of the new nurses."

"Oh, I'm not really inter—"

"Trust me, she'll eat you alive."

"Uh, I'd like to keep all my body parts tonight." I smirk as I order a cocktail from the bartender. I turn around and survey the crowd. As if on cue, a tall, voluptuous brunette in a fitted red slinky dress breaks from a group of partygoers. A tattoo sleeve of a black panther crawls from her shoulder to her elbow, looking almost 3D on her tanned, olive skin. Dark glittery eyes zero in on me. I swallow nervously as her lip curls into a snarl. I look over at JD and Nick to see if they feel like prey stalked by a lioness, but they just smile easily as she slides up to the bar.

"Hey, Genevieve. You met Nick briefly the other day, and this is Patrick."

Genevieve smiles and says hello to Nick first and then takes her red-lacquered fingernail that's more like a sharp talon and runs it down my chest. "Dr. Evans, you never told me your friends are so handsome." Her voice is smoky as her eyes devour me. Her fingernail lazily trails its way back up, and I'm suddenly feeling flashbacks of Spike the iguana. She's got me cornered against the bar with nowhere to pivot and run. I guzzle my drink as she leans in. She smells like coconut and rum. "Want to dance?"

"Uh, there's no music."

"We don't need any."

I gulp as her claw runs up the side of my face and into my hair. I try to signal my friends' help, but their backs are turned as they converse with another guy. Where's Lindsey when I need her? So much for her promise to be my wingman. I need a cake hologram signal to send up into the sky like Batman. "So, Genevieve, you're a veterinary nurse?"

"Well, the proper term is veterinary technician, but yes, I specialize in exotics," she purrs in my ear. "Does that excite you?"

I try to wedge my hand up in between us so I can take a sip of my drink. Her personal space parameters must be defunct because she's practically plastered to me. "If I could try and get a little er…space." I try to edge back, but she sways to whatever song she has playing in her head. "Are you from Miami?" I ask.

"Born and raised." She smiles, but it doesn't put me at ease. She trails her lacquered tips down my arm and clasps my hand that's holding my drink.

"My, what long nails you have." I chuckle nervously.

"The better to scratch you with." She throws her head back and laughs, a wicked gleam in her eye that some men would find sexy. I find it downright terrifying.

I try to pry her fingers off my hand, but I don't want to slosh my drink all over us. "Can I get you a drink? I need a drink. If you let go and back up a smidge, I can turn around and order us a drink because I don't know about you, but I am *really* thirsty."

"I'm thirsty for something else," she hisses in my ear before licking it. I cringe as I try to move. If Genevieve managed to separate me from my pack, she'd eat me alive.

"There you are! I lost you guys and then ended up talking to some total bore from Adventure Animals that watches the show—"

"Lovie, I'm so glad you're here. Genevieve, this is Lindsey." I pull Lindsey tight to my side and kiss the top of her head. "My girl, Lindsey. Mine."

"Stop being so awkward." Lindsey elbows me in the ribs and sticks out her hand to Genevieve, causing her to take a step back. "Hi, nice to meet you."

"Nice to meet you too. Are you and Patrick..." She points a talon at Lindsey and connects the dot to me.

"Oh, no, we're—"

"Married. Yep, she's with *me*," I say with finality as I dig my knuckles into Lindsey's side.

"Oh, I didn't see a ring on your finger."

"Yup, yeah, dang it. I always forget to wear it."

Lindsey rolls her eyes as she turns and asks the bartender for a club soda.

"Shame...you were cute," she leans in and whispers. "A little too into the drinky-drinky for my taste, but cute." She reaches out and swipes the air in front of me like a cat trying to claw its victim, and I recoil. "Next time." She winks as she sashays back into the crowd.

"Jesus Christ, I now know what it feels like to survive being mauled by a cougar."

"She was not a cougar, Trick, she was like mid-thirties."

"Not that kind of...I mean the real...you know what,

never mind. Lovie, it's time to cue up 'Careless Whisper'."

"Trick, nooo. We just got here, and I got cornered by that idiot from Adventure Animals to talk about flan for *fifteen* minutes. Do you know how much I fucking *hate* flan? It was almost as painful as the tax conversation with Kiernan. You owe me."

I wince at the mention of Kiernan and the memory of how I had tried to use him to get the truth from Kelsey. I run my hands through my hair and shake it off.

"Lovie, I almost got clawed to death by Genevieve. I swear she was this close to going for my jugular." I press my pointer finger to the pulse pounding in my neck. "She wanted me to dance with *no* music."

Lindsey folds her arms across her chest. "Trick, one more hour, please?"

"An hour?" I squeal, causing heads to turn. "I'm never going to dance again, guilty feet have got no rhythm—"

"Ugh, fine. Just stop singing, you're embarrassing me. Let me find Nick and we'll go, party-pooper."

"Good!"

"Fine!" Lindsey storms off into the crowd as I nurse my water-downed drink.

"Patrick? Is that you?"

I look up toward the sound of the familiar voice, completely gobsmacked. "Candy? What the hell are you doing here?"

Chapter 32

Kelsey

Miss Maverly's Manners

I LOOK AROUND the empty office space as I close my laptop. Most everyone around here clears out for lunch, but a few stragglers stay behind like Frank, the sportswriter, who unwraps the same peanut butter and jelly sandwich he eats every day at his desk. Or Leigh, chomping on a carrot stick across the aisle as she stares at me.

No one gets under my skin the way Leigh does. She's like a slivered piece of wood jammed under my fingernail. I always catch her staring at me, and it's downright unnerving. She has these beady little eyes behind glasses that are always slightly skewed, stringy mousy-brown hair, and I've noticed she has a penchant for turtlenecks no matter the weather. I might have thought she had a thing for me if she wasn't dating the IT guy, Kyle. Who knows, maybe she does.

On my first day, she made it crystal clear that she's "*the* reporter" for *The Ithaca Herald* and that she's the most essential team member here. I wanted to tell her that there's no I in team, but I kept my mouth shut for once—no need to make enemies on the first day. Oh, but enemies we are. When she's not staring at me, she's in my boss's office, Mr.

Pennington, with her nose up his ass.

My only friend here is fifty-year-old Marlow, who works in the Entertainment and Travel section. And to say we're friends is a bit of a stretch. She was nice to me on my first day when Mr. Pennington asked her to give me a tour and show me the ropes. Marlow isn't exactly the chatty type. In fact, she kind of scares me with her gruff demeanor and her who-gives-a-shit attitude. She said that phrase at least ten times on my brief tour. We definitely won't be getting manis and pedis during lunch together or getting cocktails after work, but I know if I have a question, she'll answer it honestly. She also thinks Leigh is a brown-nosing horse's ass. I respect that opinion.

The paper is not nearly as big as *The Miami Times*, but I wasn't expecting it to be so quiet around here during the day. It's more like a library than a busy, exciting newspaper hub. I look around and sigh as I stick my laptop in my leather carrying case my dad bought me.

"Aren't you going to lunch, Cookie?" Leigh asks as she chomps down on another carrot. "I mean, it's not like you have a pressing deadline for how to wipe down a counter using Lysol." She snorts at her own joke. I wish I could lean over and jam that carrot up her nose.

Before I can come up with a witty retort besides *shut the fuck up*, Mr. Pennington sticks his head out of his office. "Kelsey? Oh good, you're still here. Can you come into my office for a moment?"

"Do you need me in there too, sir?" Leigh calls over her shoulder.

Irritation flits across Mr. Pennington's face. "No, Leigh,

I would have called you if I needed you."

I duck my head, choosing to ignore Leigh, and grab a notepad and pen, my lips curling into a smile. I know this is driving her crazy that he's asked to speak to me privately. I can feel her scrutinizing eyes track me as I head toward the editor in chief's door, so I turn and scratch my nose with my middle finger for her to see, hoping Mr. Pennington doesn't witness my middle school behavior.

He settles back into his chair as I sit across from him, folding his hands over his stomach like he's about to take an afternoon nap. "Well, Kelsey, you've been here a couple of weeks now, and I wanted to check in to see how you're settling in. Do you like the job?"

I blink at his question, momentarily caught off guard that the editor in chief would take the time to check in on me. I would have thought Maria from Human Resources would be doing that. "Oh, yes sir, everything is great."

"Glad to hear it, glad to hear it." His chair squeaks as he looks at me thoughtfully. "Kelsey, I think you are a very talented writer, and you're certainly dedicated to your craft. You are a hard worker, and I like to reward my hard workers." He smiles as he leans forward, shuffling some papers on his desk. "As you know, Peter Brown is retiring next week."

Excitement surges in me. Peter is the writer for the local news section. Is he going to take me off the cleaning products gig? Laughter almost bubbles up as I imagine the look on Leigh's face when I tell her Mr. Pennington upgraded me to local news after a few weeks on the job.

"So, if that sounds good, we'd like you to take that over

if you think you can manage it."

Crap, I was so caught up in my daydream about sticking it to Leigh, I missed the first half of what he said. "I'm sorry sir, can you repeat that? You'd like me to take over for Peter?"

Mr. Pennington holds up his hands and chuckles. "Whoa-ho, let's not get hasty. You are an excellent writer, but you're very green. Let's see how you do with Miss Maverly's column first, and then we can chat."

I chew my bottom lip in confusion. "Sir, I'm sorry, I must have missed something. What exactly is Miss Maverly's column?"

"I need you to take over Peter's Miss Maverly's Manners column."

"*Peter Brown* wrote a manners column?" I ask incredulously. "Seventy-year-old Peter Brown, the guy who wears brown polyester pants and has a handlebar mustache...that Peter Brown?" This is not where I thought the conversation was going.

"Yes, you see, your predecessor Paige Hammond didn't want to write a Miss Manners column. If truth be told, she shouldn't have. That woman was an obstinate, rude old bat that could barely say please or thank you. God, I hated that woman." Mr. Pennington clears his throat, waving his hand. "Sorry, that wasn't very professional of me, and I'm getting off topic. Anyway, now that Peter is leaving, I'll need someone to take it over, and Leigh suggested I give it to you."

"Of course, she did. Who will be taking over Peter's job?"

"Oh…Leigh will be covering it until I can hire someone new."

"Of course, she will." I shift in my seat. This is my one opportunity, my one chance. "Sir, if I may be so bold as to ask if I can apply for the position?"

Mr. Pennington exhales loudly as he leans back and studies me. "Your dad and I go way back, Kelsey. He's a great friend, and as I said earlier, I think you've got real potential—"

"So let me prove it to you, Mr. Pennington," I press forward.

He shakes his head. "I'm sorry kiddo, but I need you on Miss Maverly's column right now." He slides his pen in between his fingers as he mulls over what he's about to say. "It's not a good time for the paper. Our numbers are down with everything going digital. I'd be crazy to put a newbie journalist in charge of the local news. I need someone with more experience. I'm sorry, Kelsey."

I shake my head feeling déjà vu. Defeated, I pick up my bag and sling it over my shoulder. "I understand."

"Work Miss Maverly's column for a year. Show me the dedication and talent I see right now, and we'll revisit this discussion down the road, sound good?"

"Yes, sir." I look toward the door. I want to run out of here so I can release the damn of tears and frustration. I'd have this experience under my belt if I hadn't given up my career for Todd.

"Get with Peter after lunch and find out everything there is to know about Miss Maverly's Manners."

"Great," I mutter as I get up and head for the door.

"And Kelsey, for what it's worth, I think you'd make an excellent local news journalist. You just need more experience. Maybe you and Leigh can work together on a couple of assignments."

Fat chance of that happening. I give him a weak smile before ducking out of his office.

"SO, YOU SEE, I get a lot of questions like, 'What should I bring as a wedding or hostess gift?' or 'When is appropriate to wear white?'" Peter scrolls through the emails directed to Miss Maverly's Manners. I eye his signature brown polyester pants and his craggy features. He looks more like a Sam Elliot than a Miss Maverly.

"Um, Peter, what if I don't know the appropriate thing to say?"

Peter chuckles. "Then you make it up." He shrugs. "Sometimes, if I have time, I'll Google it, but that rarely happens. I have more important stuff to handle than, 'How do I approach my neighbor about their dog crapping in my yard?'"

"Uh-huh."

Peter looks over at me and grimaces. "Sorry, that came out wrong. I never wanted to *be* Miss Maverly, but Paige was such a stubborn horse's—"

"I get it," I smoothly cut him off. I don't need to hear any more about my disagreeable predecessor. "No one wants to be Miss Manners. No big deal, I can handle it."

Peter smiles. "Just give them what they want to hear, and you'll do fine."

I gather up my things and walk back over to my cubicle. I have to research how to easily fold a fitted sheet by request for this week's Cookie's Cleaning column and scroll through the emails for Miss Maverly.

"So, I heard you've made it to the major leagues. Chief put you on *two* columns. Think you can handle it?" Leigh snickers as she lingers outside my cubicle. I loathe how she calls Mr. Pennington 'Chief'. Frankly, I despise anything that comes out of her mouth.

"What do you want Leigh? I'm busy."

Leigh studies her chewed fingernails and sticks one bony finger between her teeth. "Just making sure you can handle your work. I've got a lot on my plate right now having to write for the local *and* international news."

"And…" *What the fuck is her point?*

"And if you can't do your job, then I'll need to let Chief know."

I roll my eyes and turn my back to her. "Fuck off, Leigh." God, that felt so good to say.

"You know, Cookie, I wouldn't bite the hand that feeds you. I'm trying to throw you a bone, an olive branch…"

I grind my teeth as I open my laptop. Olive branch my ass. "It's Kelsey, not Cookie."

She circles back around to her cubicle. "Whatever. Hope you can meet the deadline at five tomorrow."

"It might be hard. I'm writing an article on how to break the disgusting habit of gnawing your fingernails off. Oh, that reminds me, can I take a picture of yours as an example?"

She gets up and storms off to her boyfriend Kyle's cubicle to whine about what a bitch I'm being. I know this because Marlow sits right behind him and told me it annoys the crap out of her. She doesn't understand why Leigh has such a hard-on for me, but at the end of the day, 'she doesn't really give a shit.' I wish I could adopt Marlow's attitude.

My phone rings right on time. My mom has been calling at three pm on the dot every day since I started. It's the same questions every time.

"Hi, Mom."

"Hi darling, are you busy?"

"No, what's up?"

"Well, I was wondering if you were going to be home for dinner? Or *perhaps* you might have some fun plans after work with some new work friends?"

I heave a sigh and bang my head against my desk. "No, Mom, no plans, but I don't want to put you out. I can pick something up on my way home."

"Oh no dear, no trouble at all. I just wanted to check." Like you do Every. Single. Day. I seriously need to get my own place.

"Is that all you needed, Mom?"

"Um, well…I saw Todd at your sister's place today while I was helping out at the store. He was with his new…um…person."

I rub my eye, already feeling a tension headache coming on from this tiresome conversation. "Mom, you can call her his fiancée. It's okay, I know."

"She's pregnant, Kelsey," my mom blurts out. "She

looked like she was walking around with a bowling ball under her shirt. She's due any day."

I swallow past the sudden lump in my throat. "Well, that's what happens when you get pregnant." I do the math in my head, completely blindsided by this bomb. That means she was pregnant before we declared a split. We haven't even signed the papers on the sale of our house yet. I feel sick to my stomach. *You're such a fool, Kelsey Elliot. Of course, he was banging her while continuing to throw pity sex your way. He was double-dipping, and now he's having a baby while you sit in a cubicle listening to your mother drone on about him. Why would they go to my sister's store? Why couldn't my mom have waited to tell me until after I got home instead of dropping this shitball in my lap at work?*

"Kelsey? Honey, are you there?" My mom's voice brings me back to the conversation.

"Yeah, I'm here."

"Okay, well, I wanted to make sure you're okay. I certainly didn't want you to find out the way I did today."

"Did you talk to them?"

"Heavens no! I have nothing to say to them. Mary Katherine chit-chatted with them, but they left quickly after. Your sister wouldn't tell me what she said, but I suspect it was along the lines of, 'get the hell out and don't come back.'"

"Mmm, well, it's a free country. They can go and do as they please."

"I know, honey. The nerve of them to come to your sister's store…my heart breaks for you."

I grunt, not wanting to dive back into what a poor pathetic sap I am at the moment. Out of the corner of my eye, I see Leigh stretch her neck ever so casually as she eavesdrops on my conversation. "Look Mom, I have to go."

"Yes, of course! My busy little bee! Oh, can you stop by Michelle's groomers on the way home and pick up Sasha? Oh, and my girlfriends Marty and Tish have the greatest idea for your column! They—"

"Sure, Mom, talk about it later." I hang up and glare over my cubicle wall at Leigh, who is blatantly staring at me. *Again.* "What?" Normally I can pretend like she doesn't exist, but I'm too irritable. "Don't you have a pressing article to write?" I snap as I accidentally knock my purse off my desk, my Jedi book tumbling out. I quickly snatch it up and shove it back in before memories bubble to the surface.

Leigh picks up her phone. "David, I need the article from the school demonstration on my desk, *stat*!" She looks at me smugly while holding her hand over the receiver. "Some of us have important work to do, Cookie. We can't chit-chat on the phone all day."

I give her a rude gesture as I look up a YouTube article on how to fold a fitted sheet. I've got a pretentious, overbearing, competitive co-worker breathing down my neck. My ex is flaunting his pregnant fiancée around town. I'm still living on my parents' couch and being coddled by them, and any mention of *Star Wars* makes me fall to pieces.

Dear Miss Maverly, what do you do when you feel like your whole world is imploding? Not even Peter can Google that one.

Chapter 33

Patrick

It's Complicated

I SIT DOWN in the coffee shop across from Lindsey and slide a hot herbal tea toward her. She pretends to read the magazine in front of her as I sip my coffee in silence. I glance down at my phone as it buzzes with an incoming call and silence it.

"You can't ignore me forever, Lovie."

"I don't know what you're talking about."

I slap my hand over the magazine so that she'll at least look up at me.

"I was reading that."

"Okay, I'm sorry. I really am. But I can't take the silent treatment from you too. It's been a month!"

She looks at me curiously as she takes the lid off her tea and blows on it. "Who else is giving you the silent treatment?"

"Kelsey."

"Does this mean you're back together with her?"

As if on cue, my phone starts buzzing again. "Hard to be back together with someone who won't return your calls."

"I'm not talking about Kelsey, *Pattycakes*."

I rest my leg over my knee as I sit back in my chair. I look around the busy coffee shop as I contemplate what to share with Lindsey. Although she's pushing hard for it, Candy and I are not back together. When I saw her in Miami that night at the party, I was tempted to take her up on her offer, to get lost in my own misery, but I didn't. I couldn't do that to Kelsey. But with Candy constantly needling, and Kelsey wanting nothing to do with me, maybe I should give her another chance. "It's complicated."

Lindsey snorts and rolls her eyes. "Puhlease. Complicated is Nick Elliot. Candy is…"

"Is what?"

"A mistake."

It's like a slap to the face hearing her say it so blatantly like that. She's right though, I know she's right, but still… "At least Candy acts interested in me and was sorry for how we ended things."

"How big of her," Lindsey murmurs as she turns her attention back to her magazine. She slowly thumbs through the pages, ignoring me.

Candy admitted she was jealous of my friendship with Lindsey. She was at the nightclub we walked through to get to The Green Door that night in Miami for a girls' weekend. Her friend was dating someone on the tech team of Adventure Animals, so they hopped on over to our party.

Candy called it fate. Lindsey called it serious stalking issues, and the girl should be working for the FBI. I balked at first, but after the initial surprise wore off, I started to see that Lindsey might be right. It was too convenient that Candy and I ended up at the same private party in the same city. Too convenient, she knew precisely where to find me. My phone buzzes again, so I pull it out and turn it off.

"How are you feeling?" I lean toward her and smile.

"Fine." Her bored tone scratches along my nerves.

"Patrick, is that you? Fancy meeting you here," Janice trills as she sashays up to our table, turning her back on Lindsey to face me. Great, just what I fucking need right now. Janice McKinavitch to make Lindsey's mood plummet even further.

"Uh, yeah, hi Janice. Small world."

"This is my new favorite hot spot."

"I'll never be coming *here* again," Lindsey mumbles under her breath.

"I have a new property available on Market Street if you're interested in seeing it." Janice winks at me as she perches herself on the edge of the table.

Lindsey huffs as she tries to pull her magazine out from under her butt. "Do you mind?"

"Oh, I'm sorry, I didn't even see you there," Janice dismisses Lindsey as she stands back up. "Anyway, Patrick, here's my card with my number right there. I've got a great house minutes from the beach too." She slides the card in front of me.

"Take your listing somewhere else, McKinabitch," Lindsey grumbles as she gets up from her seat. "I'm getting a refill."

I silently plead with Lindsey not to leave me alone with this woman, but she ignores me as she glares at Janice before she heads to the front counter. She tosses the card she magically swiped off the table into the trash.

"What's got her so grumpy? Sheesh."

Janice is about to take Lindsey's seat, so I hastily stand. "I'll call you, Janice, I promise…er, if you could just give me another card."

Janice looks around the table and floor quizzically as she produces another card and hands it to me. I pocket it while Lindsey's back is still turned. Her purse buzzes and she fishes out her cell. "Ooh, gotta grab this. A hot new client. Gotta run! *Ciao*!" She air-kisses me and laughs obnoxiously as she exits the coffee shop.

Lindsey sits back down. "She's so rude. Who sits on someone's table? And why does she keep trying to sell you a house?"

"I don't know. Forget about her. Ugh, Lovie, what do you want me to do?" I flap my arms in exasperation.

She looks up, her expression schooled as she quietly calculates her answer. "I want you to be happy." She shrugs. "And it's not going to be with Janice McKinabitch or Conniving Candy."

"Nice."

"You like that?" She smiles wickedly as she looks intently into her teacup, lazily drawing circles with her finger around the top. "Trick, I hate what happened between you and Kelsey. I feel partial to blame for it…" She looks up when I scoff. "Okay fine, ninety-eight-point-nine-nine percent to blame, but don't forget the yacht was your stupid idea."

"I think it's safe to say, it's over between us, Lovie," I say softly. "That ship has sailed."

"Nooo, that's where you're wrong!" She flops back in her seat. "Trick, you've got to go get your girl."

"And how am I supposed to do that when she refuses to answer my calls?"

"I don't know…Nick says she's miserable in New York."

"Is she working at the paper?"

"Yeah, she got assigned a new column called Miss Maverly's Manners where she has to answer questions sent in from the public like, should you wear pearls to tea or some bullshit like that."

I grimace. "Doesn't sound good."

"No, and her mom is driving her crazy, oh and her ex-fiancé's new fiancée is pregnant."

Lindsey's phone begins to ring. She fishes it out of her purse and looks perplexed as she slides the bar to answer.

"Hello?…Who's this?" Lindsey looks up at me, her eyebrows scrunched. "How did you get my number? Well, maybe you should try him…ugh, fine." Lindsey thrusts her phone at me. "It's for you. I'm going to the restroom."

"Hello?" I answer tentatively.

"Pat, where have you been? I've been calling you for the last half hour. Why is your phone is turned off?"

"Whoa, Candy, slow down. Is everything okay?"

"No, not when I'm trying to reach you, and I can't."

"Okay, well, you've got me. What's going on?"

"I was checking in to see how your morning is going, but then I panicked when I kept getting sent to voicemail."

"Candy, you called me three times within ten minutes."

"I was worried."

"Well, I was in the middle of a conversation."

"With Lindsey."

I rub my hand across my jaw in frustration. "Yes, with

Lindsey."

"I see."

"Look, I need to hang up now."

"Wait, Pattycakes! I thought maybe we could have dinner tonight?"

"Sorry, I can't." I hang up on her as Lindsey makes her way back to the table.

"Did you give her my number?"

"Uh, no." I drag my hands through my hair in frustration. "Think we can write into Miss Maverly and ask her how to get rid of a psychotic ex?"

Lindsey pauses from putting her phone in her purse and snaps her fingers. "Pattycakes, that's it! You're brilliant."

"What?"

"I know how to get Kelsey back!"

"How to get…What are you talking about?"

"You're going to 'Careless Whisper' Candy out of the picture and go get your girl!" She slams her hand on the table, her eyes manic.

"Lovie, you're scaring me."

"I know. That's how I know the perfect plan is coming together." She claps her hands excitedly as I wonder how the hell I'm going to get Candy to exit stage left.

Chapter 34

Kelsey

The Girl Who Runs

I SIT AT my desk and open my laptop, pulling up the email account for Miss Maverly.

"Did you know that thirty-five percent of journalists fail within the first month at a new job?" Leigh leans over my cubicle as she snacks on a piece of celery.

"Fascinating," I deadpan as I concentrate on my task at hand.

"And did you know that of those thirty-five percent, only five percent get another job in journalism?"

I shake my head as I lean back, folding my arms over my chest. "Did you know that ninety-nine percent of personal harassment in the workplace ends in firing? And did you know forty percent of harassment is from bullying?" I pull a word document up on my computer. "Don't worry, Leigh, I already have every single harassing word you've ever said to me on file with Maria. Let me add intimidation tactics to it." I start typing as Leigh huffs off to Kyle's cubicle.

I open up Miss Maverly's email and skim through the questions.

Dear Miss Maverly, how do I politely turn down an

invitation to my neighbor's Bunco party? Jenna V.

I sigh and quickly type a response for Jenna V., who needs permission from a stranger to be able to say no.

Dear Jenna V., all you have to do is politely say thank you for the invite, but that you are unable to attend. Easy-peasy lemon-squeezy. Yours truly, Miss Maverly

Dear Miss Maverly, does the fork go on the right or left? P.R.

I groan in frustration. Is this what my life has come to? Forks and Bunco invites? I quickly type up an answer.

*Dear P.R., the fork sits to the **left** of the plate, the knife to the right, and the spoon to the right of the knife. The blade of the knife should face the plate. Yours truly, Miss Maverly*

Dear Miss Maverly, I met someone. She's beautiful, funny and smart. We don't have much in common, but it doesn't seem to matter. She is it for me, my match made in heaven. My problem is, she seems oblivious to me. How do I let her know I'm interested? Any advice would be greatly appreciated. YJK

I pause as I think about how to answer. It hits closer to home than I'd like to admit. My mind automatically wanders to Patrick as I trace my lips with my index finger, thinking about how to answer. I'm definitely not the right person to give advice on relationships. I've had two tank in the past year.

Dear YJK, It doesn't matter if you don't have much in common. Sometimes finding the Yin to your Yang makes the relationship more colorful. If you truly like this woman, let her know. Send her something to show that you accept her just the way she is. Yours truly, Miss Maverly

I push Patrick to the back of my mind as I save my work and open up Cookie's Cleaning file, reading over what I wrote yesterday about when to clean your oven and which products work best. I've learned more about different cleaning products and natural ingredients you can find around your house in the last few weeks than I care to admit.

I close my laptop and pack up for the day. I'm heading to my sister's for dinner tonight, but first I have to stop off at home. My mom said a manila envelope arrived from my realtor.

I LIE ON my bed and pull apart the seal on the manila envelope. I carefully remove the sheathe of papers from the real estate agent and stare down at the black and white words as they blur together. Little tabs marked at the bottom of the page indicate where I should sign. The split wasn't drawn out or complicated. Todd gave me the sale from the house as long as I didn't try to fight him over wanting part of the practice. He pleaded with me in front of the mediator as if I wanted to exact revenge on his wife and firstborn. I didn't want anything from him. What pissed me off the most was that I lost five years of my life thinking I wanted to be with the toolbox. He's moved on with his pregnant fiancée, and

I'm here, sitting on a futon in my parents' house, signing papers for a life I never wanted.

I shove the papers away from me, my eyes filling with tears over the loss of my future and the years I wasted pretending to be someone I wasn't. For the second time today, my mind wanders to Patrick, and guilt replaces the sorrow. Patrick. I miss him so much. And at the same time, I'm still so angry about what happened. Those few weeks with him feel like a dream now, but if I let myself rewind to that time, I fall apart for what could have been, crying until my heart crumples into nothingness. But if I cling to the anger, I'm able to push my feelings for him deep down and keep them guarded. My sister Arden likes to remind me daily that keeping my feelings buried isn't healthy. But that seems to be my pattern with him.

I know I should reach out to him and return his calls, but what's the point? Why try to make a relationship work when we're at two totally different places in our life? Because I miss him. Even though he did some stupid shit, I miss him like crazy. I miss his woodsy smell, his goofy smile, I miss his skin against mine. Maybe in his own weird way, he was trying to protect me, even though he went about it all wrong. Perhaps I wasn't fair to him.

I grab my purse as I wipe my nose on my t-shirt. I pull out my book and open it up, quickly escaping into the story. Reading a fanfic *Star Wars* comforts me. It connects me to Patrick in some small strange way. My mind wanders, wondering what he's doing at the moment, wondering if he's already forgotten about me—the girl who keeps running away.

Chapter 35

Kelsey

Two Can Play at This Game

Dear Miss Maverly, thank you for your response. I took your advice and sent her flowers. She smells like garden roses in the morning dew. She hasn't responded, and now I'm worried I've screwed up. Should I write her a letter? Call her again? Thank you, YJK

I take the end of the pen I was chewing on out of my mouth, contemplating how to respond. This poor guy, he's writing to the wrong advice expert. I'm too jaded. I don't want to screw up his chance at finding true love, so I pick up my phone and call Bridget.

"Hey, Kels, what's up? I only have a minute before I go on rotation." She yawns. "I swear I haven't slept for what feels like a week."

"I'm sorry to bother you, I need help with a guy that wrote into Miss Maverly seeking love advice. I figure you're better equipped in this department than me since you have a boyfriend."

"Aw! That's so sweet he's writing in for advice. Okay, tell me what's going on."

"Okay, so he was trying to work up the courage to tell

this girl that he likes her, but they have nothing in common, so I told him to give her something she likes. He sent her flowers and told her how they remind him of her."

"Oh my god, that is adorable."

"Well, he might have scared her off because she hasn't responded, and now he's asking what he should do."

"Well, what kind of jerk ignores flowers?"

I shrink back against my chair as I think of the flower arrangement that arrived at my parents' house the other week—beautiful sunflowers with tulips and freesia. The card read, *forgive me*. I gave the flowers to my sister MK and hid the card.

"I don't know, maybe she's super busy with a new job, or maybe they had a falling out, and she didn't want to get into it with him because she's not ready to forgive him yet!"

"Oh-kay…are we talking about Miss Maverly or you?"

"Obviously, Miss Maverly, Bridget. Geez, you are sleep deprived." I look down at my notepad, stabbing it with my pen. I'm frustrated with myself for unloading all of that on her. "Maybe he's a total stalker. I mean, he is writing into Miss Maverly."

"I think it's sweet. Tell him to ask her to dinner."

"That seems boring and obvious."

"Okay, well, it also seems like the next step into asking someone out…ooh! I know. Tell him to write her a love letter, but not in a creepy way. A poem!"

"A poem?" I ask doubtfully as I stare down at the puncture wounds on my poor notepad.

"Shoot, I've gotta run. Let me know how it turns out."

Before I can utter bye, she hangs up. A poem…I guess

that would be sweet if he could do it right.

Dear YJK, try reaching out to her again. Write her a poem or quote. One like, 'She Walks in Beauty' by Lord Byron. "She walks in beauty like the night of cloudless climes and starry skies; and all that's best of dark and bright meet in her aspect and her eyes."

You've shown her, now tell her. Best of luck, Miss Maverly

Satisfied that it wasn't a generic ask her on a date response, I save it and reply to a couple more. I grimace as my cell phone starts to chime. I glance at the time in the lower right-hand corner of my laptop. Sure enough, right on time.

"Hi, Mom."

"Hello dear, I hope I'm not bothering you. I was wondering if you had plans after work with some new friends?"

"No, Mom, no plans. Thanks for the daily reminder of what a loser I am."

"Oh, Kelsey, you're so funny. You got your sense of humor from your father. I just wanted to give you an update. No new flower arrangements from anyone have arrived for you today."

Another reason I need to move out pronto. Nosy Nelly Anne Elliot read the card before I got home and has cryptically been trying to find out who sent them. She even went so far as to suggest Todd, which made me spit out my coffee all over the kitchen counter.

"No, Mom, there won't be any more flower arrangements, and yes, I'll be home for dinner."

"Okay, honey, but can I perhaps suggest that you do

forgive whoever this gentleman may be?"

"How do you know it's not a woman?"

"Well, your father and I have discussed this at great length. And honey, we want you to know we support you one hundred percent."

I'm about to pound my head on my desk when I spot Maria from Human Resources heading over to my cubicle.

"I've got to go, Mom."

"My friend Ina said that there are some attractive women in her Pilates class." Jesus, not only has she talked about it with dad but also with her tennis doubles partner, Ina.

"Oh my god, Mom, drop it," I whisper harshly and quickly hang up on her before she has me screaming to the whole office that her daughter is not gay, just heartbroken. Maria from Human Resources timidly approaches my desk.

"Kelsey, do you have time to chat in my office?"

"Oh, sure." I roll my chair back and follow her to her office. She lets me enter first before closing the door behind me. She sits down at her desk and straightens a file in front of her.

"So, you've been here a little over a month, how do you feel it's going?"

"It's going great." I smile, although my heart isn't in it. "Why? Is something wrong?"

Maria squirms in her seat as she taps the file with her hand. "Well, we've had a complaint from someone on the team."

"A complaint about *me*?" I squeal. *Who the hell could complain?* I pretty much don't talk to anyone except Marlow, and she wouldn't complain because she doesn't give a shit about anything. "If I'm being honest, Maria, this is a surprise. I keep to myself for the most part."

"Well, I think there within lies the problem. The complaint was that you're not a team player. This individual wishes you would participate and help your colleagues out more."

"Is this coming from Mr. Pennington? No one has asked me for help, but I'd be happy to contribute wherever it's needed. I'm dying to get more involved with the paper. I'm definitely a team player. I've taken over Peter's column..."

"No, it's not Mr. Pennington. He thinks you're doing great."

"Uh-huh." There's only one person who would complain.

Leigh.

"I assure you, Maria, this *individual* who's complaining is the one who should be sitting in the hot seat, not me." I ball my fists in my lap as I think of a hundred ways to exact my revenge. I'd start with the carrot sticks being shoved up her nose.

"Okay, well, unfortunately, because there was a complaint, I have to put it in your file, but I will also note that we communicated, and it seems that the problem has been rectified. Perhaps you can ask everyone in the office when you have downtime if you can help? I think that would solve this issue promptly."

I paste on a sickly smile as I get up. "Of course."

I head back to my desk. I zero in on a new Post-It note strategically placed on top of my laptop, so I can't miss it. Mr. Pennington's cramped handwriting scrawled across.

Kelsey, great job! Miss Maverly's column is getting lots of hits on the website! Keep up the great work!

I smile as I read the note. Take that, stupid-head, nail-biting, turtleneck-wearing, Leigh! As if I summoned her with my thoughts, she walks by me and dumps her bag on her desk.

"What are you smiling at?"

"Can't I just be happy?"

Leigh looks at me suspiciously as she draws her laptop out of her bag. "What are you holding?"

"Oh, this?" I wave the Post-It in the air. "A note from Mr. Pennington telling me I'm smashing it and to keep up the good work."

"Let me see that." Leigh tries to snatch the note from my fingers, but I quickly pocket it. She pulls at her turtleneck, fuming, as I smile at her like a Cheshire cat.

"Sorry, Leigh, it's a personal note addressed to me, not you."

She spins on her heels and looks around her cubicle. "Well, he must have left one for me somewhere. Did you take it?"

I snort as I roll my eyes and gather up my things. "Like I'd bother. Oh, by the way, Maria from HR stopped by to check in and see how I'm doing. That was *so* kind of you to suggest it. We had such a great talk about being a team player that she's recommending me for the five-star review."

Color leaches from Leigh's already-pallid complexion. "What's the five-star review? I've never heard of that."

"Oh yeah, well, you wouldn't. It's new. Kind of like the MVP award for football, except it's the most valuable asset at

The Ithaca Herald." I give her a megawatt smile as I pull my note out, gazing lovingly at it. I take a deep breath and exhale dramatically. "Well, I've got to run. Oh hey, if you need any help with your articles, just holler. I'm happy to help. There's a reason I'm up for the five-star review and team player award." I wink.

The sour look on Leigh's face is priceless. Steam practically blows out of her ears as she marches over to Mr. Pennington's office and knocks on his closed door.

"Chief? Hey Chief, did you leave a note for me?" She stomps impatiently when he doesn't answer and knocks again. "Chief? Is there really a five-star review? Chief, it's Leigh! I want to nominate myself for it as well as the team player award. Chief?"

I giggle to myself as I leave the office—God, what a sap. Two can play your petty little game, Leigh.

Chapter 36

Patrick

Fix What's Broken

"What's wrong with him?"

Nick looks over at me and shakes his head. "He had his heart broken by my sister a couple of months ago, and he's still floundering."

JD leans back in his chair, eyeing me over his beer bottle. "Tough break, dude. That's why I don't get involved. It's easier to have fun."

"Yeah well, it's complicated. I screwed it up."

"What did you do?" JD leans forward with a wolfish grin.

"Where do I start?" I miserably contemplate my mistakes as I take a sip of beer. JD is in town to go over the show footage with Nick, so we all met up for dinner at a local fish camp. Nick had to practically drag me out since I haven't wanted to socialize lately. I prefer wallowing in my own misery.

"Start from the beginning."

"I met her at Nick's wedding. We hit it off..." I look over at Nick and cringe. He doesn't need to hear the details. "We met up again in Miami and continued where we left off. Things were going well until…"

"Until he and Lindsey decided Kelsey was hiding something. So, they started following her, stuck their nose in business that didn't concern them, which ultimately cost Kelsey a job at *The Miami Herald*," Nick finishes for me.

"Ouch." JD taps his finger on the table. "Was she hiding something?"

"A job interview she wanted to keep secret," Nick says. "She wanted to see if she could get the job first before telling anyone."

Hearing Nick go over the details of how badly I screwed up makes me want to slide under the table. What an idiot I was not to trust Kelsey. What a fool to follow her like I was some private investigator and invade her privacy.

"Why didn't you just ask her what she was hiding?"

"That would have been the logical course of action." Nick grins. "But Lindsey got involved, and when those two hatch a plan, things get lost in translation."

"Do you love her?" JD asks suddenly.

I lift my chin, Nick's eyes lasering into mine as he waits for my answer. "Yes, I do."

JD slams his hand on the table. "Well, then you need to get back your girl."

"I've been trying, but she won't take my calls. I've sent her flowers…"

"Lindsey came up with the brilliant plan for him to write into her advice column anonymously," Nick's tone implying it was anything but brilliant.

JD grins. "How's that going for ya?"

"Not well."

"You need to fix what's broken."

"What do you mean?"

JD's eyes slide to Nick then back to me. "You cost her a job, right? So you need to get her that opportunity back."

I snort. "How do you expect me to do that? I don't know anyone in journalism."

JD drums his fingers on the table. "Well, I don't know anyone in the newspaper business, but I do know someone in the magazine industry. It's worth a shot. Give me all her info, and I'll see if Emily's sister can help."

I grunt as I look over at Nick. "This isn't one of your floozy girlfriends who knows someone who knows someone's cousin in the industry, is it?"

JD squints. "I feel like I should be offended by that, but lucky for you, I'm not." He smirks as he waves the waitress down for another round of beers. "As a matter of fact, it is someone's sister, but not one of my girlfriends. Emily is one of my patients. Her sister is the assistant to the publisher of *That Style* magazine."

I swallow my tongue. Even I've heard of *That Style*. I raise my eyebrows at Nick, asking him silently if I should give JD the go-ahead. With a shrug, he nods.

"Okay man, see what you can do." A small flame of hope ignites in me. Maybe I can right the wrong. Even if Kelsey still wants nothing to do with me, I'll at least know in my heart that I tried everything. "Even if I can fix the interview, I screwed up badly. She's lost all trust in me."

"That, my friend, you have to earn."

"Hard to do when she doesn't return phone calls."

"So, tell me about this column she writes and the poor

sucker who's writing into her."

Nick laughs as I pick up my beer and take a large gulp. "We've been going back and forth for a few weeks now. I've been asking her how to woo a girl. Her latest advice is for me to write a poem."

"Oh, this is good." JD rubs his hands together. "Let's do it."

"Let's do what?" I side-eye Nick.

"Write a poem!"

"I thought you were going to help me with her job. I don't need help with a poem."

"If this is your only open line of communication with her, then Nick and I are here to help. What's your anonymous name?"

"LSJK," Nick pipes up. JD arches a curious eyebrow. "Luke Skywalker Jedi Knight. It's a *Star Wars* thing."

"I know who Luke Skywalker is. Okay, LSJK, let's hear what you've got so far."

"Nothing," I mumble.

"What was that?"

"I've got nothing, okay? I don't even know where to start."

"Wow, clearly you've got this handled." JD shakes his head. The waitress deposits the beers on the table and collects the empties. "Hey, Katie, would you happen to have some paper and a pen we could borrow?"

"Anything for you," Katie purrs. She tears off a few pieces of paper and hands him a pen with a wink.

"Thanks." He smiles, quickly dismissing her as he turns to me. Katie slinks off, clearly disappointed he wasn't writing his number down for her.

"How do you do that?"

"Do what?"

"Have women simpering with just a smile?"

"Because he's God's gift to women." Nick throws a pretzel at JD's face.

"Because I pay attention to the details. It's not just a smile, it's learning her name when she first introduces herself. It's being polite, kind, and listening to her when she talks. Notice how the good-looking grump over here rarely gets a smile?"

I laugh as we both look at Nick, who has his arms folded across his chest, looking like he's planning someone's demise. "I get all the smiles I need and want from my hot wife, dickhead."

"Okay, so where do we start?"

"Roses are red, violets are blue, I know you don't want to talk to me, but I'm obsessed with you."

JD chuckles and shakes his head. "Clearly, Nick is not going to help."

I laugh, and it feels good. I haven't laughed like this since everything went south in Miami. I'm grateful for my two friends as they dish out lines back and forth, trying to help me win back my girl.

Chapter 37

Kelsey

The Poem

Her hair like firelight, flickering streams of golden flame;
Her eyes, the deepest blue,
Reflect back to me like stars in the sky
of timeless stories told anew.

Lips as soft as velvet;
Her skin of cream and milk.
Touching her one last time,
I could easily drown in her tapestry of silk.

Swimming into her soulful blue,
Wishing I could erase the mistakes I drew.
It must be her decision to make;
My heart forever hers to break.

I STARE AT the words that LSJK wrote until my vision blurs. They're haunting and beautiful, squeezing my soul as I long for someone to feel that consumed—to drown in her body and soul. I call Bridget and read her the poem.

"Oh my god, I want him."

"I know, me too! I've never had a poem written for me."

"Me neither. It's so romantic. What are you going to tell him to do next?"

"I don't know. I feel like if this woman doesn't respond to him after this, then she needs to jump off a cliff and let this guy find someone who deserves him."

"Yup, I agree. She needs to give him up if she can't see this knight in shining armor calling out to her."

"I think I'm going to tell him to go big or go home. Go get his girl and make her regret ignoring him all this time."

"Good plan, I approve."

"K, see you at dinner tonight."

"Just a heads-up, Mom invited the Carlisles over."

"No! Please tell me handsy Hudson won't be there."

"Why do you think she invited them? She's trying to play matchmaker."

"Ugh, can you sit next to him, please?"

"No way. The last time he came for dinner, he kept trying to touch me under the table. He's so slimy. I ended up stabbing my fork into his thigh."

"Is that why he suddenly jumped up and announced he was going to the bathroom?"

"Yup."

"I hate it when Mom does this."

"At least she's finally given up on setting you up with the lesbian Pilates instructor."

"I'd prefer her over Hudson any day of the week."

"See you soon! Bring your taser. That will make dinner super interesting." She giggles as she hangs up. Not a bad idea, actually.

I return my attention to work. The past couple of weeks since we've been corresponding, I've received emails from readers who have turned this into a local sensation. They're dying to know the outcome of LSJK and his lucky love.

Dear LSJK, if she doesn't respond to this, then she doesn't deserve you. From the hundreds of emails I've received lately, I'd say there are plenty of women who would love to date you! Now you need to plan something big. Go all out and get your girl! Best of luck, Miss Maverly

The readers will go crazy over his poem. It's prompted others to write in seeking relationship help. Miss Maverly has turned from a 'how do I tell my neighbor to mow their lawn' into a 'how do I make him or her see the real me?' It's been a challenge for me because I see myself in many of these anonymous quests for help. I've grown with them, and when they write in to tell me it worked, I cheer along with them. It's been so satisfying to help others, and I never knew it was something I'd enjoy. I always thought I wanted to chase the next story down, travel to some far-off land, and be right in the thick of the action, but my priorities, it seems, have changed.

I'm about to close my laptop when a new email appears from a EGilly@ThatStyle.com. Weird, I don't subscribe to that magazine. I click it open and scan the email. I take a deep breath, look over my shoulder to make sure Leigh isn't lurking about, and reread it more slowly, my hand trembling as I move the cursor to the top.

Dear Ms. Elliot,

An article you wrote recently for The Ithaca Herald was brought to our attention, and we'd like to discuss a possible job opportunity for you at That Style Women's Magazine. If you are interested, please reply to set up a Zoom interview with you and my boss, Elan Black. Sincerely, Elizabeth Gilly, Assistant to Elan Black, Editor in

Chief of That Style Magazine.

This can't be real. I rub my eyes and stare at the email again. I pinch myself to make sure I'm not having some cruel dream. But I realize I'm wide awake as a shrill voice pipes up behind me.

"What an insane day I've had!" Leigh trounces by my cubicle and throws her bag on her desk, looking over at me to see if I'll respond. I don't. "Chasing down the lead story has been crazy!"

She waits for me to take the bait, but I gently close my laptop and bite into my apple as I pretend to write something in my notebook. *Leigh sucks donkey turds.*

"Hey Cookie, are you listening to me? Don't you care what goes on in the *real* world? Isn't that what you want to do when you grow up? Be a *real* reporter?"

It takes all my self-control not to react to her taunts as Mr. Pennington walks by our cubicles. "Kelsey, great job on Miss Cookie's Corner last week! We've had a great response on how to make your own hand sanitizer!"

"Thank you, sir." I smile over his shoulder at Leigh, whose skin color looks as red as the apple I'm eating.

"Hey Chief, did you hear that I got the mayor's office to respond?"

Mr. Pennington turns as he acknowledges Leigh. He's a better man than me. "Uh, yes, that's great, Leigh. Glad they decided to repave the mayor's parking lot." He quickly nods and walks on toward his office. I snort as I realize her *big* story was over a parking lot getting zoned for paving.

"Well, thank God you got the exclusive on that!" I bite into my apple as I pack up my bag. My mom has already called and confirmed that I have no plans. I make a mental note to look for apartments when I get home. I look over at Leigh's cubicle as she whispers with her icky boyfriend, Kyle. He crept over from his dark hole after Mr. Pennington closed his door. They keep looking over at me and giggling. It's hard to believe we're adults trying to work, not middle schoolers eating lunch at the cafeteria. I roll my eyes as I adjust my computer bag strap on my shoulder. She chomps down on a carrot stick, her malicious little grin growing wider by the second. I wonder if her skin will start to turn orange with all the carrots she eats.

"Hey Cookie, I heard the Lifestyles column is featuring an article on Dr. Todd Fisher and his new fiancée. Apparently, he's expanding his practice. You wouldn't happen to know much about *that*, would you?"

I freeze as I try to figure out how Leigh put two and two together. Humiliation washes over me as I fight to maintain self-control. "Oh, thanks for reminding me, Leigh. I need to send them a gift."

Her face falls as if I put a needle in her balloon of hatred. "Heading out early, Cookie? I wonder what Maria from HR would say about that?" Kyle snickers like the total dweeb he is.

You know what? Fuck it. I throw off my proverbial boxing gloves and turn to Leigh, noticing that Brian from Sports, Marlow, and Peter Brown are listening from their cubicles.

"First of all, my name is Kelsey, not Cookie. Second of all, I'm tired of your bullying, Leigh. You walk around here like you own the Herald, but you're not a team player. You're a mean girl. You've made my work environment toxic, and frankly, I'm done. For some reason, you're threatened by me, but it stops right now. Go chase down whatever lame story is going on in the mean streets of Ithaca. You're not important enough for me to care about."

Leigh scoffs as I turn on my heel, leaving her and Kyle with their mouths hanging open. Peter gives me a fist-bump on my way out, and I suddenly feel free. I feel alive. I feel *clarity*. I realize that what I once thought was my dream has changed. I no longer want to be a big-time reporter chasing down the next story or a small-town journalist covering parking lots. I don't want to be a Leigh. I want to be someone who makes a difference in someone's life. I want to be someone who offers encouraging words and wisdom.

I want to be free of this sadness tethered around my neck for the life I thought I wanted. I've been carrying around so much anger ever since I left my first job for Todd. The choices I made were mine. I need to take accountability for them and stop blaming others. I never wholly opened up my heart to Patrick because I was scared. If I trusted him enough, trusted myself, I would have told him about the interview. I would have said to him that I wanted a relationship, that we could somehow make it work. I would have realized he always had my back.

The race I thought I was running isn't a sprint to the finish line. It's a marathon over hills and valleys, through woods and swamps. I've been running from my own fears without direction instead of seeing what was right in front of me.

I've been running from Patrick when all along I should have been running to him.

Chapter 38

Patrick

A Done Deal

LINDSEY LOOKS IT over, her arms folded over her chest, and shakes her head. "I can't believe you bought this. Please tell me you didn't use Janice."

"I didn't use Janice."

"Well, that's one smart decision. What if she says no?"

"Aren't you the one always saying go big or go home?"

"It is her motto." Nick rubs his jaw as he surveys the sailboat. "Do you even know how to sail?"

"Uh…no. That's why I'm hoping she'll say yes."

"Let me get this straight." Lindsey's eyes are indiscernible behind her sunglasses. "You bought a sixty-foot sailing yacht to live on, and you don't know how to *sail?* Are you insane? How much did this cost?"

"Lindsey…" Nick growls next to her.

"What? It's Trick, he's family. We don't keep secrets from each other, do we? Oh, but wait, we do. Secrets like sleeping with Kelsey and not telling us, or buying a sixty-foot sailboat!"

I shrug as I look at the boat. "It doesn't matter, it's what I wanted. I'm sorry I didn't tell you, but I knew you'd try to talk me out of it."

"Like any sane person would do," Lindsey mumbles as she chews her lip. The three of us stare at the beautiful teak wood and lines of the hull. "Is it a done deal? Can you return it?"

I snort. "I don't want to return it."

"Can we see the inside?" Nick smiles at me as he hugs Lindsey to his side.

"Sure." I walk them down the dock.

"You do know how to swim, right? And does this mean you live at the dock now?" She surveys the boat names in the slips next to mine. "Oh my god, Lady Bits is your neighbor? That's totally offensive."

"That's their last name, Bits. They're a very nice older British couple. He named it for her."

"Mrs. Lindsey Bits…Nick Bits." Lindsey says in a horrible British accent. "Might as well call it Lady Vagina. He really did not think Lady Bits through very well, did he?"

Nick and I chuckle as I unlock the door leading to underneath the boat. "Just think, guys, now I can take you out on the water when we're home."

"You mean, out on the boat in the slip, because you don't know how to sail."

"Nick knows how to sail, right, sidekick? And Kelsey."

"Oh my god, am I the only one who thinks this is completely coco-puffs crazy? She hasn't even said yes! Last I checked, you guys haven't talked, like in months! And whatever happened to Candy?" Lindsey throws her arms out as she turns in a circle, taking in the beautiful creams and navy blues and polished wood. "Wow, Trick, this is incredible! How much money *did* your parents leave you?"

· "Lindsey!" Nick shushes her, but I smile.

"A lot." I show them the galley kitchen, living room with a sectional and large-screen TV. The back bedroom with a king-sized bed and two dressers. And the master bath.

"This is way nicer than your apartment," Lindsey says in awe. "You even have a washer and dryer? Wow!"

"Yeah, I splurged on that and a larger than normal water tank. I thought I could come over and use yours, but it would be nicer to have my own." We sit down on the sectional around the coffee table. "It's cozy, right?"

"It's perfect," Nick agrees.

"So, you never answered my question. How did you get rid of Candy?"

"I met her for coffee and told her she was right. I could never love her because I was in love with someone else. She assumed it was you, and I didn't bother correcting her assumption. It made her so angry she stormed out of the coffee shop, and I haven't heard from her since."

"I could have had Nick off her…that would have been a more permanent exit."

Nick clears his throat and sits forward, scowling at his wife. "Seriously?"

"What? It's true."

"I'm not the Mafia."

"Thank god, I could never be a made wife. I'd never be able to keep it a secret."

"They're not called made—you know what, never mind."

"So, what's your plan?" Lindsey plops down on the

couch next to him.

"We've got it handled." I smile at Nick.

"Wait, *we*? As in you and Nick?"

"And JD."

"Oh really," Lindsey huffs as she folds her arms across her chest. "Do tell."

"Well, JD has this friend at *That Style* magazine. He got Kelsey's work in front of her, and she passed it along to her boss. They're looking for someone to take over the Dear Melody column in the magazine."

"Kelsey is interviewing with headquarters in Atlanta, so I told her to take a flight to Charleston for the weekend." Nick smiles at his wife.

"Were you ever going to inform me of this plan?"

"I'm letting you know right now."

Lindsey sighs deeply. "Okay, then what?"

"What do you mean?"

"How do you plan on luring Kelsey to your houseboat and convince her to take your sorry butt back?"

I look at Nick, and he shrugs. "We didn't get to that part of the plan."

Lindsey rolls her eyes. "This is why men can't plan anything. They miss the details."

"Hey! I'm excellent with details." Nick smirks, his eyes twinkling.

"Okay, yes, details are your specialty. You're very...thorough," Lindsey purrs.

"Okay, gross, you guys, can you stop eye-fucking each other and tell me how to get her here?" I glare at them as I open a bottle of water.

"Huh, what? Oh, sorry, I got a little sidetracked. Don't worry, let me handle getting her here." Lindsey smiles as she taps her fingertips together.

"Oh great, I'm doomed." I hold my head in my hands.

"Okay, I deserve that. Perhaps my track record hasn't been the greatest, but I've got this."

"Maybe we should call JD." Nick chuckles as Lindsey smacks his arm.

"Excuse me, but this is a pink-wire moment. I can cut the damn pink wire. Don't you guys trust me?"

"I'm envisioning Kelsey bound and gagged, tossed out of Lovie's minivan."

"Or held up at gunpoint with her pink Glock."

"Or tasered—"

"Okay," Lindsey interrupts. "You guys are *so* hilarious. Can I have a day to plan it out? When is she arriving?"

"Tomorrow night."

She throws her arms in the air. "For fuck's sake, that gives me no time."

"Lovie, all you have to do is get her here. I'm counting on you. Once you get her here, I can handle the rest."

She nods once before sinking back into the couch. "I won't let you down, Trick."

Chapter 39

Kelsey

Box of Condoms

I TRY TO stifle a yawn as Lindsey's sister prattles on about her delivery of twins that day. Usually, Shannon is a great storyteller, but tonight I'm exhausted and just want to crawl into clean, soft sheets. It's only seven p.m., but I didn't sleep a wink last night because I was so nervous about the interview.

I flew out of New York this morning at six a.m. after Bridget dropped me off at the airport. My interview at *That Style* went so incredibly well that the high I've been on all afternoon has suddenly plummeted into exhaustion. I really liked the magazine and loved both Elizabeth and Elan. I was a little intimidated by the busy hive of activity happening on the magazine's central floor. Who wouldn't be when coming from the crusty, sleepy little village of *The Ithaca Herald*?

Elan offered me the option of working remotely as long as I checked in weekly on their mandatory Zoom conference calls. I might have to come into the office once a month, but that's doable. I'd also be making double the salary than I am at *The Ithaca Herald*. Dear Melody's help column is very similar to Miss Maverly's, except more hip. I wouldn't be answering questions about RSVP etiquette or where to put your soup spoon. It's more a relationship advice column. They loved the saga over LSJK and hoped I could bring that magic to Dear Melody's.

I worried they wouldn't want me if they discovered I'm an imposter since my relationships have been less than stellar, and I'm the last person to be doling out advice. But, I took Peter Brown's advice, 'fake it 'til you make it,' and said yes to the job. No, it wasn't traveling the continent, hunting down the next big story like I always imagined, but I've come to learn that sometimes those dreams can be reshaped. The best part of all? No more Leigh calling me Cookie, no more writing about cleaning how-tos, and no more sleeping on my parents' couch.

"Who wants coffee and dessert?" Dan asks as he collects plates from the outdoor patio table.

"I'd love some." I smile graciously.

"Oh! That reminds me, I have something for you, Kelsey." Shannon excuses herself as Lindsey groans.

"I'm so sorry, Kels, this was supposed to be just cocktails."

"Oh, it's fine!" I try to stifle another yawn. "Besides, you are eating for two, not drinking. And Dan's cooking is amazing."

Before Lindsey can respond, Shannon brings back a box a little bigger than a shoebox and a tube of cream. "That's for your mom, and the box is for you."

Lindsey shakes her head as she reads the side of the box. "Coffee and dessert reminded you to bring your extra stash of condoms to the table?"

Shannon gives her a bemused smile. "Well, it's not like *you* guys are practicing safe sex. Kelsey can use them, right? The tube of cream is for your mom to use before sexual intercourse."

"Oh god. I'm going to go help Dan." Nick abruptly stands, practically running into the house.

I fling the tube into the box as if it's on fire. "Wow, I did not need to know my parents are still having sex."

"Kelsey, it's not like they're old! Your mom is in the prime of her life, ready to spread her sexual wings for your da—"

"Wow, okay, time's up. I've got to get Olive home, and Kelsey is beat from her day of traveling. Thank you so much for dinner, but we need to skadoodle on out of here. Can we get the desserts to go?"

"Oh, you really have to leave? Kelsey, don't forget to practice safe sex with condoms. You can never have too many."

"I think she's got a lifetime supply with the box of five hundred you generously gifted her."

"Oh, it's actually a thousand." Shannon chuckles as Lindsey rolls her eyes.

"Even better. Kels, grab your *babies aren't happening in this vagina* box. Nick, we're leaving! Wrap up that dessert and grab Olive!" Lindsey yells as we walk into the kitchen. "I'm not missing out on Dan's chocolate cake."

"Thank you so much for dinner. It was wonderful." I smile as I take the box and the magic sex tube for my parents.

"Of course! Don't forget to use them. It's not just about

babies, but diseases too." She winks.

"Oh my god, Dr. Ruth! We've got it! Enough with the safe-sex talks," Lindsey says.

"Thanks for dinner." I chuckle awkwardly as Dan hugs me.

"Sorry, she doesn't know when to turn off her doctor brain."

"I understand." I smile as I wave goodbye.

We head toward the car as Nick carries Olive and four pieces of Tupperware. "Why were we rushing out of there like the house was on fire?"

"Because Shannon doesn't know when to stop. If coffee and dessert were served, we would have been stuck there another hour listening to God knows what. She's going to traumatize her kids."

"Is that box really full of condoms?"

"Yup." I smirk as Nick fumbles the Tupperware bins of desserts he's carrying.

"That whole box?"

"And don't forget the sex cream for your parents." Lindsey laughs as she buckles Olive into the car seat. "You missed the part of your mom spreading her sexual wings."

He shudders. "Jesus, I'm sorry I asked."

"Okay, we have one more stop and then home."

"Any way you guys can drop me off at the house first? I'm beat."

Lindsey smiles at me in the rearview mirror. "Sure, no problem."

"Do you guys have plans tomorrow?"

"No plans. What would you like to do?"

"Maybe walk over and look at the houses on Rainbow Row? I don't know, I've never been to Charleston before."

"Whatever you want, Kels." Lindsey smiles as she pulls into a marina. She presses a button and my door opens up. "Get out."

"Seriously?" Nick arches an eyebrow as he looks over at her. "This is your master plan?"

"Yup, pink wire. Hurry up, Kelsey!"

"Kelsey, this was not part of the plan, I just want you to know that. Look for 'A Sunday Kind of Love'," Nick says as he starts texting on his phone. "I had nothing to do with this."

"Wait, what plan? What are you guys talking about? I'm so confused."

"Stop asking so many questions, grab your bags and condom box and get out. We're going to park the car, we'll meet you over by the boats," Lindsey instructs. I hesitate as I look out the open car door. "Now!" she barks, spurring me into action because she's scaring me. I grab my purse and carry-on and step out of the minivan.

"Lindsey, you're acting really weird. What is going on?"

She presses the button, automatically closing the door, before peeling off down the road, leaving me stranded outside the car. What the fuck? I feel dizzy and disoriented as I look around the empty marina parking lot. Did my brother and sister-in-law seriously just abandon me here? I walk down the ramp to where the boats are docked. Do Nick and Lindsey live on a *sailboat*? I feel like I would have heard about this from my sisters or Mom. Am I staying on a boat while I'm here? What did Nick say the name was?

I walk down the dock, scanning the names, admiring the beautiful sailboats, but none of them ring a bell. Lady Bits…ew, not that one. Who would name their boat that? Probably some slimy yuppy type. Why the heck am I even down here searching for a sailboat? They must be playing some kind of prank on me.

A car horn blares from the parking lot. I turn and arch my neck hoping it's Nick and Lindsey.

"Kelsey?"

I whip back around and gasp. The sun setting behind him casts a pinkish glow over everything, the waves in the water tipped with orange. The man my heart has been pining for these past few months is standing on the dock in front of me, holding a bouquet of wildflowers.

"Patrick?"

I drop my bags and box of condoms, my heart pounding as I stand there and drink him in. My feet begin moving of their own volition as I run toward him.

Chapter 40

Patrick

Home

I PANIC FOR a heartbeat as she runs toward me, hoping she's not expecting me to lift her in the air like at the wedding. I'm about to throw the flowers to the side when she stops right in front of me. Her cheeks flushed her smile wide. She looks exactly like she did the night I met her, but she's not drunk on wine tonight. It's happiness I see twinkling in her eyes.

"Hi." I smile. "These are for you."

She takes the flowers and breathes them in. "They're beautiful, thank you." She tilts her head. "What are you doing here?"

"I'm here for you."

"But, why?" Her lapis blues reflect the pink and orange of the sunset as they search my own—a thousand unanswered questions begging to be put to rest. I could answer all her questions right now, but I decide to lead with my heart.

"Because I love you." I wipe the tears that slowly trickle down her cheeks. "I love you, Kelsey. I screwed up, but I'm here asking you for another chance, hoping like hell you'll say yes."

Her lips quiver as they tilt up. "I love you, Patrick. I screwed up. I've realized that everything I thought I wanted…it wasn't me. It's who I thought I should be. I'm here, hoping like hell you'll say yes when I ask you for another chance."

My hands cup her face as I lean down and capture her lips with mine. The kiss is gentle and unhurried, as I relish every second of it. I suck on her bottom lip and then the top, savoring every part of her mouth. Her tongue tangles with mine as she deepens the kiss. I groan, missing the feel of her as I haul her up against me. She wraps her legs around my waist as I carry her onto my boat. Our kisses grow frenzied as I walk her down the steps, past the main salon into the back bedroom, where I lay her down on the comforter. She tears at my shirt, desperate to get it off. I yank it over my head as she sheds her own. I yank her jeans off and then remove my own as we desperately pant for air.

"I've never done something like this before." She smiles up at me. I kiss her, remembering when she spoke the exact words the night of the wedding.

"Liar," I rasp as I kiss a path to her breasts. I unsnap her bra and suck on her peaked nipple. She arches into me, my hand gliding down the curve of her hip. I push her panties aside and dip my fingers into her velvet heat, earning a moan as she moves with my hand. I skim kisses along her stomach, her legs quivering as she climbs higher. I taste her sweetness as she bucks into me. Her fingers thread into my hair, holding me tight as I lap her with my tongue. She comes unglued as I quicken the rhythm, her cries telling me she's close. "Come for me, beautiful."

"Patrick, yes!" she pants as she frantically clenches the sheets, her release sending her over the edge. Her eyes flutter open as she smiles. "Oh god, I've forgotten how good you are at that." I smirk as I get up and wipe my mouth. She closes her eyes again. "If you don't have a condom, I have a few hundred on the dock."

I look at her quizzically as I pull open my nightstand drawer. "I'm not sure I want to know what you mean, but I have some." I quickly sheathe myself as she watches, her eyelids heavy as she bites down on her lip. I've missed her so much.

I hold myself over her as she traces the muscle along my arms with her fingertips. I bend my head and kiss her neck, trailing down to her breasts, savoring every second with her. She wraps her legs around me, pulling me closer as I sink into her wet heat. It feels incredible, just like the first time we made love. She tries to quicken the pace, but I make myself slow down. I'm hungry for that quick release of pleasure, but this isn't the time for me to burn off some tension. I want to hold onto this moment for as long as possible. I look into her wild blue eyes as I slowly pull myself out and then push back in. A torturous steady beat.

"I love you, Kelsey. It's always been you."

"I love you too, Patrick. From the moment I first saw you." She smiles up at me, an invisible string pulled so taut between our hearts, it hurts. Her orgasm sends her into a state of bliss as I let go of the restraint I'd been holding, quickly chasing after her.

I THROW ON a pair of sweatpants as I crawl out of bed to retrieve Kelsey's things we left on the dock. I grab my phone and look over my shoulder at her sleeping form tucked under the duvet. We have a lot to talk over, but I'm just so glad she's here. I unlock my phone and shake my head when I see I have twenty text messages from Lovie and one from Nick.

Nick: *Will you please answer her so we can go home?*

I chuckle as I type out a quick message to both of them.

Me: *Lovie, please put away the binoculars, there's nothing to see here.*

Lovie: *Well, it's about time! Nick ate all my Twizzlers. What's happening? I was about to come down there, check on you myself, and use your bathroom, but Nick wouldn't let me. He had the audacity to hand me an empty water bottle. Wait, how do you know I have binoculars?*

Me: *I've been on stakeout with you before. Go home. She's fine. I'll fill you in tomorrow after we talk.*

Lovie: *What do you mean once you talk? What the hell have you been doing for the last hour?*

Me: *Tell your sister, thanks for the condoms.*

Nick: *You do realize I'm on this chat, too.*

Me: *Goodnight, Lovie, goodnight, sidekick.*

Lovie: *Goodnight, Trick. Don't fuck this up. We can only help you so much.*

Me: *Thanks for the vote of confidence.*

I haul her bags and box of condoms onto the boat and grab two bottles of water.

"You kept them."

I look up and see her standing in my Han Solo t-shirt, her hair mussed as she gazes at the paintings over the couch. "Yeah, well...I couldn't just throw them away."

She walks over to her portrait, the one I painted on our first date in Miami. Her finger traces the texture on the canvas. I hold my breath, afraid she'll shut down on me, but she surprises me with a smile. "Is this boat yours?"

"Yes," I barely breathe, afraid to move.

"I didn't think you knew how to sail."

"I don't." I smile at how crazy that sounds. Lovie was right, I'm a hopeless idiot. "I want to learn."

She nods as she looks around the room, taking in all the polished wood and soft creamy fabrics. "It's incredible. Is this an Oyster?"

"An Oyster 575. I liked the yacht we went out on in Miami, but of course, I didn't have the bank to sink into an eighty-foot yacht or pay a staff." I swallow as nerves zip up my spine. "I was hoping you could teach me."

"I'm only here for the weekend, Patrick." She sits down on the sectional, avoiding eye contact.

"I was hoping you could stay. You could live here with me. We could sail to places around the world. You could work remotely for *That Style*, and I could come back when Lindsey needs me for the show."

She looks up, her hands clasped tightly in her lap. "That was just a dream, Patrick. Sailing the world was just a stupid dream."

"But it doesn't have to be."

"This is crazy, Patrick! Can't you see that?"

"I can."

"Why the hell are you so calm about this?"

"Because even though it's crazy, it's real to me, Kels. Your happiness is real to me. It's not just a dream."

"I can't." She wraps her arms around herself, shaking her head. I don't dare try and pull her into my arms as badly as I want to, so I fold them over my chest and casually stand by the kitchen, giving her her space. "Even if I did move here, I can't live with you right now. I need my own place. I need to be independent. I jumped from my shared house with Todd to my parents' couch."

Although my heart dips in disappointment, I understand. "I'll be waiting for you when you're ready."

"Jesus, Patrick, why do you keep saying all the right things?" She cries as she scrubs her hands down her face. She sits down on the couch and tilts her head. "Wait, how did you know about *That Style*? I never told Nick or Lindsey who I was interviewing with…" Light dawns in her eyes as she puts the puzzle pieces together. "Oh my god, it was you?" She abruptly stands up and paces. "*You* set that interview up for me?"

"I had a little help, but yes. I had to right the wrong."

"Patrick…" She stands with her arms hanging at her side, looking a little lost.

"Bridget told Nick and Lindsey how miserable you were at *The Ithaca Herald*. How sad you were still living with your parents. I screwed up barging in on your interview in Miami.

I'll never forgive myself for that. I had to do something for you."

"I don't know what to say…" She looks around the boat. "You bought us a boat, and you set up a job interview for me…" Her words die off as she looks at the paintings. "You held onto our awful first-date paintings."

I shrug. "I want a love that will last past Saturday, Kels."

"A Sunday kind of love," she whispers.

I nod as I take a step forward, cupping her face in my hands. "Swimming into her soulful blue, wishing I could erase the mistakes I drew. It must be her decision to make, my heart forever hers to break."

Her mouth drops open as her eyes lock with mine. "That's from the poem. From MTFBWY's poem…how did—"

I give her a hesitant lopsided smile. "May the force be with you."

"MTFBWY from *Star Wars*…it was you? All along, it was you? Oh my god, I can't believe I didn't put that together…"

"It was the only way I could talk to you. You wouldn't return my calls."

Sadness shadows her eyes. "You eventually stopped calling."

"I'm not a stalker." I smirk. "Although I'm not making a good case for myself since I wrote into your column anonymously, bought us a boat, set up a job interview for you, and hung onto some horrible self-portraits."

"Serious stalker vibes." She smiles, chasing the shadows away. She places her hands on my chest. "But somehow, it's worked in your favor. Did you really write that poem? For me?"

I nod. "JD and Nick helped, well, mostly JD helped, but the majority was me."

She arches up on her tiptoes and kisses me. "I've never had someone write a poem for me before, much less buy me a boat, or want to make all my dreams come true. I'm not sure a simple thank-you is enough."

I wrap my arms around her. "It's enough."

"I love you, Patrick. I've been such a fool trying to push you away. I was scared you'd try and stop me from reaching my dreams."

I run my thumb along her bottom lip tenderly. "I'm so sorry I betrayed your trust in Miami."

"Let's promise each other from here on out that we won't hide anything. We need to rely on and trust each other completely."

"Deal." I seal it with a kiss. She wraps her arms around my neck as I carry her to the bedroom.

"There's only one thing missing."

"What's that?" I tenderly kiss her smiling lips.

"We'll need a cat."

"Does that mean you're staying?"

"Well, yes, but I meant what I said. I need to be on my own for a while."

"I'll be here waiting." I kiss her nose. "Are you going to help me sail this thing?"

"Someone needs to." She grins. I laugh as I shut the bedroom door with my foot. "Why are you closing the door? It's just us."

"I'm not taking any chances. There's a crazy pregnant woman out in the parking lot that needs to pee."

Kelsey looks at me oddly.

"Do you trust me?" I ask.

"With every heartbeat."

Chapter 41

Kelsey

Happiness Is Where It's At

THE SUN SPARKLES on the water as the white sail billows in the breeze. My hands leisurely turn the wheel of the boat. I smile as Patrick angles his face into the sun, his hair ruffled by the wind, his eyes hidden behind a pair of wayfarers. His hand lazily strokes the fat black cat lying on the cushion next to him. We picked up Hagrid from a local animal shelter a few weeks after moving to Charleston. He was small and scrawny and all alone in the corner of his cage. Patrick said he reminded him of himself as a kid, so we scooped him up. Hagrid stretches out in the sun. It turns out he's a Maine coon and will get up to twenty pounds. He's our baby and rules the roost.

I've never felt so incredibly happy and at peace since I moved down to Charleston six months ago. I rented an apartment in downtown off Meeting Street that I adore, although I'm over at Patrick's place most of the time. Lindsey and I have grown even closer, and we have a standing weekly Sunday night dinner with Shannon and Dan if we're in town. I miss my sisters, but I see them plenty when Patrick has to travel to New York for Lindsey's show, and I get to tag along. My mom was delighted to find out that Patrick was the mystery flower sender and has since stopped calling me every afternoon to check in on me.

I love my job working at *That Style* writing for the Dear Melody column. I love helping people sort out their problems and make their own happy-ever-afters. Sometimes I still get a letter from LSJK updating me on how happy he is in his relationship. The new readers gobble it up, so I write back and let him know his woman is very lucky.

Mr. Pennington was notably upset when I put in my resignation. He even offered me Peter Brown's column if I would stay on. I thanked him but politely declined. My dreams had changed, and I needed to change with them. According to Marlow, a week after I left, Maria from Human Resources received an anonymous envelope regarding workplace abuse at *The Ithaca Herald*. Audio recordings were attached to the file as corroboration to the claims. Last I heard, Leigh had been demoted to Miss Cookie's Corner column and was on strict probation. Marlow told me Mr. Pennington wanted to fire her, but Leigh got on her hands and knees, sobbing. He always was a better man than me. They've hired a new journalist that's doing fantastic and is a team player, but you know, Marlow doesn't really give a shit.

"Hey Kels, where do you guys keep the Ziplock baggies?" Nick calls up the stairs from me.

"If there aren't any in the drawer, check the storage closet in the hall."

Nick and I have grown a lot closer since I moved here. He's such a great dad to Olive and husband to Lindsey. He'll always be Little Dick in my heart, but I don't call him that to his face anymore…well, unless Bridget, Arden, and MK are around. Then it's game on. I love Nick dearly, and after listening to some of the stories from Lindsey and Patrick of what he endured while he was in The Syndicate, I'm also a little in awe of him.

"Seriously, Kelsey?" Nick steps up next to me, holding Olive.

"What?"

"The storage closet has five boxes of condoms in it. Are you trying to make me a therapy lifer?"

I giggle as I take Olive from him. "Woops, sorry. Shannon brings a box over every time she stops by. Patrick and I can't keep up with the demand."

"Ugh, TMI," Nick growls, shaking his head. He walks over to Lindsey and hands her a bottle of water.

Lindsey is about to pop as she sits down on the other side of Hagrid. She's due in a week, and we're so excited to welcome another little girl to the Elliot clan. I think she's adorable, but she says she feels like a beached whale. Her visit to Al's Alligator shack spiked the ratings so high that the *Food and Travel* executive producers want her to do a whole season of undesirable locations with exotic eats. She didn't talk to Patrick for a week.

JD reaches over Patrick and lays his hand on Lindsey's stomach, smiling as the baby kicks. He's visiting for the weekend to go over his show's next production with Nick. I owe JD a lot for helping Patrick set up the interview with Elan and for helping him with the poem. He's a big old softie underneath the ego and muscles.

Nick walks back over and takes Olive from me. "How far

are we going to sail today?"

"Not far. I figure I'll drop anchor in a few."

"She's getting sleepy, so I'm going—"

"Oh shit." We look over to the threesome sunning. Lindsey is standing, a puddle at her feet.

"Did she just pee on the deck?"

"Fuck, her water just broke. Kels, you better turn this boat around. We're having a baby."

Chapter 42

Patrick

Baby on a Boat

"PATRICK, I'M SO sorry about your teak deck," Lindsey cries into Nick's shirt as she lies on a cushion we put on the floor.

"Lovie, Jesus, don't even worry about it." I turn to JD and Nick. "What are we going to do?"

"Lindsey, how long have you been having contractions for?"

"All morning. I just thought they were Braxton Hicks. They would come and go."

"Her contractions are close. Everyone wash their hands thoroughly. We'll have to prepare if she has this baby on the boat."

"What? No! I don't want to have a baby on a boat!" Lindsey cries. "Someone call Shannon!"

"Have you ever delivered a baby?" I ask JD, ignoring Lindsey.

"I've delivered hundreds of puppies, a gazillion kittens, and a lion cub, should be pretty close?" He shrugs. "I'll need your help."

I swallow as I look nervously between Nick and JD. "Why can't Nick help?"

"I will be helping, but I'll also have to hold her hand. We need Kelsey to sail us back. Come on, sidekick, I need you."

I nod. "Yeah, yeah, of course."

"Just don't pull off the tail." JD smirks as he heads downstairs to wash up.

"Very funny." I rub the light scar on my forehead.

"What the hell are you guys talking about?" Lindsey cries as a contraction rumbles through her. "Oh god, that's a bad one!"

"Don't worry about it, babe. Remember to breathe through it." They do some breathing exercises as Nick talks her down from the contraction. "This is a pink-wire moment, Linds. You can do this."

"I want drugs. Shannon promised me drugs, lots of them. I don't want to deliver naturally. That was not in my birthing plan!" Her eyes blaze into JD as he crouches back down. "Don't you have any goddamn drugs?!"

"Yikes." JD nervously looks at Nick. "I wish I did. I'd give us all a sedative. We need something to clear the baby's nasal passages."

"Olive has a bulb syringe in her diaper bag. Can you clean it, Patrick? We'll need wipes from it too, and trash bags. See if Kelsey has any pads," Nick says.

"I'm on it." I grab Hagrid and pass Kelsey, who hastily brings one of the sails down. "Are you okay?"

"Just nervous for Lindsey. I'm keeping the mainsail up as we motor sail back. It will get us back faster. Thank God the headwind isn't fierce today. I'll come help when I can." Kelsey's eyes mirror the same worry in mine. We sailed for about an hour before Lindsey's water broke.

I run downstairs, wash my hands, and put a pot of water on the stove to boil. For what, I'm not exactly sure, but they always do it in the movies. I grab all of our clean towels and race back upstairs as JD checks Lindsey. I drop down next to him.

"Babe, you're going to have to go without drugs. You can do it. I've never met someone as strong as you," Nick says soothingly as he wipes her brow. "Should we move her downstairs?"

"I'm not going anywhere!" Lindsey cries through another contraction. "Fuuuuck. Where's Olive?" she pants. "Why the fuck are we out in the middle of an ocean!"

"She's in her crib napping." Nick's brow creases in worry.

"Trick, I'll buy you guys new towels and cushions, I promise," Lindsey says through clenched teeth.

"Lovie, I'm not even worried about it." I turn to JD. "I've boiled some water."

He nods in concentration. "I was wrong. This is *way* different than delivering a puppy."

Lindsey's eyes pop. "What? Oh god, oh god! *Why* is a veterinarian delivering my baby...on a boat! I want Shannon!"

"Linds, it's okay, we've got you. Kelsey is sailing us right back to the harbor where we'll have an ambulance waiting to take you to the hospital and to Shannon," Nick promises her.

Lindsey grabs Nick's polo shirt and pulls his face down to hers. "I'm not having a baby on a boat," she growls with the intensity of a woman possessed.

"She's feisty like a lioness," JD murmurs.

"She's like this even when she's not giving birth," I mumble.

Nick untangles her fingers from his shirt as he gives us a warning glare. "Babe, we don't have cell service this far away from shore. You're gonna have to be brave and do this without Shannon, okay?"

"Nick? The baby's head is crowning. Lindsey, I need you to get in the right mindset. We're going to have to do this on our own. You're having a baby on this boat whether you want to or not. I need you to push on the count of three. Patrick, help me hold her leg, Nick, you've got her hand?"

"But I'm not supposed to have this baby until next week!" Lindsey screams as another contraction hits her.

Nick nods. JD appears collected, but the waver in his voice betrays his anxiety. Kelsey rushes over with a warm cloth and a pair of scissors.

"I poured the boiling water over this towel to clean her up with afterward. I sterilized our scissors in case we need to cut the umbilical cord, and Olive is fast asleep. We should be there in twenty minutes. I've set the direction for now, so I can help for a few minutes."

Nick and I look up at her gratefully. Her steady hand passes me the pot and scissors. She crouches down on Lindsey's other side and holds her other knee and hand.

"This baby will be here in less than five. One, two, three, push, Lindsey!" JD calmly coaxes her. She screams as she bears down. "I see her head. Breathe, Lindsey, we're going to try again. One, two, three, push!"

I'm amazed by the miracle happening right in front of

me as JD pulls the baby from Lindsey.

"She's beautiful," JD says. I hand him a towel and the syringe to clear her airways. Nick and Lindsey are crying as Kelsey wipes her brow. The baby starts to cry as JD rubs her body and clears her airways. "I'm too nervous about cutting the umbilical cord, so it's best to leave it attached for now," JD says in a low voice, as he places the baby in a clean towel in Lindsey's arms. "Welcome to the world, baby girl."

Chapter 43

Patrick

Aunt Kelsey and Uncle Trick

"You did it! You delivered your first baby. How do you feel, Nurse Patrick?" Kelsey hands me a beer as I stretch out on the couch after taking a long hot shower.

"Traumatized." I watch as she plops down next to Olive and hands her a sippy cup. We're watching Olive at Nick and Lindsey's house for the next few days until Lindsey and baby Willow get released from the hospital. "JD was a lot more collected than I felt."

"I'm pretty positive he was scared shitless." She smiles ruefully. "In fact, I'd say right about now he's at the hotel bar getting drunk."

I chuckle. "That's what I'd be doing."

"Hey, Patrick? Have you changed your mind about kids after today?"

She swings Olive on her hip, and all I can think about is how beautiful she is at this moment. I choose my words carefully. "I can imagine a life with you and kids running around, but I can also imagine it just being us and being completely happy."

Her breath wooshes out as if she were holding it, waiting

for the ax to drop. "I'm not so sure I'm ready for them quite yet. I love my nieces and nephew, but I also just love spending time with you. Today was a lot."

"Today was scary as hell." I chuckle as I get up and stroll toward her. I pull her and Olive into my arms and kiss her temple. "No one says we have to. I love being Uncle Trick and Aunt Kelsey. I love you."

"Arden and MK keep asking me when I'm going to pop out a dozen—"

"Hey, who cares what others think we need to do. This is us. You and me, Kels. We're in this together. We're going to have hard days and days we wish will never end, but through it all, I'll be holding your hand."

She nods as she smiles down at Olive. "I like that."

The doorbell rings. "That's dinner."

"Oh good, I'm starving. What did you order?"

"Pizza with pepperoni and pineapple," I say. Kelsey makes a noise of disgust, and I can't help but laugh. "And Chinese for you."

"If you keep playing your cards right, Star Boy, I might let you pick out the movie."

I smirk as I bring the food into the kitchen. What she doesn't know is that I have the last *Star Wars* movie queued up. "Kelsey?"

"Yes?" Her back is to me as she slides the table onto Olive's highchair.

"I love you. A Sunday kind of love."

She looks over her shoulder at me and smiles. "A love that will last past Saturday night." She walks over to me after securing Olive, wrapping her arms around my waist, burying her nose in my neck. "I love you. Thank you for not giving up on me. A Jedi through and through."

"I'm sorry I called you a sneaky Sith."

"When?"

"When I was mad at you."

She smirks. "I took an online test. It was quite time consuming. According to the Star Wars quiz, I'm Luke Skywalker. I have a pure heart and in spite of a life of danger, I'd risk everything to save others."

"Figures, that's the best one." I squeeze her back, my love for her beating wildly in my chest. I stare into her deep blues and thank my lucky stars. "I finally found it."

"Found what?" she asks.

"Love."

Chapter 44

Lindsey

Postcards

NICK SMILES AS he pushes a very talkative Olive in her stroller. I have Willow nestled against me as we walk in the warm summer evening. We stop in front of the mailbox before heading up our driveway. I take the mail out and riffle through. A postcard falls out, fluttering down to the ground. Nick bends to pick it up.

"We got another one from them." Nick smiles as he flips it over. His grin grows wider as he reads the back.

"Oh? Where is it from?"

"Venezuela." He hands the postcard to me. I read the back and tear up. On the back of the postcard written in Patrick's scrawl reads, *She said yes!*

"I'm so happy for them. They both deserve it." I cry as Nick pulls me into his arms, kissing the top of my head. He wipes the happy tears from my cheeks. "This means we have a wedding to plan!"

Nick groans. "Please wait for them to ask for your help."

"They wouldn't even *be* together if it wasn't for my help."

Nick rolls his eyes as he lets go of me and pushes the

stroller forward. "Between you and my sisters, if they're smart, they'll elope. They're probably on their way back. Patrick said they'd meet us down in Miami next week."

"Hmm…you sure you're up for this?"

"You planning a wedding no one asked you to? No."

I whack him in the stomach. "Are you ready for another season of Dr. JD Evans and Adventure Animals?"

"No, but I'll do it for JD." His brow furrows. I know this project is stressing him. "At least I'll have you, sidekick, and Kelsey with me."

"Always." I smile as I loop my arm through his and squeeze him to me. "You're never getting rid of us."

"I wouldn't dream of it." He grins devilishly.

"I'm glad Patrick finally found love," I say.

Nick looks at me curiously. "Why?"

"Patrick loves love. He was always looking for it, but could never find it. He finally found his match with Kelsey."

"Agreed." Nick leans down and kisses my lips, tenderly tucking a lock of hair behind my ear. "By the way, Patrick booked a welcome back lunch at Alligator Al's."

My face goes slack as I think of the twenty different ways Al can cook gator. Nick wraps his arm around me and pulls me to his side, laughing at my expression.

"Never a dull moment with you, Lindsey Love."

Epilogue

Kelsey

Five years later...

I STEP INTO the enormous hotel bedroom, holding my heels and my silk clutch. I walk up behind Patrick who is fiddling with his bow tie in the mirror. His eyes meet mine and I smile.

"Wow, you look stunning." He turns around, his hands sliding up my waist. "Red is definitely your color."

"Not looking so bad yourself. Here, let me help you with that." I begin to tie the bow tie like my father taught me. "Are you nervous?"

"Nah...should I be?"

I giggle as I fiddle with the tie. "I mean, it's the Emmys. I'd be nervous."

"With you by my side, I'll be fine." He dips his head and kisses my lips, groaning. "Maybe we can just stay here."

I grab the lapels of his jacket and shuffle him back. "You'll mess up my lipstick."

"There's a lot more I want to mess up." He waggles his eyebrows.

"Maybe if you play your cards right and win another Emmy, you might get lucky later tonight."

"Remember the first night we met?"

I toss my head back and moan as he grazes his teeth against the sensitive spot under my ear. "How could I forget? You were the sexiest guy at the wedding."

"Really? Not Lindsey's second cousin, Giovanni?"

"The hairy guy with the gold chains? He had enough hair gel to make Anne Burrell jealous." I scrunch my nose. "Definitely not him. I thought my chances were dashed when you made your move on the dance floor and tried to pull down a woman's dress." I try to keep a straight face as he rears his head back.

"Aunt Mildew?" He shudders. "For the record, I slipped. You were the one who couldn't keep your eyes off me through the whole ceremony."

"I wanted you."

"Who wouldn't?"

I chuckle. "Charmer. I need to check on Rue before we head out."

Patrick nods, releasing me. I sit on the edge of the bed as I pull my cellphone out of my clutch and call my mom. "Hey mo—"

"Kelsey? Is that you?" Screaming and laughter erupts in the background. It sounds like a frat party on her end.

"Is everything okay?"

"I can't hear you, let me go out on the back deck." I hear my mom shuffle and the sliding glass door open. "I'm here."

"Is everything okay? Is Rue okay?"

"Oh Kelsey, she's fine. Your sisters stopped by with their kids, so all the cousins are together. I could use a glass of wine...or three."

"Okay, well early bedtime, Mom, she's only six."

"I raised five hellions, Kelsey, I think I can manage. Oh, I know you have to go, but did you see that Miss Cookie came out with a new stain removal formula? Olive squirted ketchup all over the suede couch yesterday and it came right up. She's fantastic!"

"Glad you're liking Leigh's products, Mom."

"She's a genius. Tell her I said so and that my friend Desiree wanted to suggest cream of tar—"

"Okay, I'll let her know. Thanks for watching Rue this weekend, Mom."

"Have fun, don't worry about us. Oh, shoot, I gotta go. Your nephew Charlie is putting something out with a fire extinguisher. MK!"

She hangs up before I can ask to speak to Rue. I slip my phone back in my clutch and take a deep breath. This is the first time we've been apart from her and I miss her like crazy. I hope she's surviving that crazy crew and isn't too traumatized. Patrick and I adopted Rue two years ago after a trip to South Africa with JD and his film crew. My friend Jem and I went to visit a local orphanage one day to volunteer and I fell in love with the little girl with the big smile named Nuru. The woman holding her told me her name meant, Filled with Light. After a very long year of trips back and forth, she was officially ours. We weren't planning on kids, but when I held Rue that day, I just knew it was meant to be. True to her name, she has brought so much light and love into our lives.

"Everything okay?" he asks.

"Apparently Olive squirted ketchup all over the couch

and Charlie was putting out a small fire, so yeah, everything's normal."

"Not it."

"Not it, what?"

"You're telling Lovie she needs to buy her in-laws a new couch. I swear, that kid and her food. Remember when she wiped red pepper hummus all over the carpet and then poured juice on top? It took three cleanings to get it out. Takes after her mom for sure."

"Well, we're both saved by Miss Cookie's cleaning products. Mom said it came right out."

"Do you regret turning down Leigh's offer?"

"I have no regrets." I wink at him. Leigh emailed me about a year ago after *The Ithaca Herald* folded and apologized for her behavior during my short stint there. She realized how obsessed and hungry she had become for the job, and admitted it was a side of herself that she wasn't proud of. She was worried I was going to take over her position, and so she'd tried to sabotage my job. She offered a peace branch and asked if I wanted to combine my self-help column with Miss Cookie. She was determined to make it a household name. I accepted her apology and wished her luck, but declined her offer. Writing for the magazine was all that I needed.

I stand and slip my heels on as Patrick waits for me by the door.

"I was thinking, since I have some time off, and your parents have Rue, maybe we should go somewhere after this."

"Where do you want to go?"

"Oh, I don't know…I hear Hawaii's nice this time of year."

I laugh. "You booked the trip already, didn't you?"

"Maybe."

"I don't have clothes for Hawaii."

"Well, it's a good thing Bridget packed a bag for you. Your parents are watching Nuru."

"I don't know how you pulled that off without me finding out from Lindsey or one of my sisters."

Patrick opens the door and ushers me out. "Some say I've got moves smoother than Han Solo."

I laugh. "No one has ever said that, Star Boy. Aunt Mildew can attest to that."

He gently dips me as he kisses me. "Go away with me?"

"I'd go anywhere as long as I'm with you."

"Remember when we first met and you asked me not to forget you?"

"Oh god, unfortunately."

Patrick's eyes twinkle. "Why unfortunately?"

"Because it's embarrassing!" I giggle. "Who says that?"

He kisses the tip of my nose. "I could never forget the most beautiful woman I'd ever met. You are it for me, Kelsey Anne Healy. I love you."

I melt into his sugar-brown eyes. "Patrick?"

"Mm?"

"I'm glad I asked you to dance."

"Smartest decision you ever made."

"Thank you for not giving up on me."

"I would never give up on love."

The End

Please read on for a snippet from JD's Book, the last in the Love series coming in 2021.

Chapter One

Jem

Dr. JD Evans

OUR SHOES SQUEAK on the linoleum floors as we walk down the bright white hallway. I can't help but stretch my neck to look into the little windows in the closed doors to see what's going on as she prattles on about the clinic.

"They're filming in the lab right now, so we'll go into the office. You'll have to sign all the paperwork and the NDA. If you don't want to be on film there's a sheet for you to fill out for that too," the brunette, Carly, says as she keeps a hand on her very pregnant belly. She holds a door open for me and I duck into the office. "Have a seat."

I sit down and nervously fold my hands in my lap as I look around the light and airy office. Everything is white with clean lines and wood beams. I smile at Carly as she pulls my file in front of her.

"So, you graduated from Florida State with a degree in veterinary science."

"Yes, ma'am. I was hoping to go on to vet school, but I wanted some experience first."

"And a recommendation." She winks. "You can call me Carly."

"I mean, that would help too, but it's not my sole pur-pose—"

"It's okay, I was just teasing. It's not easy getting a job here. Dr. Evans' schedule is chaotic, plus with the film crew, it can be a bit much. If you survive this year, the least he can do is write you a referral letter to school."

I swallow as I lightly drum my fingers along my leg. "I thought the job opening I applied for was for a veterinary technician for Dr. Summers...will I be working with Dr. Evans too?" I've heard rumors about Doctor Evans at school. All the women swooned over him when he came to lecture about dentals on large exotic animals. He was good looking, but arrogant. It's well known he's difficult to work for because he's so demanding and expects the best. I've heard he's made other visiting veterinarians and interns on his surgery rotation cry. When I saw Dr. Summers was looking for a technician I jumped at the chance. I saw her lecture once and she was very intelligent and polite.

"Oh, well, unfortunately Dr. Summers is no longer with the clinic. We're currently interviewing veterinarians. As you can tell, I'm about to pop, and well, I'm looking for someone to fill my position."

"What does your position entail?"

"Oh, a little bit of everything. You'll be Dr. Evans' assis-tant."

No, no, no, no. "What do you mean by assistant? Like veterinary assistant?"

"Um..." Carly shuffles some papers. "More like his per-sonal assistant."

"But I need—"

"I understand you want veterinary experience. You'll get that, but you'll also be his personal assistant. With the Adventure Animals show doing so well, he needs someone to help keep him organized, help with his travel, manage his appointments."

I sit back in my chair, totally flabbergasted. "I didn't sign up—"

"Look, you're the only applicant who has half a brain. Three fourths of these applications are either to get on television or to get in Dr. Evans' pants. I need someone with a good head on her shoulders, an actual goal in mind, and you are determined to get into veterinary school. Dr. Evans has a lot of pull at the University."

I worry my bottom lip between my teeth. I mean, if this job could get me to be a shoo-in for veterinary school, would I be stupid enough to pass that up? And rumors are just that, right? He can't be that bad to work for. Carly said she's been here ten years...

"What do I have to do?"

Carly beams as she gives me a list. "Welcome to the team, Jem."

AN HOUR LATER I'm standing outside his bungalow-style house in South Beach with his key in my hand. Carly assured me he wasn't home, that he was out of town. Apparently, part of being his assistant is to get his mail when he's on a trip and feed his fish. He does have two cats, but he boards them with another technician at the clinic. I stare at the silver key and shrug. The salary Carly showed me is worth driving over here to do something as mundane as getting his mail. I shove the key in and turn the lock. The door opens to a spacious living room with comfy couches and a square coffee table. It looks like a Pottery Barn set designer went apeshit in here. Everything is neat and orderly, even the colorful throw pillows are placed artfully at an angle. The walls are adorned with stunning photographs of African wildlife. I walk over to the bookshelves lined with books about animals and Africa and several photos of Dr. Evans. Dr. Evans fishing, Dr. Evans with a rhino, Dr. Evans with an African dog. I snort as I peruse. They are all pictures of him smiling cheesily at the camera. "Someone sure loves to take pictures of himself."

I turn away from the shelves. Something pink catches my eye, tucked behind a pillow on the chair. I pull on the satin and roll my eyes as a hot-pink bra dangles from my finger.

"Eww." I drop it on the chair. "I did not sign up for this shit."

I don't see the fish so I wander down the hall to the spacious kitchen which is clean and bright with a large marble island. I set his mail down on the counter and wander toward the back of the house. There's a huge screened-in back porch that calls to me. The porch furniture is comfortable, but my mouth drops open as I take in his beautifully manicured backyard with a small pool. Large elephant ears, banana plants, and tropical flowers surround the area. It's like walking upon a lagoon in the middle of the jungle. It's the most beautifully landscaped yard I've ever seen, the colors so vibrant in the early evening sun that it looks like someone photoshopped it.

I look to my left and spy a cylinder fish tank with one lone blue beta fish. "Hello, Blue. Original name." I drop in a few flakes from the food next to the tank. I know I should lock up and drive back to my apartment, but curiosity has me walking into the next room which is a quaint den. More pictures, but at least he's with other people in these. I wonder why he has all the pictures with family and friends back here. He really is handsome. This is such a cozy room. I can picture curling up in the leather armchair with a good book on rainy days.

I turn the corner and smack right into a wall. "Oof." How did I not see that? My hands reach up to steady myself, but it's not drywall I'm touching. It's hard, smooth muscle. My fingers lightly trail down a tanned eight pack as a white towel hangs loosely around hips, ready to drop with a slight breeze.

I step back in horror as my brain connects with my fingertips. JD Evans stands there practically naked, looking just as shocked to see me. Shit, shit, shit, I just felt up my new boss. And oh my god, the pictures don't do him justice at all. His dark hair is wet and slightly curling, water droplets beading on his massive shoulders. A tattoo wraps around his bicep. His lips curve up in a devilish grin as his hazel eyes glint with mischief.

"Who the hell are you?" His towel slowly starts to slip to the floor.

I let out a squeak and do what any sane woman would do in that moment.

I bolt for the door.

Acknowledgments

A big thank-you to my sister Allisson for having to read this in pieces as I'd send it. I couldn't do this without your support. Thank you to Lisa and Wendy for being amazing beta readers. Your critiques are invaluable and your support means the world to me. Thank you to Addie, who talked me off the ledge more times than I'd like to admit. Your support and ability to listen have been so incredibly helpful to me. Thank you, friend. Thank you to my ARC readers who were so excited for this book. Your support means so much to me! To my loyal bookstagrammers, thank you for always voicing your love and pushing my books. I wouldn't be here without you. I love each and every one of you. To Michelle, for having to read and edit yet another crazy book of mine. It takes a village and mine would probably burn to the ground if you weren't in charge. My writing wouldn't shine without you. Thank you to Stephany for tying up all the loose ends. To my family, for their support and insisting on reading my books, thank you and I love you. To my husband and kids for putting up with my: just give me one more paragraph, one more minute, one more second! Your patience made this book happen. To Josephine and Richard, thank you from the bottom of my heart for all your love and support.

Other Books by Sophie Sinclair

The Coffee Book Series
Coffee Girl – Coffee Book 1
The Makeup Artist – Coffee Book 2
The Social Hour – Coffee Book 3

The LLL Book Series
Lindsey Love Loves – LLL Book 1

About the Author

Sophie Sinclair lives with her husband, two daughters, and a gaggle of animals in Davidson, NC.